Liberty Crusade:
The Fight to Save the Free World

Liberty Crusade

The Fight to Save the Free World

Larry Ballard

CONTENTS

INTRODUCTION

Who Are the Financial Elite and Why Should You Care?

Most of the problems the world faces today originate from a single source, and that is the global network of central banks that enslaves the people of the world. They make us slaves without chains, forever indentured to a network of global bankers, who use their vast wealth to control the four centers of power:

1) Monetary 2) Political 3) Intellectual 4) Religious

I refer to this cabal of international bankers as the Financial Elite, which is the focus of this book. I should note that control of the global banking system goes hand in hand with control of global trade because the basis of wealth for every nation in the world is trade. Global trade and global banking are derivatives of one another! It goes like this; natural resources are mined, manufactured into finished products, and shipped worldwide. This forms the basis for the Gross Domestic Product (GDP) of individual nations and the entire world. But this is impossible without credit, so control of money and credit is the genesis of all wealth. Money is the medium of exchange that makes all this possible. As you can see, when we are talking about Globalism, we are talking about the basis of all wealth! There can be no more crucial all-encompassing topic! He who controls the money controls the world!

This book warns of the Financial Elite's plot to collapse the Free Market System, starting with the United States. As the leader of the Free Market, if America falls, the rest of the global monetary system will implode, leading to economic chaos. At that point, the Financial Elites plan is to step in and offer to fix the very problems they brought upon us. This would usher in their One-World Government Dictatorship.

Even though this book is about warning people about the dangers of Globalism, there is good news. God never lets things get too bad without first warning His people. The good news is that we are about to enter an unprecedented period of prosperity, ushered in by a political leader already on the scene. The Financial Elite are petrified of this man, but he is anointed for this time. No matter what they do, he will outwit them, and it is he who will usher in the prosperity of which I speak. The bad news is that the good times will be followed by an equally long period of bad times. So, this is a warning to prepare now while you can.

Just a little about me in closing, I am an ordinary Joe. I am a college graduate, but that in of itself is no endorsement. So why should you care what I have to say about such an important and supposedly complicated subject as global economic, political, and social affairs? My only credentials arise from an event that occurred in 1968 when I had a near-death experience. I wrecked my motorcycle and visited heaven for four hours. While I was there, I was given one heck of a download. I was told that when my hair was salt and pepper (now), I would be called to deliver a message to a world gone amuck. I was to deliver this message with *"power and clarity,"* which I construed meant to tell it like it is, with no sugar coating. The world is in serious trouble! Long story short, *"God prepares those He calls."* So, I have studied and prepared for the last 40 years, and here we are, and it is time for this message to be birthed.

Wake Up! Wake Up!
The Enemy Is at The Gate!

The hour is late
The enemy is at the gate
The enemy is not from without
The enemy is from within
The Shadow Government of the Financial Elite

They have lulled us to sleep
Transformed us while we slept
Dismantled us brick by brick
Sold us bit by bit
Stolen our wealth
Driven us into debt
Left us a shadow of our former self
And they are enslaving us bit by bit

Wake up! Wake up!
For God's sake, wake up
The enemy is at the gate.
Wake up before it is too late!

This book intends to expose the plot which Kennedy was assassinated to keep from us. Once you know the truth, I will ask you to put aside the differences that have been falsely instilled in us and come together as *"one nation, under God"* and take our country back from:

"Those Who Would Be the Masters of Us All."

CHAPTER 1

The Foundation Stones that Underpin America's Greatness!

WHAT YOU WILL LEARN IN THIS CHAPTER

- Why Did Our Forefathers Come to America?

- The Symbol of America's Founding Principles.

- The 12 Foundation Stones upon Which America Is Built and How They Are Being Undermined.

- The Economic Component of America's Greatness!

- The Financial Elite Are Real and They Are Dedicated to Destroying America

Why Did Our Forefathers Come to America?

The obvious answer is to escape economic and religious oppression in England, but there is more to the story.

The New Jerusalem: The Puritans and Separatists, known collectively as Pilgrims, who colonized America, felt they were founding *"the New Jerusalem."* They opposed the King of England as the self-proclaimed head of the church and felt that Parliament, not the King, should have the final say in all legal matters deferring to the Jewish Bible, which they held to be the highest authority in all matters. After trying to reform the Church of England by appealing to the Church and King, they finally decided that the Church of England was so corrupt that the only course of action was to separate and seek religious freedom in the New World. They saw England as Egypt, the King as Pharaoh, the Atlantic Ocean as the Red Sea, the New World as the Promised Land, and the Indians as the Canaanites. They saw themselves as the Israelites, entering covenant with God and entering the promised land. Upon reaching what they referred to as the New Jerusalem, they set about God's work. They wholeheartedly believed they were called to establish in America, *"The New World,"* a society modeled after the sacred Jewish scriptures. They believed that both individuals and nations could and should enter a covenant with God.

They Believed In:

- The righteousness and sovereignty of God in all things. God, they said, *"directed all things by exercise of His will and directed all things to an intelligent end."*

- Strict adherence to the Old Testament Sabbath.

- That man existed for the glory of God, and his first concern in life was to do God's will.

- Education was essential so they could read the Bible, which they saw as the basis of government.

- The sanctity of marriage and family.

- Husbands were viewed as the head of the household, but wives were viewed as spiritual equals of their husbands.

- They identified with the Old Testament Hebrew Bible and believed in praying and fasting before making any important decision.

The year is 1620, and the Mayflower lands in America. The first thing they did was author and signed the Mayflower Compact, a rudimentary constitution establishing Democratic rule. In 1630 their founder, John Winthrop, said that the society they were establishing would be *"as a city on a hill,"* denoting that it would be a beacon of light and inspiration to the world and that *"colony leaders would educate all."* These beliefs in the importance of education led to the founding of Harvard University.

In 1639, after the first assembly of New Haven, John Davenport declared the Bible as the colony's legal and moral foundation. *"Scriptures do hold forth a perfect rule for the direction and government of all men in all duties which they are to perform to God and men as well as in the government of families and commonwealth, as in matters of church…the word of God shall be the only rule to be attended to in organizing the affairs of government in this plantation."* Scripture formed the basis of most of the laws of early New England.

Governor Winthrop said of the colony, *"We shall find that the God of Israel is among us, but if we deal falsely with our God…we be consumed out of the good land whither we are going."* In other words, the Jewish Covenant was the centerpiece of Puritan beliefs. News flash: It seems that his words may well have been a prophetic utterance because today, the people of the United States have strayed far away from God and teeter on the brink of moral, economic, and political collapse, and we may well be taken into captivity like our Jewish forefathers. I want you to reflect on how far the U.S. has fallen and ponder what God has in store for the nation that was once *"the city on the hill—the New Jerusalem"* and has now become Sodom and Gomorrah.

The date is April 30, 1789, and George Washington is inaugurated at Federal Hall in New York City (Washington D.C. did not exist yet, New York was America's first capital) at the sight of what was to become ground zero on 9/11 and America is officially founded as a fully constituted Republic under God. In his inaugural address, Washington said,

"The propitious smiles of Heaven cannot be expected on a nation that disregards the eternal rule of order and right which Heaven hath ordained."

Our first President and the first joint session of Congress then walked from Federal Hall to St. Paul Cathedral (located on the corner of what is now ground zero), where President Washington gave a speech in which he said,

"It would be peculiarly improper to omit in this first official act my fervent supplication to that Almighty Being who rules over the universe, who presides in the councils of nations and whose providential aids and supply every human deficit, that His benediction may consecrate to the liberties and happiness of the people of the United States, a government instituted by themselves for this essential purpose."

Because America kept its covenant with God, it has been blessed as no other nation. It has become *"as a city on a hill"* and an inspiration to the world. It has been lifted high above all nations on the earth.

The Symbol of America's Founding Principles!

When people think of America, *"the land of the free and home of the brave,"* the symbol that most often comes to mind other than our flag and national anthem is the Statue of Liberty. But the Statue of Liberty didn't stand in New York harbor till 1886. Its inscription reads:

"Give me your tired, your poor,
Your huddled masses, yearning to breathe free,
The wretched refuse of your teeming shore,
Send these, the homeless, tempest-tost to me,
I lift my lamp beside the golden door."

This quote reflects the fact that by then, America had become known as *"the melting pot of the world."* This was because America was built by people, like the Pilgrims, who were seeking a better life, who wanted to take avail of the religious and economic freedom which America had by then become famous for. These were hardworking, self-reliant people who gave up their heritage and assimilated into the uniquely American culture. In the chapter on Immigration, we will discuss how the Financial Elite have used the Statue of Liberty and its inscription to justify an open borders policy intended

to collapse America from within. Without borders, there is no nation, and the Financial Elite knows this. That is what is behind our immigration policies and those of the European Union.

There is a certain irony about the Statue of Liberty representing American culture because it is modeled after the pagan goddess Ishtar, the Goddess of War and Sexuality. So, is there another statue that is more representative of America's founding principles, one that dates back to our founding, one that most Americans know nothing about? The answer is yes! It is called the Plymouth Monument, located in Plymouth, Massachusetts.

It represents America's true founding values: Liberty, Morality, Education, Law, and the Bible. We will shortly examine why these founding principles are foundational to American Exceptionalism to what has made it the greatest nation the world has ever known, the city on the hill, the beacon of hope, and inspiration for the entire world. But first, I want to lay a little more foundation by discussing:

The 12 Foundation Stones Upon Which America Is Built and How They Are Being Undermined!

In thinking of America's founding principles, I am reminded of the fairytale, *The Three Little Pigs*. As the story goes, the 1st pig built his house of straw, the 2nd built his house of twigs, and the 3rd built his house of brick. Then along came the big bad wolf and said, *"I will huff, and I'll puff, and I will blow your house down."* And as the story goes, he blew down the house of straw and the one of twigs, but when he got to the house built of brick, he huffed, and he puffed, but he couldn't blow the house down.

This story has many parallels to America. Our house is built of bricks, and it rests on a strong foundation built on 12 founding principles. As long as those foundation stones remain in place, America is virtually invincible. It has endured two World Wars, so it is capable of withstanding virtually any external assault. But it is susceptible to collapse from within. In the case of America, the big bad wolf is the Financial Elites who patiently work from within our own government, corporations, schools, news media, Hollywood, unions, community organizing groups, etc. to systematically undermine and remove our foundation stones till the day comes when our house topples (as to how exactly they do that is a subject for another chapter). But if the people are vigilant, they can keep the wolf at bay. But today in America, our people have been fed a never-ending stream of lies and half-truths coming from the big bad wolf and his minions. Their propaganda has brainwashed many and polarized the nation, creating so much dissension and outright hatred that the nation founded on *"life, liberty and the pursuit of happiness"* is so divided, so fractured that its foundation is in jeopardy of imploding in on itself. It is not an exaggeration to say that the Financial Elite are behind a political coup of the sitting President. Just in case that fails, they are trying to ferment so much racial tension that they can spark the kind of civil disobedience and riots that topple governments.

One of this book's primary purposes is to ring the fire alarm and let the American people know exactly what is being done to collapse America from within, who is behind it, and how they carry out their stealth, undercover operation. I believe President Abram Lincoln was right when he said,

> *"I firmly believe in people, if given the truth, they can be depended on to meet any crisis. The great point is to bring them the real facts. America will never be destroyed from the outside. If we falter and lose our freedoms, it will be because we destroyed ourselves."*

So here are the 12 foundation stones that underpin America's greatness. This entire book focuses on examining these founding principles and why they have made America the greatest nation the world has ever known. Regardless of what the Financial Elite may say, America is Exceptional, and it shines the light of Liberty for the entire world. Should America ever fall, the entire world would be the poorer for it, both economically and culturally. As America goes, so goes the rest of the world!

The 12 Foundation Stones That Underpin America's Greatness!

1. **Government:** A Republic serves the people, but all other forms of government are self-serving, resulting in an elite ruling class with a perverted shadow government that operates behind the scenes!

2. **Borders:** Territory over which a nation is sovereign. Erase the borders, and there is no sovereignty!

3. **Military:** Provides safety and security, but if perverted, it becomes a means of domination and oppression!

4. **Legal System:** Provides order and defines the people's rights, but if perverted, it oppresses them!

5. **Patriotism:** Source of national allegiance and strength. Undermine it, and the nation falls from within!

6. **Property Rights:** A Republic protects property rights, but other forms of government allow the government to take rights, leading to Socialism!

7. **Monetary System:** Medium of exchange, but if perverted, it becomes a means to enrich the ruling class at the expense of the public!

8. Natural Resources: Basis of all wealth and the necessities of life, or if perverted, becomes the ultimate control mechanism!

9. Trade and Commerce: The conversion of natural resources into useful goods and a basis of wealth, but if intentionally restricted, it becomes a means by which to bankrupt a nation!

10. Educational System: Essential to a Republic because it forms the basis for voters' informed decision-making and the basis for the innovations that drive economic growth! If perverted, it becomes a weapon to sow social discourse and insight revolution!

11. Religion and Family Values: Forms the basis of the moral system which determines a civilized society, but if perverted, society collapses from within!

12. Media: Informs the public or, if perverted, becomes propaganda used to brainwash!

Our Founding Fathers referred to America as *"The Great Experiment."* Why was that? It was because America represented a unique form of government. It was not a Monarchy. It was not a Democracy. It was not Socialism or Communism. It was a Republic, which is the only form of government ever designed to limit the power of government and allow the people to govern themselves in a manner they felt best served their needs. The American Republic was founded on three coequal branches of government, the Executive, Legislative, and Judicial, which was intended to give control of the government, not to an all-powerful Federal Government, but to the States and the People who were to be responsible for keeping their freedom intact.

As the story goes, Ben Franklin left the Constitutional Convention when he was met by a woman who inquired, *"Sir, what form of government have you given us?"* to which he responded, *"A Republic Madam, if you can keep it."* That may seem a strange response, but it gets to the heart of what a Republic is. A Republic is unlike any other form of government because it truly gives the people the power of self-government, but with that privilege comes responsibility. Let's take a look at precisely what a Republic is and what makes it unique. A Republic is a government *"of the people, by the people, and for the people."* It requires an educated, well-informed public. That is why education is one of the founding principles on the Plymouth Monument, and that is why President John Adams said,

> *"Liberty cannot be preserved without general knowledge among the people."*

Knowing this to be true is why the Financial Elite have hijacked the education system and the media in America. Under a Republic, the people must be willing to abide by the Constitution (the rule of law). Leaders must pass laws in the people's best interest, not special interest groups or the Financial/Political Elites. By contrast, a Democracy is based on majority rule and our Founders referred to it as *"Mobocracy."* James Madison famously said of Democracies,

> *"Democracies have ever been spectacles of turbulence and contention; have ever been found incompatible with personal security or the rights of property; and have, in general, been as short in their lives as they have been violent in their deaths."*

Why would that be? Democracies invariably degrade into chaos when those least willing or least able to work realize they can vote themselves handouts. For this reason, Democracies invariably morph into Socialism and Communism, which is exactly what is happening in America today. As Jefferson said,

> *"The democracy will cease to exist when you take away from those who are willing to work and give to those who will not."*

In a similar sentiment, Thomas Jefferson said,

> *"I place economy among the first and most important virtues and public debt as the greatest of dangers. To preserve our independence, we must not let our rulers load us with perpetual debt."*

This concept of taking from the public treasury (taking money from Peter to give to Paul) is what we today call *"Redistribution of Wealth,"* which digresses into Socialism and ultimately financially collapses a nation, plunging it into chaos, anarchy, and Communism. That is exactly what the Financial Elite are trying to do to America and all the world's sovereign nations. Their goal is to collapse America to birth their New World Order. Please pay attention; we are on a slippery slope. Obama, with his (redistribution of wealth), amassed more debt than the 43 Presidents, which preceded him. As I write this, the national debt is a staggering $26 trillion, which doesn't even count the unfunded entitlements. America teeters on the brink of financial collapse, but as you will soon learn, God has given America a second chance. The best is yet to come.

Under President Trump, we are seeing the early stages of an economic recovery. In another chapter, we will examine how Trump's policies all relate to restoring the 12 foundation stones that made America Great in the first place. So, our economic recovery is not a complicated matter requiring egghead economists to explain it to us. All we must do is look at our 12 Foundation Stones and see where they have been undermined, perverted, or removed and restore them to their original condition.

We also need to look at how the Constitution has been perverted to give control of our government to the special interest Financial Elites. Now, I have a question to ask you. Have you read the Constitution? For those who say yes, I have a big surprise for you; that beautifully succinct document written by our Framers is no longer our Constitution. That beautiful document has been perverted by a judicial system gone amuck, which legislates from the bench and by legislators who pass legislation they never bothered to read. These actions undermine the Constitution and have systematically stripped power from the States and the People and transferred it to an all-powerful Federal Government, which is the exact opposite of what our Framers intended. One hundred fifteen years of tampering has ballooned the Constitution into a 2,738-page book. There is a way we can get back control of our government, which is the subject of a later chapter in this book.

America: God's Nation of Destiny!

There once was a nation of destiny
A nation dedicated to God
A nation founded on liberty
A nation which embraced the world's refugees
A nation most glorious to see

People the world over flocked to its shores
All were welcome, and none were forlorn
Their hopes and dreams they brought with them
The promise of a better land

A land where men could raise their families
A land where they could worship as they pleased
A land of freedom and liberty
A land most glorious to see

Then came men from foreign shores
The old oppressions to restore
Moneylenders to enslave
And bind the people with invisible chains

A decision the people have to make
The fate of the world was at stake
Submit or fight and restore liberty

Putting It All Together: America's founding principles, as depicted on the Plymouth Monument, have been undermined by the Financial Elite in an effort to collapse it. They control the global monetary system and use their vast wealth to buy media outlets, endow universities, control corporate and political leaders. Through tax-exempt 501c's, they even control our pulpits. What this means is that the Financial Elite have effectively hijacked.

The Four Centers of Power:
Monetary, Political, Intellectual, and Religious

These are the basics of any civilized society. Undermine them, and society will collapse from within. I should note that what they are doing to America, they are doing to all the world's sovereign nations so they can birth their *"New World Order."* In addition to the founding principles inscribed on the Plymouth Monument, America's greatness is underpinned by our Patriotism, Christian, and Family Values. Undermine these core values, and the nation becomes divided, and a nation divided cannot stand!

The Economic Component of America's Greatness!

I have another question for you. Exactly how it is that America, the world's youngest superpower, came to prominence? Oh, not another history lesson. Sorry, but if we know history, it can often keep us from making the same mistakes over and over. In this case, it will show us why our fair-trade agreements, as they are falsely depicted, are a major cause of America's debt crisis and why President Trump is renegotiating them, so they are, as he says, *"reciprocal."* Congressman Duncan Hunter (R-CA), in an interview with Human Events, December 4, 2006, told us the truth about America's fair-trade policies when he said,

> *"We practiced what I call 'Losing Trade'—deliberately losing trade— over the last 50 years..."*

It is no accident that ever since we opened trade with China, the U.S. Economy has contracted while China's economy has skyrocketed. Our economic contraction has been caused by intentionally losing free trade agreements intended to gut U.S. manufacturing capability, destroy our balance of trade (the basis of wealth), drain the wealth from America, and redistribute the wealth to China and other emerging economies. This is happening because the Financial Elites see a vibrant U.S. economy as an insurmountable obstacle to establishing their long dreamt New World Order. America must fall that China may arise, and the New World Order can be birthed. The Financial Elite introduced Chinese Free Trade to the world under President Carter. Its primary purpose was to bankrupt the U.S. through intentionally losing trade deals!

Intentionally Losing Trade Agreements Are Intended to Gut U.S. Manufacturing and Drive Us into Bankruptcy!

It took over 200 years to accumulate a $660 billion national debt. All of a sudden, thanks to intentionally losing free trade agreements, it has skyrocketed to $26 trillion as of July 2020.

What Better Way to Collapse the U.S. Economy?

National Debt by U.S President				
President	Start Date	National Debt	End Date	Nation Debt
Carter	1/20/77	660 Billion	1/20/81	997 Billion
Reagan	1/20/81	1.029 Trillion	1/20/89	2.684 Trillion
Bush Sr.	1/20/89	2.953 Trillion	1/20/93	4.117 Trillion
Clinton	1/20/93	4.536 Trillion	1/20/01	5.662 Trillion
Bush Jr.	12/31/01	5.934 Trillion	1/20/09	10.700 Trillion
Obama	1/20/09	12.311 Trillion	1/20/2017	19.500 Trillion

America on the Eve of Greatness: Let's take a journey back in time and see where all this started. The year is 1869, and the Transcontinental Railroad is completed! America becomes the first nation in the history of the world to fully exploit its economic potential by connecting the country from North to South, from East to West, from border to border, and from coast to coast. The moment the last spike was driven, signaling the railroad's completion, the U.S. became the greatest threat *"The British Free Trade System"* would ever experience. Having developed a domestic policy of tariff protection and transporting goods from coast to coast, America was free from exploitation by the British Free Trade System. It was poised to experience the most significant economic growth in the history of the world. *"The American System"* was launched, and it would soon be embraced by a world eager to escape the slavery of the British.

The American System of Economics!

The year is 1876, and the United States is hosting the U.S. Centennial Celebration exhibiting the marvels of American technology! America's high tariffs and technological innovations had made America the world's youngest and most prosperous nation. President Trump understands the power of tariffs to protect U.S. domestic markets, create fair trade agreements, and stoke the U.S. economic engine! He is reversing our decades-old policies of intentionally losing trade policies imposed on us by every President since Carter to Obama!

1876: The Civil War is over, and Henry C. Carry has organized The United States Centennial Celebration. The world is invited to witness the technological marvels of human ingenuity and see how America, the youngest nation in the world, had become the most prosperous. Nine million visitors attend, including official foreign delegations of scientists, engineers, industrialists, and economists. They saw the potential for uplifting the human condition, such as had never been seen before. It was all attributable to *"The American System of Economics,"* which prized human creativity as the key to material wealth, as opposed to control of natural resources. It imposed high tariffs as a form of protectionism necessary to allow economic development to flourish in opposition to the British Free Trade System.

Change the name from British Free Trade to Chinese Free Trade, and you can see that we have gone full circle, and the Financial Elite are once again up to their old tricks, and America is their primary target. Perhaps now you can see why President Trump has imposed tariffs on Chinese goods! Seeing America's success, the world realized that they could emulate the American System, escape from the British Free Trade System's oppression, and transform their national economies. With that realization, American technology was exported worldwide, and the world held the promise of a better tomorrow.

In Russia: The Russian Transportation Minister imposed a system of high tariffs and worked with American engineers to construct a Trans-Siberian rail system modeled after the American Transcontinental rail system.

By 1890, there were plans for a Bering Strait bridge to connect by rail to America.

In France: Tariffs were also imposed, and plans were made to develop the Nile River area, and perhaps most important was a plan to connect to the Russian Trans- Siberian project.

In Germany: German Chancellor Otto Von Bismarck wholeheartedly embraced the American System and transformed Germany into Europe's leading industrial power. He also began plans to connect to the Russian Trans-Siberian rail system and develop a rail line from Berlin to Baghdad.

The world was changing. Instead of fighting over natural resources, nations were cooperating in developing rail systems to connect the four corners of the earth. The world saw the promise of the American System to *"elevate while equalizing the condition of man throughout the world."* The future held the promise of an era of prosperity and peace as nations joined together in cooperation and mutual benefit. Once completed, the rail systems network promised a cheap, efficient way to transport goods worldwide and significantly diminished the world's dependency on maritime shipping.

While the rest of the world rejoiced at the prospects for the future, the powers behind the British Empire laid plans to make certain that no such future would ever be realized. The world's dependency on naval power had to be maintained, and nations couldn't be allowed to develop their technological potential. Should such plans ever be realized, it would mean the demise of the British Empire's stranglehold on world resources, labor, and commerce and with it the end of their ability to pillage the wealth of other nations. There was only one hope for the British. It was risky, but they were desperate. They would orchestrate WWI.

The True Cause of WWI

WWI was to maintain England's dominance of trade by sea from the threat of a transcontinental rail system connecting the four corners of the globe. On June 14, 1914, the heir to the Austro-Hungarian throne, Archduke Ferdinand, was assassinated. As history accounts, it started World War I, but few people realize that the groundwork for the war had been in the making for over twenty years, ever since plans were announced in 1890 to build a Trans-Siberian Rail System.

The American Economic System held the hope of a better world for all, but that hope threatened England, *"The Empire on which the sun never set, the Founders of Globalism."* Henry C. Carey, the Economic Adviser to Abraham Lincoln, had this to say about the American Economic System and its hope of making the world a better, more peaceful, and more prosperous place,

> *"Two systems are before the world. One is the English System; the other we may be proud to call the American System. The only one ever devised the tendency of which was that of elevating while equalizing the condition of man throughout the world...."*

The American System was based on the belief that the single *"most important resource is human creativity, which it saw as the basis of material wealth."* Thus, the American System did not struggle to control resources, as did the British System. Instead, it sought to encourage creativity as the basis of technological advancements, which can enrich the nation, which invents the technology while simultaneously raising the standard of living for the country which embraces the technology. Thus, unlike the British System, which oppresses people, the American System is seen as using technology to elevate the standard of living for all.

The key to allowing a nation to withstand the cheap goods of the British Free Trade System was to *"impose high tariffs"* as a form of domestic protection that protects wages while allowing for the development of manufacturing capability and long-term infrastructure projects, all of which led to economic stability and a higher standard of living. That is the exact opposite of what our last several Administrations have done. Along comes President Trump, the *"Disruptor,"* the *"Billionaire Businessman,"* and common sense reemerges.

Trump's Policies Are Reinventing the American Economic System, and the U.S. Economy Is Once Again Flourishing!

The Failed Policies of the Past: Read this next quote and ask yourself if this isn't exactly what has happened to the American worker since Chinese Free Trade was implemented under President Carter. Actually, it started when the Financial Elite took over the printing of our currency in 1913, but that is a story for the next chapter.

> *"We are opposed to British political economy...Free Trade shaves down (the workingman's labor first, and then scales down his pay by rewarding him in a worthless and depreciated State currency"* (Henry C. Carey, Economic Adviser to Abraham Lincoln).

Would you like some proof that tariffs work, that President Trump's policies are working? If so, then read on. On September 5, 1901, President McKinley made a speech at the Pan-American Conference in Buffalo to 50,000 North and South Americans espousing the American plan's virtues. The quote below is from that speech.

> *"Thirty years of protection have brought us to the 1st rank in agriculture, mining, and manufacturing development. We lead all nations in these three great departments of industry. We have outstripped even the United Kingdom, which had century's head start on us.....31 years the protective tariff policy of the Republicans has by any test, measured by any standard vindicated itself."*

I will touch on this briefly in closing this chapter because this topic overlaps with the next chapter. I want to leave you with an idea of just how deeply the Financial Elite have infiltrated our system of government. There truly is a Deep State Shadow Government, and they have in truth hijacked both political parties. Congressman Ron Paul has this to say on the subject,

> *"I think there are 25,000 individuals that have used offices of powers, and they are in our Universities, and they are in our Congresses,*

and they believe in One World Government. And if you believe in One World Government, then you are talking about undermining National Sovereignty that you could well call a Dictatorship-and those plans are there" (Congressman Ron Paul at an event near Austin Texas on August 30, 2003).

I want to leave you with a few quick quotes to ponder. In the Financial Elite, we face an enemy more dangerous than the Nazis in WWII because they have infiltrated virtually every aspect of our society. They use their vast wealth to buy power and influence and systematically undermine the core values we have discussed in this chapter, particularly our patriotism, Christian, and family values, because they know they constitute the glue that holds our society together. You will notice that several of the quotes below are from Communist Leaders. That is because the Financial Elite are Communist. Their version of a utopian society is a highbred Capitalist/Communist Dictatorship with no middle class and no inalienable rights. That is slavery without chains, which is what Communism is!

Undermining Our Core Values:

"America is like a healthy body, and its resistance is — its patriotism, its morality, and its spiritual life. If we can undermine these three areas, America will collapse from within" (Russian Leader Joseph Stalin).

Academia as a Propaganda Tool:

"Give me four years to teach children, and the seed I have sown will never be uprooted" (Vladimir Lenin, founder of Soviet Union).

Why the Financial Elites Propaganda Machine Is So Powerful:

"The organized minority will beat the disorganized majority every time" (Vladimir Lenin, founder of the Soviet Union).

The Danger of International Bankers:

> *"The one aim of these financiers is world control by the creation of inextinguishable debt"* (Henry Ford, Industrialist).

> *"... The super-national sovereignty of an intellectual elite and world bankers is surely preferable to the National Auto-determination practiced in past centuries"* (David Rockefeller Council Foreign Relations).

The Gradual Assault on Our Sovereignty:

> *"The New World Order will be built...an end-run on national sovereignty, eroding it piece by piece will accomplish much more than the old-fashioned frontal assault"* (Council on Foreign Relations Journal 1974, P558).

How Communism Creeps Into Society and Destroys It:

> *"Communism succeeds because most people who support Communist causes are not Communists. The Useful Idiots, as Lenin called them, give Communism an air of legitimacy it would never have if it were identified with Communist and Communism"* (Whittaker Chambers).

> Russian leader Vladimir Lenin put it this way, *"We can't expect the American people to jump from Capitalism to Communism, but we can assist their elected leaders in giving them small doses of Socialism until they wake up one day to find that they have Communism."*

These quotes reflect a Global Shadow Government intent on destroying America and all sovereign nations to birth their New World Order Dictatorship.

God's Secret Bible Code Revealed!

As at the beginning so, at the ending
Life's answers are woven in the fabric of time

The knowledge you seek, your ancestors do keep
Their victories and losses reveal the divine
To those who are obedient the path they shall find

One came before you to show you the way
His virtue the key to unlocking the way
Walk-in his footsteps and go not astray
Endure to the end and righteousness will enter in

No enemy will prevail against you
The promise land shall be before you
Peace and prosperity shall prevail in the land

CHAPTER 2

Unmasking the Deep State Global Agenda!

WHAT YOU WILL LEARN IN THIS CHAPTER

- Who Are the Financial Elite and How Did They Originate?

- How Did the Financial Elite Get Control of the Global Monetary System?

- The U.S. Declared Bankruptcy in 1933: How That Event Birthed the Deep State!

- Wars for Profit: What They Have Done to Our Country!

- The Plan to End All Sovereign Nations and Establish 10 Servile Trading Blocs!

- Comments From the Rich and Powerful.

Who Are the Financial Elite and How Did They Originate?

I am about to launch an all-out attack on the most powerful family in the world. Their estimated net worth is over $500 trillion, which is more than ½ the world's total wealth. As you can imagine that much money buys secrecy and makes their crimes go away. So, it is difficult to validate their actual wealth or prove their many crimes. No matter how much evidence points to their wrongdoing, there is an army of bought and paid for news outlets and politicians to cover their tracks. One way or another, their problems are made to go away, and their skeletons are kept in the closet. When accused of anything, they deny, deny, and deny. They either slander their accusers or call them conspiracy theorists. Blackmail, bribery, extortion, and murder on an unimaginable scale are necessary if one wants to be the master of the world.

In the book *Confessions of an Economic Hit Man* (2005), author John Perkins relates how the Financial Elite employed him and men like him to collapse small resource-rich countries in order to get control of their natural resources. In the preface of the book, Perkins says,

> "Economic hit men (EHMs) are highly paid professionals who cheat countries around the globe out of trillions of dollars. They funnel money from the World Bank, U.S. Agency for International Development, and other foreign "aid" organizations into the coffers of giant corporations and the pockets of a few wealthy families who control the planet's natural resources. Their tools include fraudulent financial reports, rigged elections, payoffs, extortion, sex, and murder. They play a game as old as empire, but one that has taken on new and terrifying dimensions during this time of globalization. I should know I am an EHM."

Hopefully, this sets the stage for our journey into the dark recesses of global domination and the kind of things one must be willing to do if one wants to be the master of the world. Because the family I am about to profile is so powerful and shrouded in such secrecy, I am not going to come at them straight on. Instead, I will tell you some stories, including a couple of fairytales and layout some critical global events, and then let you decide if what you read is fact or just a work of fiction. Then I will follow up with several quotes from people who themselves are in positions of power and influence and see if what they say convinces you that these men are indeed the masters of the world, and they are truly evil. I will lay out the events and let you decide what they mean. Instead of saying that the man who wanted to be the master of the world committed any specific crime, I will lay out the historical events and let you draw your own conclusions.

Before this chapter is over, things will get pretty intense because we will be looking at the greatest crimes in all history, so I want to ease into things by telling you a couple of fairytales. By the way, there is much symbolism hidden in our little story. See if you can figure it out. Maybe you can even figure who the central character is before I tell you.

The Pauper's Wish

There once was a poor but ambitious man who would often fanaticize that he was rich and powerful. One night he had a dream in which a mysterious figure, which he described as a *"Wizard,"* came to him in a soft voice and whispered, *"That which you desire can be yours."*

The Wizard identified himself as *"The ancient of days – the bringer of light – the all-knowing eye."* He continued, *"I once offered the Judean what I now offer you, and he foolishly refused me and ended up hated and hung on a cross. Are you wiser than He? Will you have dominion over all the earth and all that dwell therein?"* The Wizard said, *"I am called away for there is a war in heaven, but think about what you truly want, and I will revisit you tomorrow in the midnight hour."*

That night as the man laid with his head on his pillow, the clock struck 12 and, he heard the wizard whisper. Faintly at first, then louder and louder till he thought his head would burst. He heard these words. *"What do you truly want, and how much is it worth to you?"* The man's thoughts drifted away to faraway places and future times, and then he replied, *"I want that! My descendants and I shall rule the earth, and Kings shall bow before us!"*

At that moment, the Wizard appeared over his bed and told him a story. He said: *"As God told Abraham that his descendants would be as the sands of the sea and be a blessing to all the earth, I, this day, offer you and all your descendants' dominion over all the earth and all that dwell therein."* "Excellent," the man thought, as his mind pondered what would be required to be master of all the world. Then came his response, *"Whatever is required, I will do it!"*

The Wizard told the man, *"I shall give you a cloak of invisibility that you may walk among the councils of men and know their plans in advance, that you may stifle their every hope, dream, and aspiration. They will marvel at you because you will always be one step ahead of them. They shall think you are a genius and fear to defy you. And any that dare will suffer greatly for it. I shall give you a magic wand with which you can control the affairs of men. And I shall give to the magical incantations that you may blind the eyes of men and fog their minds that they may see not the truth and may do those things which are inconvenient. In so doing, you shall bind them in chains of their own making, and they shall be none the wiser for it. All men shall give you a portion of all that they earn as the fruit of their labor, and if it is not enough, I shall give to the power to take all that they have. I shall give to thee a potion that will turn man against man, nation against nation that you may rule them with an iron fist. You shall say to the leaders of the nation's go and conquer in my name, and so it will be done. Their kings in their folly shall seek your council thinking you to be wise, not knowing it is you who cause the very problems they seek to solve. In this manner, you shall bring chaos upon humankind so that they surrender to you. You shall be the most powerful man on the earth, and all I ask for granting all this is that as you ask that men bow before you, you bow before me."*

Instantly the man replied, *"Of course, my Lord,"* and bowed down. There came a searing deep within the man's soul, and at that instant, the man's wish was granted. The man was so jubilant at the thought of what was to come that he gave no thought to the searing deep within.

The next morning, he arose to a knock on his door. It was the executor of the estate of his only wealthy relative. It seemed he had died at the stroke of midnight last night, and he had bequeathed his estate, vast holding, and money counting business to him. As the Wizard had promised, he was rich. The man feigned grief, but inside he was jumping with joy. Instantly his thoughts wandered, and he said to himself, *"but what of the power to make men bow before me?"*

The next night the man had another dream. This time he had a burning sensation and a sense of dread deep down in his soul? He thought to himself: *"How could this be for I am rich?"* The man cried out, and again the mysterious Wizard appeared, but this time his voice was harsh and frightening. *He shouted, "Why do you bother me? I gave you what you asked, did I not?"* The man trembled and hesitated, and in a sheepish voice, he mumbled these words, *"My Lord, why did I have such a disturbing dream? Why do I dream of a place that torments me? What does it mean?"* With that, the Wizard turned his back and then vanished into thin air, but these words lingered in the air! *"Did you not agree to bow before me as men bow before you? As you are to have a kingdom on earth and men are to bow before you and tremble in fear of your wrath, so shall you bow before me and kneel at my feet and tremble before me."*

THE END

So How Did the Man Become the Master of All the Earth?

The Genesis of the Global Network of Central Banks: Well, let's find out. Our story begins in Europe during the 100 Year War between France and England. The British treasury is empty, and without money to fund the war effort, France will defeat England, and the empire will fall. As the story goes in desperation, the King of England calls on the Rothschild's (the wealthiest family in England) and asks them for a loan. Opportunity knocks, and a plan is hatched. Barron Rothschild will loan the King all the money he needs, but there is a condition. The Barron will subsequently control the Bank of England and print its currency! The empire will be saved but at what cost?

Our true-life story has many parallels to another fairytale, *Rumpelstiltskin*. The story of Rumpelstiltskin has an interesting twist, and so does our true-life story. The fairytale goes like this: A miller had a beautiful daughter, and he bragged to the King that she could spin straw into gold. The King had the girl put in a room full of straw and told her that she would surely die if the straw were not spun into gold in the morning. She lamented; the miracle of miracles along came a little man to the maiden's rescue, and he spun the straw into gold.

For three nights, the King had the girl spin straw into gold, but on the 3rd night, the little man made a demand of the maiden. He knew the King had promised to marry her, so having no children, he demanded that he be given her 1st child when she was Queen. With her life depending on his help, she agreed (just like the King of England, having no choice, agreed to turn over control of the Bank of England to Barron Rothschild).

A year passed, and the maiden now Queen has a child, and the little man demands the child as payment. The Queen pleaded with the little man not to take her child, and he told her that if she could tell him his name within three days, she could keep her child. The Queen sent spies into the land, and she found out the little man's name, and she lived happily ever after.

But that is where our fairytale and our real-life story diverge. You see, in our real-life story, the King of England wasn't as lucky as the Queen in the fairytale, or should I say the King's subjects weren't so fortunate. They didn't live happily ever after because the King's deal with Baron Rothschild had indentured them and their future generations.

How Did the Financial Elite Get Control of the Global Monetary System?

Rothschild's deal with the King of England made him realize that it was far more profitable to loan money to governments than individuals. By conditioning the loan of money to governments on printing their currency, the Rothschild's had literally mastered the art of alchemy! The simple act of printing fiat currency backed by nothing would generate an interest charge that would directly create wealth out of thin air! The best part was that the interest charges just keep accruing potentially forever. Today, through their control of the World Bank, billions of people labor and give a portion of their earnings to the Rothschild's. The Rothschild's truly own the world, and we are their indentured slaves.

But wait, it gets better, or should I say worse. The Wizard had indeed given the Rothschild's a magic wand which they could wave and cause economic crashes any time they pleased. By controlling, 1) the issuance of currency, 2) the money supply, and 3) the interest rates, the Rothschild's could create an unending cycle of economic crashes that would allow them to crash the economy of any country whenever they desired. In so doing, they could steal the life savings of hardworking men and women the world over, making them unknowingly slaves without chains forever in debt and oppressed by a banking system that controlled them from the cradle to the grave! The graphic explains just how this magic is performed.

If the Financial Elite want to cause an economic crash, here is what they do. They increase the money supply, so there is plenty of money available to borrow. Then they lower the interest rate, so it is cheap to borrow, then drive investors toward a specific market, stocks, bonds, or real estate (whatever they want). This increased demand drives up the price and causes a buying frenzy, which pushes the prices ever higher. Then at a time and manner of their choosing, they dry up the credit, which crashes the market. So, the

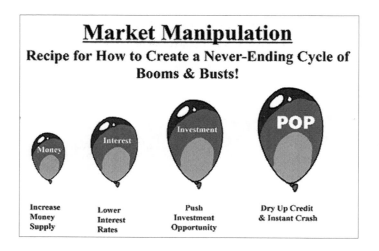

Financial Elite make money in three ways: 1) They make money off their loans. 2) They own the assets that are the target of the market boom, so they make money selling them at inflated prices. 3) When the market crashes, they buy back their assets for pennies on the dollar. The lucky investors who get in early and manage to get out before the crash make money, but the vast majority of people see their life's savings devastated by such events. The 1929 Great Depression and 2008 financial collapse are prime examples of this heinous crime against humanity. I want you to grasp the gravity of what I just said, so let me quickly tell you how they pulled off one of the biggest white-collar crimes in history and, in the process, ruined the lives of millions of people.

1929 - The Great Depression: The Industrial Revolution was in full swing. The decade leading up to the crash was referred to as the roaring twenties. The auto industry was booming, the radio had just been invented, and people were anxious to invest in these and other modern marvels. Opportunity knocks, J.P. Morgan, and other front men for the Rothschild's would create a stock market boom by loaning people money at low-interest rates and allowing them to buy stocks on margin with just 10% down. It was like taking candy from a baby. People jumped at the opportunity, and the stock market went up and up and up till it didn't. Why, you ask, did it stop going up? Because the money manipulating Financial Elite sprung their trap. They colluded to dry up the credit market and crash the stock market. On a single day, they called all their margin loans in. Having put only 10% down and with the credit dried up, people defaulted on their loans, and the markets crashed. The wizards had just pulled off the greatest heist in world history!

The Financial Elite got richer, and the masses were destitute. Here's how it worked; the Financial Elite had funded the Industrial Revolution, so they held major stock positions in virtually every company traded on the stock exchange. When the market peaked, they sold, which made them a fortune. Of course, the stocks plummeted. When they hit bottom, they repurchased their stock for pennies on the dollar, but wait; it gets better. With the money they made, they were able to get the controlling interest of most of the company's traded on the stock market.

So, the outcome of the stock market crash was that the common man lost his investment. But that was just the beginning of their woes. Entire companies went out of business, and with the credit market intentionally dried up, global commerce came to a screeching halt. The world was plunged into a depression that lasted twelve long years. The people suffered, but the Financial Elite made out like bandits. They already owned the banks, but they now owned the corporations as the result of the stock market crash. Their grip on the U.S. economy was complete. The worst is yet to come, but that will have to wait for a second while I tell you about the plight of the average American during the Great Depression. You need to hear this, so you understand just how evil these men are.

By 1932 the depression was in its 4th year, and no matter what the government did, it didn't seem to work. Over ten million people, approximately 20% of the population, were unemployed and locked in the grips of depression, despair, gloom, and the inevitable loss of self-esteem, which besets a person when they have no hope, and their nightly companion is fear of starvation. No matter where you turned, it was bleak. There was not only an army of unemployed, but there was also an army of underemployed, as nationwide the combined effects of unemployment and involuntary part-time employment left 50% of the American workforce unutilized for a decade.

I found this quote by Frank Walker, President of the National Emergency Council (1934), to be especially heart rendering.

> *"I saw old friends of mine – men I had gone to school with – digging ditches and laying sewer pipe. They were wearing their regular business suits as they worked because they couldn't afford overalls and rubber boots. If I ever thought 'there but for the grace of God go I' it was right then."*

I remind you that this misery was no accident. It was inflicted on the American people by the Rothschild Fed.

Comments From the Rich and Powerful

Though these men will not be indicted in a court of law, hopefully, we can indict them in the court of public opinion, and hopefully, we can learn from what they did and guard against their evil in the future. The worst is yet to come, but before we go there, let's see what the people of the time had to say about the Great Depression and the men who intentionally caused it.

> *"…This is an era of misery, and for the conditions that caused that misery, the Fed is fully liable. This is an era of financed crime, and in the financing of crime the Fed does not play the part of a disinterested spectator"* (Congressman Louis T McFadden).

The Great Depression would never have happened had it not been for the traitorous actions of President Woodrow Wilson. His election campaign was funded by Rothschild agents in America, who wanted to establish the Federal Reserve Bank (the Rothschild Central Bank). Wilson promised the American people there would be no Central Bank under his presidency (he lied!) He later made the following confession,

> *"We are no longer a government by free opinion, no longer a government by conviction and the vote of the majority, but a government by the opinion and duress of a small group of dominant men. Our great*

industrial nation is controlled by its system of credit. Our system of credit is privately centered. The growth of the nation, therefore, and all our activities are in the hands of a few men. Who necessarily by very reason of their own limitations chill and check and destroy genuine economic freedom. We have become one of the worst ruled, one of the most completely controlled and dominated governments in the civilized world" (President Woodrow Wilson – the traitor who imposed the Fed on America).

Believing that the Federal Reserve had brought the Great Depression on the American people on purpose, Congressman Louis McFadden, a longtime opponent of the banking cartels, began bringing impeachment proceedings against the Federal Reserve Board saying of the crash and depression,

"It was a carefully contrived occurrence. International bankers sought to bring about a condition of despair so that they might emerge the rulers of us all."

By the way, this is almost exactly what President Kennedy said just before he was assassinated shortly after signing executive order #11110 to disband the Fed.

"There is a plot in this country to enslave every man, woman, and child. Before I leave this high and noble office, I intend to expose this plot" (President John F. Kennedy).

In the book *FDR My Exploited Father-In-Law* (1967), Author Curtis Dall said of the depression,

"It was the calculated 'shearing' of the public by the World-Money powers, triggered by the planned sudden shortage of call money in the New York Market."

What follows are quotations from several speeches made on the Floor of the House of Representatives by the Honorable Louis T. McFadden of Pennsylvania.

"Mr. Chairman, we have in this Country one of the most corrupt institutions the world has ever known. I refer to the Federal Reserve Board and the Federal Reserve Banks, hereafter called the Fed..."

"This evil institution has impoverished and ruined the people of these United States, has bankrupted itself, and has practically bankrupted our government. It has done this through the defects of the law under which it operates, through the maladministration of that law by the Fed, and through the corrupt practices of the moneyed vultures who control it."

"Some people think that the Federal Reserve Banks are United States Government institutions. They are private monopolies which prey upon the people of these United States for the benefit of themselves and their foreign customers; foreign and domestic speculators and swindlers; and rich and predatory money lenders. In that dark crew of financial pirates, there are those who would cut a man's throat to get a dollar out of his pocket; there are those who send money into states to buy votes to control our legislatures; there are those who maintain international propaganda for the purpose of deceiving us into granting of new concessions which will permit them to cover up their past misdeeds and set again in motion their gigantic train of crime."

"These twelve private credit monopolies were deceitfully and disloyally foisted upon this country by the bankers who came here from Europe and repaid us our hospitality by undermining our American institutions. Those bankers took money out of this country to finance Japan in a war against Russia. They created a reign of terror in Russia with our money in order to help that war along. They financed Trotsky's passage from New York to Russia so that he might assist in the destruction of the Russian Empire. They fomented and instigated the Russian Revolution and placed a large fund of American dollars at Trotsky's disposal in one of their branch banks in Sweden so that through him, Russian homes might be thoroughly broken up

and Russian children flung far and wide from their natural pro-
tectors. They have since begun breaking up American homes and the
dispersal of American children. "Mr. Chairman, there should be no
partisanship in matters concerning banking and currency affairs in
this Country, and I do not speak with any."

Congressman Louis McFadden said that in 1913 when the Federal Reserve Act was passed,

"A world banking system was being set up here…a super-state con-
trolled by international bankers…acting together to enslave the
world for its pleasure. The Fed has usurped the government."

And Congressman Charles Lindberg added,

"Under the 'Federal Reserve Act, panics are scientifically created. The
present panic is the first scientifically created one, worked out as we
figure a mathematical equation."

It had taken 137 years, but in 1913, with the signing of the Federal Reserve Act, the likes of J.D. Rockefeller, J.P. Morgan, Paul Warburg, and Barron Rothschild had managed to seize control of the nation's money supply and could proceed unabated with their plan for economic enslavement! During the great depression, President Franklin Roosevelt warned us saying,

"The real truth of the matter is that a financial element in the large
centers has owned the government since the days of Andrew Jackson."

This next quote is particularly enlightening because it is from the director of the bank of England, the very evil institution we have been talking about. So, you are about to hear the truth, as they say, from the horse's mouth. As the director of the Bank of England, Baron Josiah Stamp was one of the wealthiest men in England, and he was undoubtedly in a position to know the evil that the bankers do. Here is what he said about the Bank of England controlled by the Rothschild's.

"Banking was conceived in iniquity and was born in sin. The bankers own the earth. Take it away from them, but leave them the power to create money, and with the flick of the pen, they will create enough deposits to buy it back again. However, take away from them the power to create money, and all the great fortunes like mine will disappear and they ought to disappear, for this would be a happier and better world to live in. But, if you wish to remain the slaves of bankers and pay the cost of your own slavery, let them continue to create money" (1st Baron Josiah Stamp, Director of the Bank of England).

The Financial Elite Will Fall! They Are Not Invincible!

So, with this quote from Josiah Stamp, we know how to utterly destroy the Financial Elite and their minions implanted in the world's governments and institutions! We take away their ability to print money. Before you finish this book, you will know precisely how we do that. Or, as President Trump might say, *"WE DRAIN THE SWAMP!"* I don't care how rich or powerful they are; sunlight is a great disinfectant!

I ask your indulgence a little longer on the subject of the Fed. I want to give you some quotes from our Founding Fathers. This is important because, in large part, our Founders fled England to escape this same corrupt banking system, so, from the days of our founding, they warned us what would happen to our freedom if we ever allowed the banks to take over the issuance of our currency.

Note: I feel we may soon have an opportunity to finally do what President Kennedy died trying to do, which is to get out from under the oppression of the Rothschild Central Bank (the Fed). We will discuss how we do that a little later! Now to the words of our Founding Fathers:

"History records that the money changers have used every form of abuse, intrigue, deceit, and violent means possible to maintain their control over governments by controlling money and its issuance" (James Madison, 4th President of the United States).

"We can either have democracy in this country or we can have great wealth concentrated in the hands of a few, but we can't have both" (Louis Brandeis, Supreme Court Justice).

"The Central Bank is an institution of the deadliest hostility existing against the principles and form of our Constitution…if the American people allow private banks to control the issuance of the currency, first by inflation and then by devaluation the banks and corporations that will grow up around them will deprive the people of all their property until their children wake up homeless on the continent their fathers conquered" (President Thomas Jefferson).

Isn't this precisely what is happening? The following graphic shows how our wealth and property are being insidiously devalued and stripped away.

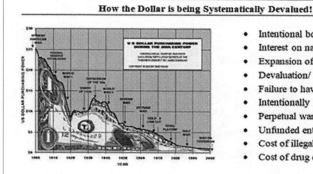

"There are two way to conquer and enslave a nation. One is by the sword, the other is by debt" (President John Adams).

"The government should create, issue, and circulate all currency. Creating and issuing money is a supreme prerogative of government and its greatest creative opportunity. Adopting these principles will save the taxpayer immense sums of interest and money will cease to be the master and become the servant of humanity" (President Abraham Lincoln).

"A wise and frugal government, which shall leave men free to regulate their own pursuits of industry and improvement and shall not take from the mouth of labor the bread it has earned – this is the sum of good government" (Thomas Jefferson).

"I sincerely believe...that banking establishments are more dangerous than standing armies, and that the principle of spending money to be paid by posterity under the name of funding is but swindling futurity on a large scale" (Thomas Jefferson to John Taylor, 1816).

"Since I entered politics, I have chiefly had men's views confided to me privately. Some of the biggest men in the United States, in the fields of government and manufacturing. They know there is a power somewhere, so organized, so subtle, so watchful, so interlocked. So complete, so perverse, that they better not speak above their breath when they speak in condemnation of it" (President Woodrow Wilson).

The U.S. Declared Bankruptcy in 1933: How That Event Birthed the Deep State!

I told you that we weren't done, that things would get worse. Buckle up because what I am about to expose will shock you and explain once and for all how a Shadow Government controls the U.S. and, in the same way, the entire world. Today all but three countries in the world have been inflicted by a Rothschild Central Bank, which means that just like America, the halls of their governments have been infiltrated. This is what President Trump calls the *"Deep State"* and what I call *"The Rothschild Global Shadow Government,"* which is the true *"Masters of the World."*

The end game of the 1929 Great Depression was to drive the U.S. into bankruptcy so as the receivers of the bankruptcy (the Rothschild's) could orchestrate a coup of the U.S. Republic and put in its place a communist government. This allowed them to place Rothschild operatives in virtually every government agency so they could work from then till now to insidiously destroy America from within.

Why if the Pledge of Allegiance Says America Is a Republic Is It Routinely Referred to as a Democracy?

The Pledge of Allegiance:

> *"I pledge allegiance the flag of the United States of America and to the Republic for which it stands one nation under God indivisible with liberty and justice for all."*

The U.S. Declares Bankruptcy and Becomes a Democracy: A Socialist-Communist Order

> *"All United States Offices, officials and departments are now operating within a de facto status in name only under Emergency War Powers. With the Constitutional Republican form of government now dissolved, the receivers of the bankruptcy have adopted a new form of government for the United States. This new form of government is known as a Democracy, being an established Socialist-Communist order under a new government for America"* (United States Congressional Record, March 17, 1933, Vol. 33, Page H-1303).

At that moment, the Republic fell, and America was taken over from within by the Shadow Government. Both Houses of Congress became irrelevant, and the Fed and IMF controlled America! Let's fast forward to today and see where all this has taken us. Congressman Ron Paul says he believes that as the result of the U.S. bankruptcy in 1933, there are upwards of 25,000 people that have been embedded in our government and positions of influence. This is *"The Deep State Shadow Government,"* which Trump has pledged to expose so that *"We the People"* can reestablish our Constitutional Republic.

Our founding fathers called Democracy *"Mobocracy"* because instead of being based on the Constitution, it is based on majority rule controlled by those least willing or least able to work. **Translation:** Democracy is just another name for Socialism, which is just another name for Communism, which is just another name for slavery without chains!

Let's take a step back and see how the Rothschild's created the Deep State Shadow Government in the U.S. Rothschild agent Jacob Schiff was sent to America with orders to establish a banking network for the explicit purpose of gaining control of the United States Government. By the way, they do the same thing in every sovereign nation in the world because their master plan calls for the ending of all sovereign nations. We will get to that in a minute, but for now, let's look at their master plan for America.

The Rothschild's Master Plan:

- Gain control of America's monetary system in order to control the four centers of power: monetary, political, intellectual, and religious.

- Recruit men (who would for a price support the Rothschild agenda) and place them in high places in the Federal Government, the Congress, Supreme Court, and all Federal Agencies!

- Create racial, ethnic, and class strife to create division and tear the country apart from within!

- Create a movement to destroy religion, patriotism, morality, and the family!

- Buy media outlets to control public opinion!

- Endow universities to control their curriculum and steer them toward Socialist-Progressive ideologies.

- Create wars for profit: and fund both sides!

- ✓ **Done – Done – Done – Done - Done & Done! Mission Accomplished**

Wars for Profit: What They Have Done to Our Country!

This brings us to the topic of wars for profit. Referring to the story of the 100 Year War, the Rothschilds had learned more from loaning money to the King of England and taking control of the Bank of England (which represented the creation of the world's 1st Central Bank.) As I said, today, all but three nations in the world are repressed and indentured by a Rothschild Central Bank. They truly own the world! So how did that come about?

Based on their experience with England, the Rothschild's realized that if they could somehow bankrupt a nation as England had been bankrupted, they could take over the printing of their currency and indenture their people just like they had done in England. So how do you bankrupt a nation? We just learned how the Rothschild's bankrupted America in 1933, but they also realized that a prolonged war could bankrupt a nation as well.

But how do you get a nation to go to war, and then how do you drag the war out in order to drive the nation into unmanageable debt? It isn't as hard as you might think if you have enough money. You use your vast wealth to buy the influence of news outlets, politicians, and whoever else proves useful, and you ferment division (real or staged) between political, religious, economic, and ethnic factions. Then you create an event, a violent event, a *"false flag"* event, and then use your bought and paid for mouthpieces to agitate the situation, and the next thing you know, you have a war.

The quote below will give you insight into exactly how those in power orchestrate events and, yes, provoke wars. When contemplating such actions, we have to realize that in such instances, our political leaders are just pawns being manipulated by the Financial Elite who control the global monetary system. It is as I have said, he who controls the money controls the world, and I would add these are evil people!

> *"Naturally, the common people don't want war: Neither in Russia, nor England nor for that matter in Germany. That is understood. After all, it is the country's leaders who determine the policy, and it is always a simple matter to drag the people along, whether it is a democracy, or a fascist dictatorship, or a parliament, or a communist dictatorship. Voice or no voice, the people can always be brought to the bidding of the leaders. That is easy. All you have to do is tell them they are being attacked and denounce the peacemakers for lack of patriotism and exposing the country to danger. It works the same in any country"* (Reichsmarschall Hermann Goering at the Nuremberg Trials).

Having staged a false flag event and having used their political and news cronies to whip up support for the war, all that remains is to drag the war out as long as possible to maximize profits and inflict optimal damage on the economy. We have two real-life examples of how to do that in recent American history: The Vietnam War and, more recently, the Iraq War.

The Truth About Vietnam: The Vietnam War was intentionally drugged out for two reasons 1) To enrich the Financial Elite and 2) to drive the U.S. into debt. It was the Vietnam War that started America's economic debt spiral! For several years the war raged on, and our boys continued to be sent home in body bags, their flag-draped coffins to be greeted by grieving parents, wives, children, and other loved ones. But then one of the biggest scandals' in history broke onto the front pages of newspapers. The war was a scam! Our boys died for nothing! They were slaughtered in the rice patties of Vietnam so the Shadow Government could get rich and drive America deep into debt. I start this discussion with a quote from President Dwight Eisenhower:

> *"We must guard against the acquisition of unwarranted influence....
> by the military-industrial complex. The potential for the disastrous
> rise of misplaced power."*

It was only later in the closing months of the Vietnam War that the significances of Eisenhower's warning became clear. Here is what happened. Just before his assassination, Kennedy was taking steps to limit the CIA's authority, and he had ignored pressure from the military-industrial complex to commit additional troops to the war. But Johnson conspired with the CIA and the Financial Elite, and immediately following Kennedy's assassination, Johnson reversed Kennedy's policies and committed additional troops to the war, knowing full well we couldn't win. His actions benefited the Financial Elite and did gross injustice to the American people.

Classified documents named *The Pentagon Papers* obtained from a whistleblower disclosed that Eisenhower, Kennedy, and Johnson knew the Vietnam war couldn't be won. Yet, under Johnson, the war was escalated, and over 100,000 of our sons and daughters were sent to the jungles of Vietnam to be killed and maimed for nothing except pure greed! A government that will do that will do anything!

Once the scandal broke and the people found out what had been done, a protest broke out all across the country. Had it not been for the whistleblower, who knows how long the needless killing would have gone on! The Financial Elite and their willing pawns like Johnson are truly evil!

The Vietnam War could have been ended any time we chose. War is about logistics. What that means is no supplies, no war. The world's most acclaimed military strategist Sun Tzu, author of *The Art of War* (5th Century A.D.), says you never engage in a prolonged war because it drains national resources and destroys morale, but that was exactly what the Financial Elite wanted.

They could have ended the war whenever they wanted. Here's how. Our generals knew that the Ho Chi Minh Trail couldn't supply the Vietcong's war effort. They depended on the Haiphong Harbor for supplies. So, it was simple, close the harbor and end the war. Guess what? When President Nixon finally ended the war under pressure from U.S. protesters, he mined the harbor. No harbor, no supplies, no war. How simple!

The worse thing was that the war turned out to be based on a false flag event. Following President Kennedy's assassination, President Johnson needed a pretext for committing more troops to the war. Then came the now-infamous Gulf of Tonkin incident where U.S. Naval ships were supposedly under fire. This was Johnson's justification for committing more troops to the war. The only problem is that it turned out to be a hoax. It would take too long to prove what I am about to say, but all of our wars have been based on false flag events. WWI was the (Lusitania), which was carrying munitions, so it was a legitimate war target. This was long speculated but was proven when the shipwreck was found. Then there was WWII and the bombing of Pearl Harbor. It turns out that Roosevelt had an 8-point plan designed to provoke the Japanese into attacking us. He needed a target to give them, so he ordered the 7th fleet into Pearl Harbor, where it was a sitting duck. Then there were reports that Australian shore watchers spotted the Japanese fleet in rout and reported it, but it was ignored. Lastly, the U.S. had broken the Japanese code and had decipher machines, one of which had been sent to Pearl Harbor, but it was mysteriously lost in transit. Go figure! If you do a little research, you can confirm everything I just said. War is a business, and our soldiers, our loved ones, are expendable. It is as Henry Kissinger so famously said:

> *"Military men are dumb, stupid animals meant to be used as cannon fodder."*

Were it not for perpetual war, America would be a far different place. We wouldn't be teetering on the brink of financial collapse. We would have money for social programs, to rebuild our infrastructure, and much more. The next time our leaders tell us we have been attacked and have to go to war, we better think long and hard, and I hope we will remember all the times they have lied to us in the past.

The Iraq War: It's time to ask the unimaginable question, could 9/11 have been a false flag event? Yep! Could the Iraq War have been a war for profit or other political purposes? Yep! I urge you to watch the movie *Shock and Awe* (2017), directed by Rob Reiner and written by Joey Hartstone. It points out what any expert on the Middle East knows: there exist centuries-old hatreds between rival Muslim sects. That fact has underpinned U.S. Middle East policies for decades. That knowledge is why, for example, tyrants like Muammar al-Gaddafi in Libya and Saddam Hussein in Iraq were allowed to remain in power for so many years. U.S. leaders knew full well that if these strongmen were removed from power, these centuries-old revelries would result in bloody civil wars that would drag out for years and destabilize the entire Middle East. In my opinion, that knowledge is what prompted President Bush Jr. when announcing the Iraq War, to say that it would be a generational war lasting 30 years or more. This fact is clearly supported in the movie *Shock and Awe* (2017). The movie also supports the fact that:

- Because of these centuries-old hatreds, there would never have been any joint attack hatched between Osama bin Laden and Saddam Hussein.

- There were no weapons of mass destruction, just like in the instance of the Vietnam War, there was no Gulf of Tonkin incident. It was a hoax.

- Military assets were pulled from Iraq, where Osama was pinned down, allowing him to escape to a safe haven in Pakistan. Because to justify the war, the U.S. needed Osama on the loose as the face of terror where he posed an ongoing threat. That is why President Bush Jr. more than once refused the surrender of Osama.

- One last tidbit: We now know that the Iraq War's battle plan had been written a year before 9/11. Go figure!

"A crisis is an event that forces democracies to make decisions they wouldn't otherwise make" (Timothy Wirth, former U.S. Senator D-Colorado).

*"The interests behind the Bush administration, such as the CFR, the Trilateral Commission (*founded by Brzezinski for David Rocke-feller) *and the Bilderberg Group have prepared for and are now moving to implement open world dictatorship..."* (Dr. Johannes Koeppl, Former Official of the German Ministry for Defense, and advisor to NATO).

The Plan to End All Sovereign Nations and Establish 10 Servile Trading Blocs!

There is one last step in the Rothschild's master plan that we have yet to discuss. They want to end all sovereign nations and establish ten servile trading blocks. Why? I refer you back to a passage from this book's introduction for the answer to that question.

> *"Control of the global banking system goes hand in hand with control of global trade because the basis of wealth for every nation in the world is trade. Global trade and global banking are derivatives of one another! It goes like this; natural resources are mined, manufactured into finished products, and shipped worldwide. This forms the basis for the Gross Domestic Product (GDP) of individual nations and the entire world. But this is impossible without credit, so control of money and credit is the genesis of all wealth. Money is the medium of exchange that makes all this possible. As you can see, when we are talking about Globalism, we are talking about the basis of all wealth! There can be no more crucial all-encompassing topic! He who controls the money controls the world!"*

To control the wealth of the world, the Financial Elite must control money, credit, and global trade; what better way to do that than to end all sovereign nations and establish ten servile trading blocs (more on this shortly).

> *"...The super-national sovereignty of an intellectual elite and world bankers is surely preferable to the National Auto-determination practiced in past centuries"* (David Rockefeller, Council Foreign Relations).

Translation: David Rockefeller is calling for an end to the national sovereignty of all nation-states. The following quote will give you an idea of how evil Rockefeller and his fellow Rothschild Financial Elite truly are.

> *"Whatever the price of the Chinese revolution, it has obviously succeeded not only in producing more efficient administration but also*

in fostering high morale and community of purpose. The social ex-
periment in China under Chairman Mao's leadership is one of the
most important and successful in human history" (David Rockefeller,
New York Times).

What kind of man praises a regime that killed 60 million people? Let me ask you this. Can there be any limit to the atrocities such a man, and the organization he represents (the Financial Elite), would commit? What is the difference between killing millions and killing, say, billions? By the way, I have not yet told you what the Rothschild's end game is. It is heinous beyond imagination, and I guarantee you had I not prepared you as I am. You would never be able to believe that any individual or group of individuals could be that evil.

All of humanity has but one enemy, and that is the Financial Elite. Unless the people of all nations come to this realization and come together as one people, with one voice, with one resolve, I guarantee you the Financial Elite will end all sovereign nations and set up their Global Dictatorship. If they get that power, there will be no limit to the atrocities they will commit. They will make the Holocaust look like nothing. The U.N. has announced plans to end all sovereign nation-states and replace them with ten servile trading blocs modeled after the European Union.

The European Union started as 1) A Trade Agreement (just like NAFTA). 2) Then, a common currency was issued. 3) Then, the individual countries' constitutions were done away with and replaced by a Socialist Constitution. 4) Then, nonelected bureaucrats in Brussels set about passing laws and writing regulations, which constituted a Shadow Government, the real ruling power in Europe. This realization is what is behind the *"Brexit"* moment in England. The British want their freedom and their Constitution back.

Now let's look at what is happening in the U.S., and we will see that they are endeavoring to do the same thing here. To understand what they are doing, we have to go back to the Presidency of *"Globalist"* George H. W. Bush and a secret meeting he had with the Presidents of Mexico and Canada, but first, a couple of quick quotes to validate that he is a Globalist.

"But it became clear as time went on that in Mr. Bush's mind the New World Order was founded on a convergence of goals and interests between the U.S. and the Soviet Union, so strong and permanent that they would work as a team through the U.N. Security Council" (Excerpt from A. M. Rosenthal in the New York Times, January 1991).

"On Nov. 9, 1989, The Berlin wall fell & just days later Communist Pope Paul II, Russian Leader Mikhail Gorbachev and U.S. President George H. W. Bush meet to declare the birth of the New World Order."

"It is the sacred principles enshrined in the United Nations Charter to which the American people will henceforth pledge their allegiance" (President George H.W. Bush addressing the U.N.).

Why would a Russian Communist Leader, a Polish Communist Pope, and a U.S. President all meet to announce the birth of the Globalist-New World Order? I'll tell you; the Rothschild banking cartel truly controls the global monetary system and with it all the supposed leaders of the world (Communist Governments and Democracies alike). They truly are the masters of the world. Maybe our fairytale of *The Pauper's Wish* wasn't a fairytale after all. You decide! Now, do you see why Trump got us out of NAFTA? He is Pro-America and Anti-Globalism!

The bottom line is that nonelected Financial Elite Bureaucrats in Brussels and Washington are writing regulations intended to undermine both the U.S. and European governments in order for their Deep State Shadow Government to do an end-run on our national sovereignty. They are doing the same thing on every continent in the world! They must be stopped, or the entire world will become one huge Communist Dictatorship, and as Kennedy warned, we will all become their slaves!

The Globalist U.N. uses the false narrative that our carbon footprint causes climate change to justify their push to establish their One-World Government. In a subsequent chapter, we will discuss the real cause of climate change, but the truth doesn't help their narrative, so they lie.

Understanding the U.N.'s Hidden Agenda:

"Isn't the only hope for the planet that the industrialized civilization collapses? Isn't it our responsibility to bring that about?" (Maurice Strong, Founder of the U.N. Environmental Program during his opening speech at the Rio Earth Summit, 1992).

The Elite's Plan to Collapse the U.S. by Force If Necessary:

"We shall have world government whether or not you like it. The only question is whether world government will be by conquest or consent" (James P. Warburg, Representing Rothschild Banking Concern while speaking before the United States Senate, Feb. 17, 1950).

The Globalist – Financial Elite plans on collapsing the U.S. from within to force it into the New World Order. But if that fails, they have a plan (b), to utterly destroy the U.S. Still having problems believing this could be true? Ok! I want you to think back to our fairytale about *The Pauper's Wish.* Just in case you didn't make the connections, the story was about the Rothschild's, and the Wizard was the Devil. Do you believe in God? Do you believe in the Devil? I believe in both. What you are about to read strongly suggests that the Rothschilds and the Financial Elite are in league with the Devil. If that is the case, then there is no limit to the evil they are capable of. You decide! Are they evil and capable of committing any atrocity in pursuit of their dream of being masters of the world?

Who Are the Rothschild's Really?

- They are the wealthiest family in the world.
- They are worth an estimated $550 trillion or half the world's total wealth.
- The family's patriarch was born in Frankfurt, Germany, the son of a money counter, Moses Amschel Bauer.
- The sign over the door of his business was a red hexagram.

- Following his father's death, Mayer Amschel Bauer took over his father's business. He recognized the significance of the red hexagram and changed his name from Bauer to Rothschild after the red hexagram sign (Rothschild is derived from the German *"Zum Rothen Schild,"* which translates to *"with the red sign".*

- The significance of the red hexagram is that it translates geometrically and numerically into the number 666, which we know biblically to be the mark of the beast.

- George J. Laurer, an employee of the Rothschild's controlled IBM, invented the Universal Product Code (UPC).

- It just so happens (no coincidence) that the entire global trading system of the world utilizes that barcoded, which is identified by the number 666.

- The hexagram was also used to represent Saturn, which has been identified as the esoteric name for Satan.

- The Book of Revelation, Chapter 13, Verse 17 – 18 states the following concerning the number 666, *"And that no man might buy or sell, save he that had the mark, or the name of the beast, or the number of his name. Here is wisdom. Let him that hath understanding count the number of the beast: for it is the number of a man, and his number is Six hundred threescore and six."*

- The Bauers are from Khazaria, which is between the Black Sea and the Caspian Sea. They claim to be Jews because in 740A.D., under the direction of the King, they converted to the Jewish faith, but that doesn't change their genealogy, which is Asiatic Mongolian, not of Jewish descent. Given this, they are not actually Jews because Judaism is both a faith and ethnicity. So that makes them false Jews. Why is that significant? Read on.

- The Book of Revelation, Chapter 2, Verse 9 states, *"I know thy works, and tribulation and poverty, (but thou art rich) and I know the blasphemy of them which say they are Jews, and are not, but are the synagogue of Satan."*

So, we just learned that according to the Bible, the Bauers (Rothschild's) are false Jews and are of the *"synagogue of Satan."* Back to the fairytale of *The Pauper's Wish*. Is my story just a fairytale?

Is It True That He Who Controls Money Controls the World?

- Have I convinced you that there is one family, the Rothschild's, which literally controls the world's global monetary and trade system?

- Have I convinced you that they have used their vast wealth to buy power and influence to control all the governments of the world?

- Have I convinced you that that family is the Rothschilds?

- If this is true, doesn't it go a long way toward explaining that there really is a *"Deep State Shadow government"* that pulls the strings of our politicians and tells them what to do?

- Have I convinced you that the global network of Rothschild Central Banks extorts money from literally every person on the planet by charging us interest for printing worthless fiat currency backed by no more than the paper it is printed on?

- Have I convinced you that the Rothschilds have intentionally caused every financial crash since they got control of the global monetary system? That includes the 1929 Great Depression and the 2008 Financial Collapse.

- Have I convinced you that literally, every person in the world is little more than an indentured servant of the Rothschilds (slaves without chains)?

- Have I convinced you that the Rothschild Globalists buy mouthpieces in the media, academia, politics, and our churches that feed us a never-ending stream of lies and half-truths with which to blind us to the truth?

- Have I convinced you that they have hijacked the four centers of power: Political, Monetary, Intellectual, and Religious?

- Have I convinced you that the Rothschild Financial Elite are behind an attack on the Family, Morality, Christianity, and Patriotism (The glue which binds any nation)?

- Have I convinced you that they pit Blacks, Whites, Hispanics, Liberals, Conservatives, Rich, and Poor against one another to divide us because a nation divided cannot stand?

- Have I convinced you that they create false flag events in order to foster wars for profit?

- Have I convinced you that Gutle Schnaper, Mayer Amschel Rothschild's wife, was telling the truth when she said, *"If my sons did not want wars, there would be none."*

- Have I convinced you that WWI, WWII, Vietnam, and the Iraq wars were all wars for profit fostered on us by false flag events perpetrated by the Rothschild's?

- Have I convinced you that they prolonged those wars because it was profitable for them to do so, and they didn't care about the millions killed and maimed because to them, *"military men are dumb, stupid animals meant to be used as cannon fodder."*

- Have I convinced you that the Rothschild's are the spawn of the Devil, and there is no atrocity to heinous for them to commit?

- Have I convinced you that the Rothschild-Globalist's New World Order/ One-World Government is intended to be a dictatorial repressive government that will take away your freedom and that of your children?

- Have I convinced you that you will never be free as long as the Rothschilds control the global monetary system?

Have I convinced you that we have, but one enemy, the Rothschild's, and as the military strategist Sun Tzu would say, *"We are on death ground."* Which is to say our freedom, happiness, prosperity, and our very lives are at stake? I still have not divulged to you the end game of the Rothschild's. When I do, I guarantee you; you will be horrified. It is so vile it goes beyond the veil of human understanding. It is truly a work of the Devil. But there is hope! Before you finish this book, you will know what the Rothschild's end game is. More importantly, God has warned us so we can prepare. But more importantly, God is removing the scales of deception from our eyes so we can fight the evil!

The Shadow Government Revealed

The enemy lives amongst us
He is rich, powerful, and cunning
He is charismatic, charming, and ruthless

He comes at us from above and below
He uses the rich and the poor as pawns
He divides us and pits us against one another

He uses propaganda and brainwashing to deceive us
He is patient and strategic, attacking and withdrawing
He wants the hearts and minds of our children to enslave them

He is cunning, deceptive, and a liar full of guile and deceit
He creates crisis after crisis to keep us in a state of fear
He controls us by making us dependent for the necessities of life

He intends to use chaos to make us surrender to his tyranny
In his arrogance, he sees himself as superior to us in every way
He believes it is his destiny and his right to rule over us
He tells us what we want to hear and does as he pleases
He gives us what we want and then takes it away
He comes to kill, steal, destroy and enslave us

He is the Shadow Government of the Financial Elite!

CHAPTER 3

How the Financial Elite Control the World from the Shadows

WHAT YOU WILL LEARN IN THIS CHAPTER

- The U.S. Must Fall to Birth the New World Order!

- The Organizational Structure of the Financial Elite's Global Empire!

- How the Financial Elite Systematically Infiltrated the Halls of Power!

- Congress Is Irrelevant Because the Bankers Are Their Puppet Masters!

- Our Presidents Are Selected, Not Elected!

- The Five Manchurian Candidates That Betrayed America!

The U.S. Must Fall to Birth the New World Order!

It is imperative we understand that America must fall in order to birth the New World Order. As America goes, so goes the rest of the world!

> *"The New World Order can't happen without U.S. participation, as we are the most significant single component. Yes, there will be a New World Order, and it will force the United States to change its perceptions"* (Henry Kissinger, [CFR] World Affairs Council Press Conference, Regent Beverly Wilshire, April 19, 1994).

So, if the Financial Elite want to collapse the U.S., is there a country they are grooming as its replacement? You bet! The quote below points us in the direction of that country.

> *"The Rockefeller File… may be the most important story of our lifetime – the drive of the Rockefellers and their allies to create a one-world government combining Super-capitalism and Communism under the same tent, all under their control… the Rockefellers and their allies have been carefully following a plan to use their economic power to gain political control of first America and then the rest of the world…"* (Congressman Larry P. McDonald 1975).

Now we know that the replacement for the U.S. as the economic superpower of the world is to be a hybrid Capitalist – Communist economy. That narrows things down appreciably. As a matter of fact, there is only one country in the world that fits that description, and that is The People's Republic of China. So, if they are intended to be the archetype for the New World Order, we better know more about them.

For openers, China has arguably the worst record of human rights violations of any country on the planet! But wait, before we get into that, let's make sure it is China we should be looking at. So, is there any indication that the Financial Elite have raised China from 3rd world status to be the leading economic superpower in the world? You bet! Let's take a quick look at China's extraordinary rise to superpower status. When Nixon entered office, he was tasked by the Financial Elite to open trade with China, but he was impeached, so that task fell to Carter. Did anything unusual happen during Carter's Presidency, which might account for China's stellar rise to superpower status? You Bet! What was it? It was a little thing called the 1973 Oil Embargo. Remember, Roosevelt said: *"There are no accidents in politics. If it happened, it was planned."*

The oil embargo gave the Rothschild's Fed the excuse they needed to intervene in the U.S. economy and bring it to its knees. Here is what happened. The U.S. conveniently went into an economic deep freeze known as stagflation, where all of Carter's term in office interest rates and inflation were a staggering 18% or more. This economic phenomenon allowed China time to gear up for its assault on U.S. manufacturing and trade. Also, for the first time in U.S. history, perfectly sound corporations were bought only to be sold off in pieces. This phenomenon was referred to as corporate raiding. It saw perfectly sound companies bought and sold off in pieces making way for China to take over the markets they had dominated.

Only one thing remained, use the U.N.'s World Trade Organization to create free trade policies assured to create staggering U.S. trade deficits to drive the U.S. into unmanageable debt! Since Carter's Presidency, the U.S. economy has suffered from intentionally losing trade policies, and our national debt has skyrocketed from a scant $660 Billion to a staggering $26 trillion. This was no accident. That is why President Trump is renegotiating all our trade deals and turning them into fair trade and reciprocal agreements so America can stop the bleeding and rebuild our economy. Now we know that the U.S. must fall to make way for the New World Order and whom our replacement is intended to be China, not Russia, is the country we need to be on the lookout for.

What exactly will the New World Order look like? It will be pure hell! It will be a totalitarian regime where people have no rights except those given to them by their oppressors. It will be a place where dissenters are put in work camps or simply taken out and shot. It will be a place where there is no such thing as civil rights or human rights. It will be a place where your invisible chains are exchanged for real chains. It will be a place where the state decides if you can have a child, if you can go to college, where you will live, what job you will do, and under what conditions. It is a place where you either submit or suffer the consequences. How do I know this to be the case? Because of all the things I just described exist in China today. For example, The People's Republic of China is a place where the organs of people in work camps are harvested and sold to the highest bidder. As hard as that may be to believe it is true. Read on.

> *"A Chinese military surgeon had eight Chinese citizens killed to supply a single foreign patient with a new kidney... The incredible thing is that the doctor would...go down the names on a sheet of paper looking for blood types and tissue types and so on, and he (the patient) would point at names on the list..."* (Former Canadian Secretary of State for Asia–Pacific David Kilgour).

Let's move on and examine how exactly the Financial Elite are organized to rule the world. We know that they control the world monetary system through their network of central banks, and they dominate world trade through the World Trade Organization (WTO). Still, there has to be a lot more to their organizational structure for them to truly control all of the governments of the world from the shadows. So, let's get into it.

The Organizational Structure of the Financial Elite's Global Empire!

Let's start with the organization chart below. Because there are so many entities involved, I had to use abbreviations, and I have supplied a legend that follows immediately after the graphic. Once we see the breadth and scope of their global network, it will become clear that they truly do have the ability to orchestrate global events, to groom people for positions in the governments of the world, to control the global economy, media, and academia, and in so doing, script our world view and thereby pit us against one another. They have the means to create false flag events and drag us into unending wars for profit. They truly are the Puppet Masters who pull our government leaders' strings and control the world from the shadows.

The Organizational Chart of the New World Order

Legend

Global Oversight Organizations:

(**B.G.**) **Bilderberg Group** - The central command center of the global cabal is comprised of the wealthiest globalist families in the world (the Financial Elite).

(**NATO**) **North Atlantic Treaty Organization** - A military compliance organization that masquerades as peacekeepers.

(**IMF**) **International Monetary Fund, (W.B.) World Bank, & (US-AID) U.S. Agency for International Development** - Are all banking organizations, which in concert with central banks such as the Fed, control the world's monetary system on behalf of the Financial Elite. Their job is to drive sovereign nations into unmanageable debt so they can eventually be forced to accept the New World Order.

(**WTO**) **World Trade Organization** - Controls global trade. It is used to reintroduce The British Free Trade Slavery System repackaged as Chinese Free Trade. Its job is to collapse the Free Market System by driving major industrialized nations, particularly the U.S., into unmanageable debt by creating trade imbalances.

(WHO) World Health Organization - Is responsible for establishing global health accords favoring major corporations owned by the Financial Elite and is designed to reduce the population in 3rd world countries through malnutrition, disease, and starvation.

Implementation Organizations:

(CFR) Council on Foreign Relations & (T.C.) Trilateral Commission - They can be thought of as the feet on the ground that carry out the day-to-day initiatives of the Globalists organization. Their meetings and those of the Bilderberg Group are conducted under what is referred to as Chatham House Rules, which specify that nothing discussed in the meeting is repeated or quoted outside the meeting or in the press. In other words, they hide in the shadows. All three entities are in one way or another committed to ending national sovereignty and establishing a One World Government. The Bilderberg Group comprises the wealthiest and most influential power brokers in the world (approximately 125 people).

(Fed) Federal Reserve Bank - A private U.S. Central Bank which prints our currency and charges us interest by creating worthless paper currency out of thin air. Remember, all but three countries have a Rothschild Central Bank that rules their economy and controls their government officials.

(MEDIA) T.V., Newspapers, Magazines, Etc. - Owned by the Financial Elite and used to control public opinion (brainwash us) and pit various factions against one another to cause a never-ending cycle of crisis. They create racisms where none ought to exist. They incite wars where none should be. They are the ultimate propaganda machine because they feed us a never-ending stream of lies and half-truth masquerading as news. They are indeed, as Trump calls them, *"FAKE NEWS!"*

(CORP) Politically Connected Corporations - Given sweetheart deals to line the pockets of the wealthiest families in the world. Also, companies like Google, Facebook, and YouTube are used to control our access to the truth.

(GOVT) Government Agencies - Politicians at local, state, and federal levels, as well as nonelected bureaucrats used to write regulations that favor

Globalist policies. Also, high ranking political figures are placed in office by the Financial Elite to make sure both political parties are nothing, but political theater staged to make us think we have a say in our government when it is the Financial Elite who decide all the fundamental policies. Such policies keep us their indentured servants or slaves without chains controlled by the world's money powers.

(COMM ORG) Community Organization Groups (i.e., ACORN, SEIU, Etc.) - They are used to organize minority groups to push their agendas up from the bottom disguised as public opinion so our politicians can champion those policies (from the top down), claiming them to be the will of the people when in fact they are using the minority groups to create a constant state of tension between opposing groups.

UNIONS - Politically connected unions such as SEIU.

(ACADEMIA) Educational Systems, particularly Ivy League Universities - Used to brainwash our children into believing, for example, that Socialism is good, same-sex marriage is okay, Christianity is racist, progressivism is good, etc.

How the Financial Elite Systematically Infiltrated the Halls of Power!

It is the Financial Elite's money that pays for the lobbyist, which represents the special interest groups that buy legislation favoring special interest groups in deference to the best interest of the people. By virtue of their vast wealth, they virtually control all the power centers of the world. By virtue of their control of the world's wealth, we are their slaves, and they are our slave masters. President James Madison warned us saying,

> *"The day will come when our Republic will be an impossibility because wealth will be concentrated in the hands of a few. When that day comes, we must rely upon the wisdom of the best elements in the country to readjust the laws of the nation."*

That day is at hand; this book will show you exactly how we change those laws and take our country back. Please be patient. Now is not the time to get into that. Let's start our discussion of the Halls of Power with the CFR and T.C. I want to impress on you just how deeply the CFR and T.C. are embedded in Washington and why it is, as President Trump says, *"WE MUST DRAIN THE SWAMP!"* I wholeheartedly believe we must root out the CFR and T.C. members in our government, along with other subversives in other organizations. We will discuss how to do that in a subsequent chapter.

The Shadow Government: CFR & T.C. Members in Washington!

- **Presidents & Vice Presidents:** Every President and or Vice President since Carter through Obama

- **Secretaries of State:** 7 of 12!

- **Secretaries of Defense:** 9 of 12!

- **Secretaries of Treasury:** Henry Paulson (CEO of Goldman Sachs appointed Goldman employees to top positions in Treasury!)

- **World Bank Presidents:** 6 of 8.

- **Chairman Economic Recovery Advisory Board:** Paul Volker (Former Fed Chairman & North American Chairman for the Trilateral Commission!)

Given the CFR & T.C. is dedicated to establishing a New World Order, how is it so many politicians are Members?

> *"Council on Foreign Relations is the establishment. Not only does it have influence and power in key decision-making positions at the highest levels of government,* [i.e., Washington and the Office of the President], *to apply pressure from above, but it also uses individuals and groups to bring pressure from below,* [i.e., unions and community organizing groups, etc.] *to justify the high-level decisions for converting the U.S. from a sovereign constitutional repub-*

lic into a servile member state of a one-world dictatorship" (John Rarick (D), Representative from Louisiana).

"The New World Order will be built…an end-run on national sovereignty, eroding it piece by piece will accomplish much more than the old-fashioned frontal assault" (Council on Foreign Relations Journal, 1974, P558).

"The Trilateral Commission [T.C.]: is intended to be the vehicle for multinational consolidation of the commercial and banking interest by seizing control of the political government of the United States… They rule the future" (Felix Frankfurter, Justice of the Supreme Court).

"The Trilateral Commission represents a skillful, coordinated effort to seize control and consolidate the four centers of power—political, monetary, intellectual, and ecclesiastical (Religious). *What the Trilateral Commission intends is to create a worldwide economic power superior to the political governments of the nation-states involved* (a dictatorship). *As managers and creators of the system, they will rule the future"* (Senator Barry Goldwater).

They Do This By:

- Printing our currency at interest and driving us into unmanageable debt

- Controlling the basis of wealth, i.e., natural resources, global manufacturing, and trade

- Controlling the necessities of life: food, water, energy, money, jobs, and healthcare

- Selecting, grooming, and financing key political figures and corporate executives

- Imbedding a Shadow Government rendering both political parties irrelevant

- Using the media, Hollywood, and the education system as a propaganda machine

- Undermining national patriotism so we will accept their One-world Government

- Open borders to undermine national sovereignty (no borders = no sovereignty)

- Using crisis' (climate change, war, and terrorism) so we will relinquish our freedom

- Undermining Christian and family values because they are seen as a threat

- Using 501c tax exemption legislation to muzzle religious freedom

- Using race, religion, sexual preference, and socioeconomic status to divide us

By the way, once you know what is being done to collapse us, you have your counter strategy readymade. You undo what they have done by opposing all these things, pretty simple, right? Let me ask you a question. Given what you just read about the CFR and T.C., would you think it odd for our highest-ranking political figures to belong to such subversive organizations given that their stated goal is to collapse the U.S. in order to drive it into the waiting arms of the New World Order? For my part, I would consider it downright treasonous for our elected officials to belong to such organizations. But the fact of the matter is that anybody who is anybody in Washington belongs to one or both of these subversive organizations. I find that to be shocking! I wouldn't blame you for doubting what I just said, so let's take a look at the inner workings of Washington. I think you will see that it is as I said, *"anybody who is anybody in Washington belongs to the CRF and or the T.C."* Remember, he who controls the money controls the world, get ready to be shocked; this is just the tip of the preverbal iceberg.

The Shadow Government! CFR & TC Members in the Government			
Zibgniew Brzezinski	Security Advisor to five Presidents & Founding Member of TC	CFR	TC
Colin Powell	Chairman Joint Chiefs of Staff	CFR	
George H. Bush	U.S. President	CFR	
William Clinton	U.S. President	CFR	TC
Jimmy Carter	U.S. President	CFR	
Walter Mondale	U.S. Vice President		TC
John McCain	Senator (Arizonian) Presidential Candidate	CFR	
Albert Gore Jr.	U.S. Vice President	CFR	
Hillary Clinton	Secretary of State (Obama Administration)		TC
Condoleezza Rice	Secretary of State (Bush Administration)	CFR	
John Kerry	Senator & Chairman, Foreign Relations Committee	CFR	
James Woolsey	Director of the CIA	CFR	
Robert Gates	Secretary of Defense & Former Director of the CIA	CFR	
Henry Cisneros	Secretary of Housing & Urban Development	CFR	
Dick Chaney	U.S. Vice President	CFR	

"The case for government by elites is irrefutable"
(William Fulbright, U.S Senator).

"I think there are 25,000 individuals that have used offices of powers, and they are in our Universities, and they are in our Congresses, and they believe in One World Government. And if you believe in One World Government, then you are talking about undermining National Sovereignty, and you are talking about setting up something that you could well call a Dictatorship—and those plans are there!" (Congressman Ron Paul at an event near Austin, Texas, on August 30, 2003).

Did you ever wonder how so many politicians go to Washington as middle-class Americans and in no time are multimillionaires? Let's see, if you were in charge of writing a bill that would benefit a Globalist Corporation and you knew that that would cause its stock to go through the roof, would you want to invest in it? Of course, you would! But if you were going to get rich off such a transaction, you would need a lot of money to invest. Wouldn't it be nice if some friendly Globalist banker just happened along and offered to loan you a lot of money at a very low-interest rate? Gee, you might be a millionaire overnight. It happens all the time in Washington. It is called insider trading, and if you or I did it, we would go to jail, but politicians do it all the time, and nobody does a thing about it. Or let's say you leave Washington with your Rolodex and security clearance in hand. What do you think are the odds you could get a job paying millions as a Lobbyist? It happens all the time! That is the real reason high ranking government officials like former FBI Director James Comey need their security clearances. They are like money in the bank. And oh yes, Comey is a millionaire. This process is called the revolving door. Become a politician, leave, become a lobbyist, and magically they are rich. That is why I call our Washington Politicians *"Political Elite,"* which is why most of them serve the Financial Elite and not the American voters.

The Global Elite Bankers Own Washington

Is it possible that, as I have said that our politicians in Washington have by in large sold out? That Washington politics is just Political Theater? If so, then who really runs the country? Would you be surprised if it was the bankers? When appearing on PBS' *Lehrer Report,* Fed Chairman Alan Greenspan was asked,

> *"What is the proper relationship between the Chairman of the Federal Reserve and the President of the United States?"* Greenspan said, *"Well, first of all, the Federal Reserve is an independent agency, and that means basically that, uh, there is no other agency of government which can overrule actions that we take. In so long as that is in place…what that relationship is, uh, don't frankly matter."*

The bottom line is that Greenspan arrogantly says that the relationship between the Federal Reserve Chairman and the President of the United States doesn't matter because no government agency, not even the President, can tell the Fed what to do. Translation: The Fed runs the government, and both political parties are their puppets. Trying to take back the reins of power from the Fed is what, in all probability, got Kennedy killed. Appearing before Congress, President Kennedy referred to the Fed as,

> *"This establishment that virtually controls the monetary system; That is subject to no one; That no Congressional Committee can oversee; and that not only issues the currency, but loans it to the Government at Interest."*

JFK was so outraged at this usurping of power by the Financial Elite that he signed Executive order # 11110 to dismantle the Fed. To accomplish this, he issued U.S. silver certificates to replace the U.S. dollar. He was also taking action to limit the CIA's power, and he refused the Military-Industrial Complex's demands to commit more troops to Vietnam. Johnson reversed all three of Kennedy's initiatives. You don't oppose the Fed and the Financial Elite and live! The fact that the Fed (Shadow Government) runs the country is further supported by the following quote from Robert Reich (a member of President Clinton's Cabinet).

> *"The dirty little secret is that both houses of Congress are irrelevant. U. S's domestic policy is now being run by Alan Greenspan and the Federal Reserve (Fed). U.S.'s foreign policy is now being run by the International Monetary Fund (IMF)."*

The bottom line is that the Fed and IMF run the U.S. government on behalf of the Financial Elite. They select, groom, and finance key political candidates, most importantly, presidential candidates. Is there any proof that the Financial Elite actually selects, grooms, and finances political candidates and even presidents? You bet there is! The precedent for selecting and funding U.S. Presidents dates back to the election of President William McKinley and his rival William Jennings Bryan.

The Buying of the First U.S. President

Here is what transpired that made the Financial Elite understand once and for all that they had the power to place in office whomever they wanted. Long story short, McKinley was pro-big business, and Bryan was anti-monopoly. The three richest men in America (Rockefeller, Carnegie, and Morgan) decided that if Bryan was elected, he might break up their empires, so they colluded to use their money and influence to get McKinley elected (from the documentary, *The Men Who Built America*, 2012). With that, the Financial Elite knew that as their ancestors had bought Kings, they could buy Presidents and other politicians and rule over an elected Democracy in the same manner their ancestors had ruled over the Monarchies of the past. By the way, the Financial Elite always hedge their bets. For example, that is why they fund both sides of a war on the condition that the victor honors the debts of the vanquished, and that is why they back more than one candidate in most elections. This is why they hate Trump; he wasn't for sale!

The Five Manchurian Candidates That Betrayed America!

| Carter | Bush Sr. | Clinton | Bush Jr. | Obama |

We have already talked about how under Carter's Presidency, the U.S. economy was intentionally stagnated while China geared up its manufacturing capability in order to gut the U.S. manufacturing base and how President Carter allowed the Globalist World Trade Organization to inflict the U.S. with intentionally losing trade deals that drove the U.S. deep into debt!

We also talked about how President George H. W. Bush is a Globalist and how he pledged his allegiance to the U.N., which actively supports ending all nation-states in order to form a One-World Government. That, of course, means the U.S. would cease to exist! And we talked about how in 1989, he met with Communist Pope Paul II (a Globalist) and Russian President Gorbachev (a Globalist) to announce the birth of the New World Order. How could there be anything more traitorous than selling out our country by openly endorsing the very entity sworn to its destruction? So, I want to focus on the fact that the 2008 financial collapse could never have happened had it not been for the actions taken by Presidents Bill Clinton, George W. Bush, and Barrack Obama. Is it possible that these men sold out American homeowners to further the Financial Elite's interest and to further plans to establish a One-World Government? The answer is a resounding YES! Remember, *"There are no coincidences in politics. If it happened, it was planned."*

2008 Subprime Real Estate and Stock Market Crash: The 2008 financial collapse resulted in $3.3 trillion in lost real estate value and $6.9 trillion in stock value for a total of $10.2 trillion. Predatory lending practices lead to the collapse of the housing market and the ensuing stock market crash. The crash resulted in the largest transfer of wealth in the history of the world as American taxpayers were forced to bail out the corrupt banking industry, which then turned around and bought their homes at bargain prices.

The Role of Presidents Obama, Clinton, and Bush Jr. in the 2008 Financial Collapse

President Obama: In the years leading up to the crash, Obama sued Citi Bank on behalf of ACORN for racial discrimination, forcing lenders to lower their lending standards. For the first time in the world's history, it was possible to purchase a home with no income verification and no money down. This was the basis for the predatory subprime mortgage practices which followed.

President Clinton: Repealed the Glass-Steagall Act. Glass-Steagall was the firewall that protected the real estate market by prohibiting mergers of insurance companies, security firms, and conventional banks because such mergers would allow the formation of banks that were too big to fail. So, when the 2008 financial collapse happened, we, the American taxpayers, bailed out the banks because mergers of banks, insurance companies, and security firms had created banks that were, you guessed it, too big to be allowed to fail.

President George W. Bush: Well in advance of the collapse, the Governor of Georgia, who had been a banker before going into politics, saw the impending crash and took measures to protect the residents of Georgia by passing an anti-predatory lending bill. Seeing what he had done to protect Georgia's residents, other state legislatures began drafting their own anti-predatory bills modeled after Georgia's.

Then Bush stepped in and sent a planeload of Washington lawyers to Georgia and got the legislation thrown out. He told the Governors and States Attorneys that anti-predatory lending legislation fell under the federal government's jurisdiction and should cease and desist. When they did, the federal government took no action to pass such legislation. The result was that the real estate market suffered a catastrophic collapse that could have been obverted. Millions of Americans lost their homes and life savings. But that wasn't the end of it. The high-risk, zero down, and subprime loans had been bundled with conventional 20% down mortgages creating Collateralized Debt Obligations (CDO's). In turn, the rating companies gave these high-risk investments AAA ratings, and the banker gangsters proceeded to sell them all over the world. So, when the crash came, its effects were felt worldwide, just like was the case in the 1929 Great Depression. The following quote refers to actions taken by President Bush, which were clearly intended to keep lawmakers from passing anti-predatory laws that could have prevented the 2008 financial collapse.

> "In 2003, during the height of the predatory lending crisis, the OCC invoked a clause from the 1863 National Bank Act to issue formal opinion preempting all state predatory lending laws, thereby rendering them inoperative. The OCC also promulgated new rules that prevented states from enforcing any of their own consumer protection laws against national banks. The federal governments' actions were so egregious and so unprecedented that all 50 states attorneys general, and all 50 state banking superintendents, actively fought the new rules" (Eliot Spitzer, former New York Governor).

Allegations: President Bush intentionally stood by and allowed the 2008 Housing Collapse to occur when he had it in his power to prevent it by allowing anti-predatory lending legislation to be passed! Former New

York Governor Eliot Spitzer accused Bush of causing the financial collapse saying,

> *"When history tells the story of the sub-prime lending crisis and recounts its devastating effects on the lives of so many innocent home-owners, the Bush administration will not be judged favorably. The tale is still unfolding, but when the dust settles, it will be judged as a willing accomplice to the lenders who went to any length in their quest for profit. So, willing, in fact, that it used the power of the federal government in an unprecedented assault on state legislatures, as well as on state attorney generals and anyone else on the side of consumers."*

Similar charges were made against the Fed following the 1929 crash when Congressman Louis McFadden brought articles of impeachment against Fed officials saying,

> *"It was the calculated sheering of the public by the world money powers triggered by the planned sudden shortage of call money in the New York Market."*

As President Kennedy said, *"There is a plot in this country to enslave every man, woman, and child..."* That plot is real. It is not a conspiracy theory, but a real conspiracy orchestrated by the Financial Elite, who are some of the evilest people ever to walk the earth. They are harbingers of misery, destitution, and poverty; as to whether Obama, Clinton, and Bush were unwittingly used by the Financial Elite, or were they coconspirators, I leave that up to you.

In the next chapter, we will explore how the Financial Elites have laid the groundwork for yet another financial collapse. But something is different this time. We may be able to stop it from happening, and if we can, President Trump's agenda will play a vitally important role. He has a trump card that may stop them cold in their tracks.

CHAPTER 4

How and Why the Public Has Been Intentionally Divided!

WHAT YOU WILL LEARN IN THIS CHAPTER

- Fake News Is Real: The Financial Elite Own the News Outlets!

- Why the Nation Is So Divided!

- Brainwashing 101: The Mechanics of Brainwashing!

- Examples of How We Are Intentionally Divided!

- Time to Organize and Take a Stand for Freedom!

Fake News Is Real: The Financial Elite Own the News Outlets!

This will be hard to believe, but our opinions, beliefs, and prejudices are all scripted by those who would be the masters of us all. They control us in almost unfathomable ways. If we can accept this fact, it will go a long way toward defusing the animosity, angst, mistrust, bias, and downright hatred that our would-be masters intentionally propagate to bring us to the precipice of chaos and anarchy!

They use T.V., movies, and our education system to debase society by calling those things which are good and wholesome evil and those things which are evil and debasing good. For example, in the 1950s and '60s, we had wholesome programs like *Father Knows Best* (1954), but today the Financial Elite champion single mother families because they know that not having a male role model in a family leads to increased school dropout rates, increased drug abuse, and gang activity which is exactly what they want. The Financial Elite want to break down morality, family, Christian values, and national patriotism. If we're going to keep America from falling, we can't let them get away with what they are doing. We all have a common enemy in the Financial Elite. We are not each other's enemies.

Fake News Is Real: U.S. Congressman Oscar Callaway informs Congress that J. P. Morgan is a Rothschild front and has taken control of the American media industry. He states,

> *"In March 1915, the J.P. Morgan interests, the steel, shipbuilding, and powder interest, and their subsidiary organizations, got together 12 men high up in the newspaper world and employed them to select the most influential newspapers in the United States and sufficient number of them to control generally the policy of the daily press. They found it was only necessary to purchase the control of (25) of the greatest papers. An agreement was reached. The policy of the papers was bought, to be paid for by the month, an editor was furnished for each paper to properly supervise and edit information regarding the questions of preparedness, militarism, financial policies, and other*

things of national and international nature considered vital to the interests of the purchasers."

That was then, and this is now. Things worked out so well for them that they expanded their lock on the information that defines our world view by buying major Hollywood movie studios, and they own three of the major news outlets. Their control of information has spread to the internet with Facebook and Google rigging search results. Like a computer, our brains reach conclusions based on the data that is imputed. As the saying goes, *"garbage in, garbage out."* We are being programmed with pure garbage! The Financial Elite have been hiding their plans of global domination from us for decades, as the quotes below expose.

> *"We are grateful to the Washing Post, the New York Times, Time magazine, and other great publications whose directors have attended our meetings and respected their promises of discretion for almost forty years. It would have been impossible for us to develop our plan for the world if we had been subjected to the lights of publicity during those years"* (David Rockefeller, speaking at the June 1991 Bilderberger meeting in Baden, Germany).

Rockefeller went on to say,

> *"But the world is more sophisticated and prepared to march toward a world government. The supranational sovereignty of an intellectual elite and world bankers is surely preferable to the national auto-determination practiced in past centuries."*

How Is This Not Treason?

Remember, in 1915, the Financial Elite bought the 25 largest newspapers in the U.S. in order to control public opinion. That worked so well that they then purchased Hollywood studios, and today we see the search results of Google and Facebook skewed to the progressive left Socialists. How is this not brainwashing when they control all the information that influences our perception of reality? Let's not forget that they endow our universities so that they will support left-leaning curriculums!

> *"Those who manipulate the unseen fabric of society constitute an invisible government which is the true ruling power of the country... In almost every act of our lives, whether in the sphere of politics or business in our social conduct or ethical thinking, we are dominated by the relatively small number of persons who understand the mental process and social patterns of the masses. It is they who pull the wires and control the public mind"* (Edward Bernays, Father of Modern Advertising).

Why the Nation Is So Divided!

Simply put, we are polarized because we are denied the truth and fed an endless stream of lies by those who, according to President Kennedy, *"want to be the masters of us all."* They hide behind a veil of secrecy and orchestrate events designed to lead the mass of humanity in directions and to conclusions carefully scripted by them. They orchestrate events intended to create so much division that it will eventually tear the nation apart, resulting in chaos and a crisis that will allow them to seize power and impose their New World Order! We want to think that our belief system was formed by open-mindedly analyzing the facts and, after careful reflection forming the opinions which constitute our world view. But what if the facts which we based our decisions on were tainted? What if they weren't facts at all? What if they were a carefully orchestrated compilation of emotional triggers coupled with the truth, half-truths, and flat out lies designed to lead us to certain conclusions? What if our perception of reality was based on false information? What then? Is it possible; is it even conceivable that brainwashing and mind control could be a reality? Is it possible the mass of society is scripted in such a way as to polarize them to such an extent that they hate each other? If you keep reading and if you can set your preconceived beliefs aside, for the time being, I think you will be shocked to learn that the mass of society has, in fact, been scripted to think in certain ways that are intended to polarize us, to set us against one another and to divide the nation to such an extent that it threatens to tear the nation apart.

If what I just said is proven to be true, we are sleeping with the enemy without knowing it. That makes us what Lenin called *"Useful Idiots"* in a global chess game where the winner rules the world! What is central to this mind control process is that the Financial Elite know and take advantage of this simple fact! It isn't easy to see another person's perspective when we have a vested interest in maintaining our current perspective or when we have a significantly different frame of reference.

The Enemy Within: The Financial Elite constitutes a Shadow Government that threatens our nation's very existence! Unless we embrace this fact, America will fall from within. We are facing an enemy more dangerous than we faced in WWII when we were fighting Nazi aggression. In order to fight back, we have to know who and what we are fighting.

Fundamental to the brainwashing process is the requirement to segment people into different camps based on various circumstances. The rich are pitted against the poor. Blacks, Whites, and Hispanics are pitted against each other. Different religious groups are pitted against each other. Another component of this mind control process is the need to keep one segment of the population in some fashion oppressed and point the finger at another segment of society and blame them for that oppression. When in truth, that segment doesn't have the power to oppress anyone. Then who does? The Financial Elite! They control the source of all the information upon which we base the decisions which constitute our belief system. They control the monetary system, and with their vast wealth, they buy power and influence. This allows them to control the media, Hollywood, academia, and enough politicians to make a sham of our political system rendering it little more than political theater. Democrats and Republicans appear to oppose each other vehemently, but in reality, this supposed polarization is simply the pretext that allows them to account for the political gridlock that assures that nothing gets done in Washington. No, that isn't exactly true. Nothing is done unless it favors the special interest groups that allow politicians to come to Washington as middle-class Americans and leave multi-millionaires.

The Financial Elite alone have the resources to control the necessities of life, a living wage, food, water, energy, and access to healthcare. They alone have the means to organize the various factions that they've created and weaponized by sending them out into the streets to cause the conflict that is intended to create such division that it breaks down the very fabric of society, degrading it into the kind of chaos that topples governments and gives rise to totalitarian regimes. If we are to save America from collapse from within, we must awaken to the fact that we have but one enemy, and that is the Financial Elite!

Brainwashing 101: The Mechanics of Brainwashing!

If we understand what is being done to us and by whom, then we can stop being their *"Useful Idiots"* and take our country back and, in the process, once again become *"one nation under God, indivisible, with liberty, and justice for all."*

Brainwashing 101: Finally, we are ready to learn exactly how the Financial Elite go about brainwashing billions of people, morphing us into useful idiots. By buying into their lies and half-truths, we become weapons of the Financial Elite used to destroy America and birth the Communist-New World Order without realizing it. But the good news is that if we know what is being done to us, we are no longer susceptible to their propaganda machinery. Here's how the propaganda machine works.

The Objective: To cause so much chaos that society is destabilized, ushering in the New World Order. They do that by creating situations that cause anger, frustration, hopelessness, fear, radicalism, division, racism, violence, and or apathy. They so convolute the truth that there are no absolutes. Without absolutes, society degrades into chaos, and that is their intent.

The Mechanics of Brainwashing

Tell a Big Lie: Adolf Hitler once said, if you are going to tell a lie, tell a big one because it is more readily believed than a small one!

"The size of the lie is a definite factor in causing it to be believed, for the mass of a nation are in the depths of their hearts more easily deceived than they are consciously and intentionally bad. The primitive simplicity of their minds renders them a more easy prey to a big lie than to a small one, for they themselves often tell little lies, but would be ashamed to tell big lies" (Adolf Hitler, Mein Kompf, 1925).

Tell the Lie Over and Over Till the Masses Believe It: Repetition is important. If you tell a lie frequently enough, over time, people tend to accept it as fact. This is particularly true where the Financial Elite control virtually all of the media outlets, even including the education system. In the absence of a competing narrative, a lie, no matter how ridiculous, becomes a reality to most people.

Use Different Sources to Spread the Propaganda: If a lie, no matter how ridiculous, is spread by Hollywood, the media, the schools, virtually every available source of information, it becomes the de facto truth.

It is a psychological fact that most people are uncomfortable holding an opinion that the majority does not accept. For example, in one study, a lone person is placed in a group of people who are all instructed to say 2 plus 2 is 5. In almost every case, the lone dissenter would eventually acquiesce and go along with the majority opinion. That doesn't necessarily mean the person actually believes that 2 plus 2 is 5. It merely means that it is uncomfortable to disagree with the majority opinion, so they are silenced. For example, those who oppose same-sex marriage have been silenced in this manner. Under President Obama, many Christians stopped saying *"Merry Christmas"* because it was portrayed as offensive. The new norm was to say *"Happy Holidays"* instead. Hollywood, the media, and the greeting card companies pushed this narrative hard. Thank goodness Trump made it okay to say *"Merry Christmas"* again. It doesn't matter if the person's opinion changes. All that matters is that the person is silenced, so there is no dissenting voice to the Financial Elite's brainwashing narrative. So over time, their narrative becomes all that remains.

Convolute the Truth So the Masses Can't Tell What Is True: Turn on the news, grab a newspaper. It is virtually impossible to get the facts about a news story. Those days are gone. What you get instead is opinion news designed to lead you to a particular conclusion or claiming to be fair and balanced. You get a panel of dissenting and contradictory panelists who make certain that by the time they are done pontificating, every bit of the truth is shredded, clouded in contradiction, or obliterated by flat out lies. Journalism in America is dead. It is now nothing more than a propaganda arm of the Financial Elite.

Build Bottom-up Support for Minority Causes: The Financial Elite carries out the transformation of America, the destruction of our core values through a carefully coordinated bottom-up - top-down strategy. Did you ever wonder how the minority opinion always seems to prevail over the majority opinion, and in the process, our core values are always diminished? It is as Vladimir Lenin said,

> *"The organized minority will beat the disorganized majority every time"* (Vladimir Lenin, Founder of the Soviet Union).

Why is that? How is that possible? Reflect on the following quote, and then we will examine how the Financial Elite carries out their strategy to inflict the minority opinion on the silent majority.

> *"Council on Foreign Relations is the establishment. Not only does it have influence and power in key decision-making positions at the highest levels of government, [i.e. Washington and the Office of the President], to apply pressure from above, but it also uses individuals and groups to bring pressure from below, [i.e., unions and community organizing groups etc.] to justify the high-level decisions for converting the U.S. from a sovereign Constitutional Republic into a servile member state of a One-World Dictatorship"* (John Rarick (D), Representative Louisiana).

The Financial Elite build bottom-up support by eliciting grassroots organizations like special interest groups, unions, gay rights organizations, environmental groups, or community organizers like President Obama did before he became President. They organize protests and marches. The media covers them and pleads their case, generally portraying those that oppose

their position as racist, unpatriotic, or cast them in some other uncompli-
mentary light. Before long, it appears that whatever the cause these special
interest minority groups are pushing has a groundswell of support when in
reality all they have is the support of a crooked media and other minions of
the Financial Elite. But never mind. The truth doesn't matter. This perception gives them the momentum to push their cause up the food chain to
Washington.

For example, if you turn on the nightly news, pick up a magazine, go to
the movies, watch T.V., in virtually every instance, you will encounter a narrative endorsing same-sex marriage and condemning anyone who opposes it
as racist. After thousands of years of defining marriage as the union of a man
and a woman, that core value has been supplanted virtually overnight. How
did it happen? For decades, gay rights groups (minority groups) pushed for
recognition without gaining much traction. Then came President Obama,
and the narrative changed, which brings us to phase two of the Financial
Elite's strategy: top-down pressure.

Impose Top-Down Support for Minority Causes: When an issue has
gained enough exposure, it becomes a social mandate. The politician's step
in, saying it is now their responsibility to do something; after all, the people
have spoken. It doesn't matter if, in reality, the issue is the mandate of a very
small special interest group. All that matters is that the agenda of the Financial Elite is furthered.

Back to our example about same-sex marriage, after years without getting any traction, President Obama chimes in (top-down pressure is exert-
ed). Almost overnight, same-sex marriage is the law of the land. This bottom-up – top-down strategy is employed over and over. We see it not only
with gay rights but with immigration, sanctuary cities, removal of national
monuments, refusal to stand for the National Anthem, etc. It doesn't matter
what the cause is. They all have one thing in common. They undermine our
Constitution, patriotism, family, or Christian values because the Financial
Elite know that these things constitute the glue that binds the nation. Destroy them, and America will fall from the within.

Special Interest Groups: Like the ones mentioned above, are used to bring an issue to the public's attention where the bottom-up – top-down strategy discussed above is brought to bear.

Organizers: Their job is to circulate petitions, organize marches and protest rallies, etc.

Financiers: They provide funding for the movement. The funding source can be a financer like George Soros, a political donor with a vested interest, a political party, etc. It doesn't matter where the money comes from. Remember, the Financial Elite controls the global monetary system so they can marshal support from anywhere, including Communist nations like China and Russia. Remember, China is the model for their New World Order. Historically, the unorganized majority hasn't stood a chance championing their causes when they can be outspent 10 to 1. Money buys power and influence and drives political agendas. But that can change. The scandals which are unfolding in Washington might awaken the unorganized majority from their apathy. If we come together as one voice, we would represent a force to be reckoned with. I can only hope we wake up and make our voices heard before it is too late. I honestly believe that God is calling his people. He doesn't want us to fall victim to the Financial Elite and those that seek to be the masters of us all.

Influencers: They focus on controlling public opinion. Their numbers include educators endowed by the Financial Elite (now teaching our children that Capitalism is evil, and Socialism is good etc.). They include the media that bombards us with their pseudo-news intended to draw our conclusions for us. Hollywood is a particularly effective influencer because they come at us subliminally through propaganda disguised as entertainment. Other influencers can include politicians, religious leaders, and community organizers. They can be anyone in a position of authority, especially if the Financial Elite funds them.

Demonstrators: Are what Charmin Mao called *"Useful Idiots."* In Mao's case, they were the 60 or so million peasants who supported his Cultural Revolution only to meet their death at his regime's hand after he gained power. I am not saying we shouldn't stand up and speak out. I am saying we should know what we are standing for, so we don't end up being pawns of the Financial Elite.

Agitators: Do you remember the recent disclosure that shortly after Trump's election, there were two rallies in New York on the same day. One was pro-Trump, and the other was against him. As it turns out, they were both funded by the same source. The point here is that the Financial Elite want to pit us against each other because they know a nation divided cannot stand.

Illegal Activities: Where the Financial Elites are concerned, anything goes. It is like what President Bush and Henry Kissinger said in the quotes below.

> *"The Constitution is just a God damn piece of paper!"* (White House Blues, George W. Bush).

> *"The illegal we do immediately. The unconstitutional takes a little longer"* (Henry Kissinger, Secretary of State & CFR Member).

Spin Doctors: Their job is to spin the news and confuse the issues that there is no absolute right or wrong, no moral absolute, only opinion, angst, anger, frustration, and apathy.

Detractors: They are tasked with discrediting and belittling the Financial Elite's opposition, i.e., Hillary called Conservatives *"deplorable."* The media called Christians *"mentally ill."* Obama called Christians *"radicals."* The media called Trump *"mentally unfit."* Anyone against illegal immigration is labeled a *"racist,"* and on and on the attacks go.

Intimidators: During the Presidential campaign, there were paid protestors at Trump rallies who not only disrupted the rallies but also intimidated and assaulted Trump supporters. At Berkley, masked demonstrators staged a full-scale riot. In Ferguson, violent thugs were bused in to ensure the protest was violent enough to get maximum media coverage. Again, the objective is to cause chaos and division and to focus our attention on these staged events so attention will be taken off of the real problems we are facing, like going broke.

Political Theater: Both political parties are polarized. Enough politicians have sold out to assure that Congress is irrelevant. It is just political theater designed to make us think we have a voice in our government. Each party takes opposing positions and claims the moral high ground as the excuse for the gridlock that assures that very little is accomplished. And most of what is accomplished benefits the special interest groups, not the people. As President Trump says, *"we need to drain the swamp."*

The End Game: Impose the agenda of the Financial Elite's organized minority on the silent majority in order to insidiously undermine patriotism, family, and Christian values, drive the nation into unmanageable debt, and cause division and chaos. All intended to culminate in the fall of the U.S. and the entire Free Market System to be replaced by a Highbred Capitalist-Communist New World Order Dictatorship. I remind you that in order for the New World Order to rise, America must fall, and when it falls, we will lose our freedom and our way of life. Communism is the organized implementation of oppression!

Examples of How We Are Intentionally Divided!

What follows are several graphics that punctuate the various ways the Financial Elite are intentionally pitting us against each other in order to tear the fabric of our great nation! There has never been a time in our history, whereas many different and varied disruptive events have occurred in such a short timeframe. The Financial Elite are making a push to cause so much division that it erupts into violence and builds to the point that it literally tears the fabric of society apart. Their goal is to create chaos to create, as they say, *"the right crisis"* to usher in their New World Order.

Ask yourself this, what is underpinning all the conflict, all this division, all this violence? It is caused by economic oppression, which is stirred up by the Financial Elite, by the feeling among a growing segment of the population that they are downtrodden. They feel that there is little hope for a better future and, even worse, that things are getting progressively worse. The Financial Elites have created these circumstances, and now they are taking the very despair that they created and focusing it on various segments of society to create hatred and division. In other words, our anger and frustration are being focused on our fellow Americans. But the truth is that we are all victims of the Financial Elite. Unless we wake up and see what they are doing to us, we will fall victim to their propaganda, manipulation, and mind control.

The graphics that follow are a compilation of images that are right out of the pages of our recent news stories intended to create social hysteria, hatred, and chaos. They are propaganda! But they punctuate the fact that the Financial Elite are desperate. For the 1st time in decades, the American electorate woke up, and they managed to elect a billionaire businessman who couldn't be bought. God anointed this man for just this time. His assignment from God is to wake up the people to the corruption so America and the world can stand up to the forces of evil that have taken over the world.

Daily News calls Trump voters "Mindless Zombies!"

Sows discord and confusion among school-age kids and military personnel!

Destroy Patriotism, And You Destroy America!

Why would Sanctuary cities protect gang members and other criminals?

Those that wish to collapse America know, *"a nation divided cannot stand!"*

UC Berkeley: The Bastian of Free Speech No Longer!

It quells the voice of conservatism!

As President Kennedy said,

"There is a plot in this country to enslave every man, woman, and child..."

The Rothschild's Master Plan:

- Gain control of America's monetary system in order to control the four centers of power: monetary, political, intellectual, and religious

- Recruit men (who would, for a price, support the Rothschild agenda) and place them in high places in the federal government, the Congress, Supreme Court, and all federal agencies!

- Create racial, ethnic, and class strife to create division and tear the country apart from within!

- Create a movement to destroy religion, patriotism, morality, and the family!

- Buy media outlets to control public opinion!

- Create wars for profit and fund both sides!

✓ **Done – Done – Done – Done - Done & Done! Mission Accomplished!**

The Plan to Make America Great Again

- Time for the *"silent majority"* to make their voices heard!
- Time to vote out the carrier politicians!
- Time to make sweeping election reforms!
- Time to say no to Socialism!
- Time to take back the printing of our currency!
- Time to take back the media, our schools & Hollywood!
- Time to stand up for Christian values!
- Time to pledge allegiance to the flag!
- Time to stand up for family values!
- Time to demand border security!
- Time to demand fair reciprocal trade!
- Time to stop driving America into debt!
- Time to end the division that is tearing the nation apart!
- Time to establish energy independence!

Our Just Reward

The harvest is at hand
The spotless lamb cometh
In righteousness and virtue
His ways to show to a lost world

But woe to this wicked generation
That hears his word and hearkens not

But to those with ears to hear
The mysteries of the ages will be revealed
That they may divine his word
That they be no longer deceived

Wicked doers will be exposed
Their evil schemes for all to see
Their just reward they will receive

Yet I am God that loveth thee
Therefore, have I provided a way for thee
Repent and turn from your wicked ways
That you may yet be with me
Repent not, and your just reward you will receive

The kingdoms of man will fall
And the wicked with them
But to those who endure to the end
A crown of righteousness' they will receive
And communion with the Lamb their just reward

CHAPTER 5

He Who Controls the Money Controls the World?

WHAT YOU WILL LEARN IN THIS CHAPTER

- Pivotal Turning Points That Changed the World Forever!

- Why America Must Fall in Order to Birth the New World Order!

- Russian, Chinese, and American Leaders Are All Controlled by the Financial Elite and Are Pushing to Establish the New World Order!

- Why America Needs to Liberate Itself from the Tyranny of Globalism!

- The Truth about America's Open Borders Policy!

- The Financial Elite Are Preparing to Start WWIII!

- Why President Trump Is the Key to Stopping the Next Financial Collapse!

The End Game Agenda of the Financial Elite

"We shall have world government whether or not you like it. The only question is whether World Government will be by conquest or consent" (James P. Warburg [Representing Rothschild Banking Concern] while speaking before the United States Senate, February 17, 1950).

We Can Stop Them if We Stand United:
One Nation – One People – Under God

Do you remember when we started this journey several chapters ago, I told you that when dealing with the ultra-rich and powerful, they can do things, illegal things, horrendously horrible things, and the evidence of their crimes never sees the light of day? One way or the other, they maintain their cloak of invisibility! Do you remember that I said at some point I would ask you if you believed my story of *The Pauper's Wish* to be just a fairytale or a true story about a family that is pure evil? Well, that time has come.

In this chapter, I will summarize everything we have discussed so far, and I have compiled a list of true/false questions that will assist you in deciding if this is just a fairytale or a work of non-fiction. If you decide that this is a work of non-fiction, then I am going to invite you to join the *"Army of Light"* and take action to take our country back so our children and their children and their children for generations to come can live in freedom because we broke the chains that bind us. We are in a war that is every bit as real and every bit as dangerous as WWII. Now, as then, the stakes couldn't be higher. As the military strategist Sun Tzu said, *"we are on death ground,"* so we have to defeat this enemy or else!

The Financial Elite thought they would finally collapse America and birth their New World Order under a Hillary Presidency, but God had other plans. In President Trump, he gave us a Cyrus to stand in the gap. America's best days do not have to be over. We have been given a second chance at greatness, but it will require something of each of us. As the Israelites did so many times before, we are expected to stand and be counted. Every time the Israelites prayed to God, repented, and put on the armor of God, He went into battle with them, and no matter what the odds, they were victorious.

We can defeat this Goliath. We can defeat an army of Goliaths. No weapon forged against us will prevail. God gave me the assignment to write this book so that, as with Saul, the scales could be removed from his people's eyes, so they be deceived no longer, so we have reprobate minds no longer, and so we no longer do those things that are inconvenient. If we stand up and slay the giant of Globalism, not only will God break our chains of bondage, but God will honor our obedience by pouring out the latter-day rain that he promised. God is not a man that He should lie!

An Ode the Rothschild's

There once was a family of royal descent
Who thought themselves deserving to rule the land
And all that dwelled therein
The people were to submit to their royal hand
And bend their knees and bow their heads
The sweat of their brow was theirs to command.
The earth and its riches they did demand
And none dare challenge their every command

In the shadows, they did reside
Their plots and schemes there to contrive
Hidden away from prying eyes
Their witches brew they would contrive
There was one to which they did submit
For he gave them the power their sins to commit
But one demand did he have
A sacrifice must be made to him
The blood and tears of billions
Upon his alter must be laid

Then the earth and all there in
Would travail under their heavy hand
Their yokes and burdens of no concern
To those that would rule over all the land!

Finally, their plan they could unleash
Against one another, the people must be turned
Old hatreds kindled and wars unleashed
Invisible chains to be forged
Control of money a weapon most grand
To be used to control all in the land
The earth's bounty to be stolen on their command
None to buy nor sell save those under their command
Whoever defies them to the worms they must be fed!
Then shall they rule over all the land

Pivotal Turning Points That Changed the World Forever

In preparation for our review of the pivotal points that changed the world, I need to refer you back to the paragraph below from the introduction. It will give you the appropriate perspective for the rest of this chapter.

I should note that control of the global banking system goes hand in hand with control of global trade because the basis of wealth for every nation in the world is trade. Global trade and global banking are derivatives of one another! It goes like this; natural resources are mined, manufactured into finished products, and shipped worldwide. This forms the basis for the Gross Domestic Product (GDP) of individual nations and the entire world. But this is impossible without credit, so control of money and credit is the genesis of all wealth. Money is the medium of exchange that makes all this possible. As you can see, when we are talking about Globalism, we are talking about the basis of all wealth! There can be no more crucial all-encompassing topic! He who controls the money controls the world!

As you read what follows, think about what President Franklin D. Roosevelt said,

"In politics, nothing happens by accident. If it happened, you can bet it was planned that way."

Pivot Points that Changed the World:

- **The 100 Year War Between France and England:** England declared bankruptcy, and the Rothschild's loaned the King money conditioned on printing England's currency at interest. This is the birth of the 1ˢᵗ central bank and the genesis of the plan to rule the world!

    - The Rothschild's understand that if they can bankrupt a nation, they can take over their monetary system and run the government from the shadows.

    - **Note:** All but three nations in the world now have a Rothschild central bank which controls their government from the shadows

    - The Rothschild's also understand that financing wars are not only enormously profitable, but it can drive a nation(s) into unmanageable debt, allowing them to be taken over.

    - This evolves into the strategy to create false flag attacks as a means of starting wars for profit!

- **The American Revolutionary War:**

    - **Why It Happened:** *"The inability of the colonists to get power to issue their own money permanently out of the hands of King George III and the international bankers was the prime reason for the Revolutionary War"* (President James Madison).

- **War of 1812:**

    - **1811:** The charter for the Rothschild's 1st Central Bank of the U.S. expired, and Congress elected not to renew it.

    - Nathan Mayer Rothschild threatens, *"Either the application for renewal of the charter is granted, or the United States will find itself involved in a most disastrous war."*

- Congress ignores his threat, at which point he issues a second threat, *"Teach those impudent Americans a lesson. Bring them back to Colonial status."*

- **1812:** The British, backed by Rothschild money, declare war on the United States. The plan was to drive the U.S. so deep into debt that they would be forced to renew the bank charter.

- This was known as the 2nd American Revolution.

- **1861 - The U.S. Civil War Begins:**

    - President Lincoln approaches New York Bankers to obtain loans to fund the war. Under the Rothschild's thumb, the banks made him an absurd offer of 24% to 36% interest.

    - Lincoln decided to print his own debt-free money, the Green-back, and upon its distribution, he says, *"We gave the people of this Republic the greatest blessing they ever had, their own paper money to pay their own debts."*

    - In response, The Times of London publishes the following, *"If that mischievous financial policy, which had its origin in the North American Republic, should become indurated down to a fixture, then that government will furnish its own money without cost. It will pay off debts and be without debt. It will have all the money necessary to carry on its commerce. It will become prosperous beyond precedent in the history of civilized governments of the world. The brains and the wealth of all countries will go to North America. That government must be destroyed, or it will destroy every monarchy on the globe."*

- **1865** - Shortly before his assassination, President Lincoln makes the following statement to Congress, *"I have two great enemies, the Southern Army in front of me, and the financial institutions in the rear. Of the two, the one in my rear is my greatest foe."*

- **April 14, 1865 - President Lincoln is Assassinated:**
  - Subsequently, eight British spies are hung for their part in his assassination.
  - *"The death of Lincoln was a disaster for Christendom... I fear that foreign bankers with their craftiness and tortuous tricks will entirely control the exuberant riches of America and use it systematically to corrupt modern civilization. They will not hesitate to plunge the whole of Christendom into wars and chaos in order that the earth should become their inheritance"* (Otto von Bismarck, 1st Chancellor of the German Empire).

- **1869 - The U.S. Completes the Transcontinental Railroad:**
  - Ends U.S. dependency on British Free Trade Slavery System.
  - America embarks on developing its natural resources and manufacturing capability.

- **1876 - U.S. Centennial Celebration:**
  - Celebration of America as the youngest nation in the world becoming an economic superpower.
  - Rise of the U.S. to economic superpower status based on high tariffs on British goods in order to allow domestic development of U.S. manufacturing base.
  - The American Economic System, based on human ingenuity, proves superior to the British Free Trade System, which is based on control of natural recourses and suppression of wages. The American System uplifts the condition of humankind while the British System enslaves them.
  - The world embraces America's Transcontinental Railroad. England seeing it as a threat to their dominance of trade by sea, hatches a plan to start WWI and destroy all the nations of Europe, especially Germany who is emerging as their primary European rival.

- **1897 - Buying of 1ˢᵗ U.S. President:**

  ○ The three richest men in America (Carnegie, J.P. Morgan, and Rockefeller) back pro-business candidate McKinley against anti-monopoly candidate Bryan and get their man elected.

  ○ Rothschild's now understand they can buy Presidents and other politicians to control Democratic governments.

- **1913 - Federal Reserve Is Established:**

  ○ President Wilson (put into office by Rothschild front man J.P. Morgan) breaks his campaign promise not to impose a central bank (the privately-owned Fed) on the American people.

  ○ The Fed is established and takes over the printing of our currency at interest. From that point, the government is controlled by the Fed and IMF, and our elected politicians are little more than figureheads.

  ○ Not even the President can challenge decisions made by the Fed Chairman.

  ○ Remember, "He who controls the money controls the world."

  ○ Vladimir Lenin is also on record as having stated, *"The establishment of a central bank is 90% of communizing a nation."*

- **1915 - Rothschild Interests Start Takeover of Media Outlets:**

  ○ They buy the 25 largest newspapers in America and put in their own editors in order to control public opinion.

  ○ Editors were to influence public opinion regarding militarism, war preparedness, and financial policies, etc. This was in preparation for WWI.

  ○ This was the 1ˢᵗ step in taking over Hollywood, TV, news outlets, the education system, and most recently, their influence is seen in rigged search results on the internet.

- **1917 - The U.S. Enters WWI on the Side of Rothschild Controlled England:**

  ○ The war destroyed Europe, which ended the building of the Transcontinental Railroad system and destroyed the emerging industrial revolution in Germany, whose success threatened England.

  ○ **Note:** As with most things, America entering the war that was orchestrated by the Rothschild's. They wanted a homeland in Palestine for the Jews, so a deal was struck; America would enter the war on the side of England, and the Jews would get a homeland. This was known as the Balfour agreement.

  ○ Rothschild's fund both sides of the war conditioned on the winner paying the debts of the vanquished.

- **1929 - The Great Depression:**

  ○ Impeachment charges were brought against the Fed for intentionally causing the depression.

  ○ *"Whoever controls the volume of money in our country is absolute master of all industry and commerce…and when you realize that the entire system is very easily controlled, one way or another, by a few powerful men at the top, you will not have to be told how periods of inflation and depression originate"* (President James A. Garfield, stated two weeks before he is assassinated).

- **1933 - U.S. Declares Bankruptcy During the Heart of Depression:**

  ○ A bank holiday is declared.

  ○ All safety deposit boxes are opened, and any gold in them is confiscated.

  ○ The public is told to surrender all gold on penalty of 10 years in prison and/or a $10,000 fine.

  ○ Receivers of bankruptcy declare all U.S. government agencies to exist in name only.

- ◦ The U.S. Republic is ended. Receivers of the bankruptcy establish a new government, a Democracy, a Socialist-Communist order.

- ◦ This marks the Shadow Government's takeover of the U.S. Government, with an army of nonelected bureaucrats put in the government to write regulations undermining the Constitution and controlling the economic system.

- **CFR Plotted to Cause WWII:**

  - ◦ CFR set up a committee on *"post-war problems"* prior to the end of 1939, before the war even started. In other words, the CFR orchestrated the start of the war (State Department Publication 2349, submitted by Secretary of State and CFR member Edward Stettinius).

  - ◦ **1939:** Rothschild controlled I.G. Farben (the world's leading producer of chemicals and Germany's largest steel producer) increases production so Germany can build its military in preparation for WWII.

  - ◦ During the war, I.G. Farben used slave labor in the concentration camps.

  - ◦ They created the lethal Zyklon B gas used to exterminate the Jews.

  - ◦ At the end of the war, it was reported that I.G. Farben plants hadn't been targeted in bombing raids on Germany. Their plants had only sustained 15% damage.

- **1941 - President Roosevelt Lays Plans to Take America Into WWII**

  - ◦ He has an 8-point plan intended to force Japan to attack the U.S., giving him an excuse to enter the war.

  - ◦ As part of that plan, the U.S. refused to sell Japan scrap steel or oil.

  - ◦ He also staged what was called *"pop-ups,"* where U.S. Naval ships would make incursions into the war zone in hopes of inciting a conflict.

- Japan needed a tempting target, so Roosevelt gave them one. Against the advice of his Admirals, he brought the 7th Fleet into Pearl Harbor, where they were sitting ducks.

- Over 3,000 Americans lost their lives that day, but as planned, America entered the war under a false flag event!

- **1941 - America Enters WWII:**

  - The U.S. needed a spy network, and it just so happens that the Financial Elite CFR happened to have a vast spy network.

  - CFR's spy network was embedded in the U.S. Government. It became the CIA and infiltrated the Department of Justice. Have you ever wondered why top-level FBI and Department of Justice's heads seem to be corrupt?

- **1942 - Prescott Bush's Company Seized Under the Trading With the Enemy Act:**

  - He was funding Hitler while American soldiers were being killed in Germany.

  - Prescott Bush is the father of President George H. W. Bush and grandfather of George W. Bush.

  - By the way, both Bush Presidents belonged to Yale Universities' *"Skull and Bones"* secret society, which is known for grooming people to be placed in positions of power in the government.

- **1945 – The United Nations is Established:**

  - Dedicated to establishing a One-World Government.

  - The CFR is involved in establishing the United Nations. They state the following in their own handbook, *"The New World Order will be built...an end-run on national sovereignty, eroding it piece by piece will accomplish much more than the old-fashioned frontal assault"* (Council on Foreign Relations Journal 1974, P558).

  - The U.N. provides an umbrella organization for all global governance organizations, i.e., World Bank, IMF, NATO, World Trade Organization, World Health Organization, etc.

- ○ **Note**: There were two previous attempts by the Rothschild's to establish a global governance body.

- **1963 – President John F. Kennedy is Assassinated:**
  - ○ JFK had issued Executive order #11110 to end the Federal Reserve's Charter, putting them out of business.
  - ○ He issued silver certificates to replace the Fed's printed dollar.
  - ○ He refused efforts of the Rothschild controlled military complex to commit more troops to the Vietnam War.
  - ○ If the Rothschild's were to maintain control of the U.S. government, Kennedy had to die.
  - ○ Once Johnson became President, he reversed all three of the initiatives listed above. Had Kennedy lived, America would be debt-free, and the American people would be free.
  - ○ *"It is well enough that people of the nation do not understand our banking and monetary system, for if they did, I believe there would be a revolution before tomorrow morning"* (Industrialist, Henry Ford).
  - ○ *"The one aim of these financiers is world control by the creation of inextinguishable debts"* (Industrialist, Henry Ford).

- **1964 - The Vietnam War:**
  - ○ The Vietnam War was a false flag event perpetrated by the Rothschild Global Shadow Government.
  - ○ The Gulf of Tonkin event, which was President Johnson's provocation for committing troops to the Vietnam War, was proven to have never occurred. It was a hoax, a false flag event!
  - ○ Pentagon Papers disclose the Vietnam War could not be won, yet it was drug out in order to drive the U.S. into debt.

- **President Carter Opens Trade with China:**
  - U.S. economy has years of 18% interest rates and inflation rates coupled with an unprecedented period of corporate raiding, which saw many major corporations bought only to be broken up and sold off in pieces.
  - This cleared the way for the reintroduction of the British Free Trade system rebranded as Chinese Free Trade.
  - This led to intentionally losing Free Trade Deals, which gutted the U.S. manufacturing base and created a devastating trade imbalance for the U.S., which is a major cause of our debt crisis.
  - Henry Kissinger said NAFTA *"was a steppingstone to a One World Government."*
  - NAFTA was also intended to model the U.S. after the European Union, which started as a trade agreement, then a common currency, and finally a common Socialist Constitution.
  - Our open borders policies have nothing to do with human rights (it is a smokescreen) and has everything to do with merging the U.S., Mexico, and Canada into a servile Socialist trading bloc modeled after the European Union.

- **The Iraq and Afghanistan Wars:**
  - NBC News reported May 2002: A former National Security Presidential Directive *"submitted two days before the 9/11 attacks"* had outlined essentially the same war plan that the White House, the CIA, & the Pentagon put into action. In other words, they knew what was going to happen before it happened. Another false flag event, just like Pearl Harbor and the Gulf of Tonkin!
  - According to NBC, on October 14, 2001: Seven days into the bombing, the Taliban offered to surrender Osama Bin Laden to a third country for trial if the bombing was halted, and they were shown evidence of his involvement in the September 11 terrorist

attacks. This was their second offer to surrender Osama, and it was also refused by President Bush, who declared, *"There's no need to discuss innocence or guilt. We know he did it."* They needed Bin Laden on the loose as the face of terror in order to prolong the war. This is another example of wars for profit!

- **Project for the New American Century (PNAC):** The report written in 2000 outlines three major U.S. military objectives: 1) The need for strategically positioned military bases worldwide. 2) The need to bring about regime change in countries unfriendly to U.S. policy. 3) The desire to increase military spending by upwards of a trillion dollars..." Then came 9/11, and they got everything they wanted, go figure!

- The wars in Iraq and Afghanistan cost the U.S. over $7 trillion.

- **The 2008 Financial Collapse:**

  - Just like the 1929 Great Depression, the 2008 financial collapse was orchestrated. It was the largest theft of money from the public coffers in world history.

  - Had it not been for the actions of Presidents George W. Bush, Bill Clinton, and Barack Obama, the collapse would never have happened.

- **2016 - Trump Elected as President:**

  - 1st U.S. President in decades not put into office by the Financial Elite.

  - He immediately begins reversal of the policies listed above, and the U.S. economy begins a remarkable recovery.

The chronology we just went through contained a lot of information and exposed some eye-opening events, but there is more to the Rothschild story, much more. Still, we need to move on, so I will take you into the stratosphere and give you the 60,000-foot overview of the important stuff, the big picture stuff.

Why America Must Fall in Order to Birth the New World Order!

First, I want to make it absolutely clear that America is the #1 target of the Rothschild's global takeover scheme. From our founding, we have represented their biggest threat. Why do you think that is? Think about that a second before you read on. It has to do with light vs. dark! Their global takeover model has always been about taking. They swindle 3rd world resource-rich countries out of their resources and then suppress wages in order to produce finished goods at the lowest possible price. If that wasn't bad enough, they pay workers in depreciating fiat currency controlled by their manipulation of the global banking system.

By contrast, America's model has always been to encourage human ingenuity as the basis of economic progress. That is why in less than 50 years after completion of the Transcontinental Railroad, America surpassed England as an economic superpower despite the fact that they had hundreds of years' head start.

Light vs. Dark:

The British Free Trade Slavery System with its cheap labor & low tariffs was diametrically opposed to *"The American System of Economics"* with its high tariff & shared technology!

The Darkness:

"It, [The British System Free Trade System] is the most gigantic system of slavery the world has yet seen, and therefore it is that freedom gradually disappears from every country over which England [The Free Trade System] is enabled to obtain control" (Henry C. Carey, Economics Adviser to Abraham Lincoln).

"Free trade shaves down the workingman's labor first, and then scales down his pay by rewarding him in a worthless and depreciated State currency" (William McKinley, October 4, 1892).

"…Slavery is but the owning of labor and carries with it the care of labors, while the European plan [British Free Trade System] is that capital shall control labor by controlling wages…" (Hazard Circular, July 1862).

This is the system of slavery we labor under today. Change the name from *"British Free Trade"* to *"Chinese Free Trade,"* and you will begin to understand that the Financial Elite controls America, Russia, China, and virtually the entire world. The various global ideologies exist in order to give us enemies to focus on instead of our real enemy, the Financial Elite.

The Light:

"The Republic is the only form of government which is not eternally at open or secret war with the rights of mankind" (Thomas Jefferson, Founding Father).

Remember, our Republic was morphed into a Democracy, *"a Socialist-Communist Order,"* in 1933 when we declared bankruptcy and the Financial Elite Shadow Government was imbedded in our government to begin the process of dismantling the Republic bit by bit from the inside out!

"Two systems are before the world. One is the English System; the other we may be proud to call the American System of Economics, the only one ever devised the tendency of which was that of elevating while equalizing the condition of man throughout the world" (Henry C. Carey, Economics Adviser to Abraham Lincoln)

"Thirty years of protection have brought us to the 1st rank in agriculture, mining, and manufacturing development. We lead all nations in these three great departments of industry. We have outstripped even the United Kingdom, which had century's head start on us.....31 years the protective tariff policy of the Republicans has by any test, measured by any standard vindicated itself."

This is the economic system President Trump is fighting to restore!

Russian, Chinese, and American Leaders Controlled by Financial Elite Are Pushing to Establish the New World Order!

(This is the system President Trump's predecessors colluded to establish!)

To say that we are all Socialists is not as crazy as you might think. The following quotes from world leaders all pledge their allegiance, not to their respective countries but the Financial Elite's U.N. and or to establish a New World Order. In the next chapter, we will find out why our leaders would make such a pledge.

I start you off with a quote from Karl Marx, which reminds us what Socialism – Communism is really about and follow it up with a quote from Financial Elite David Rockefeller so you can see that our political leaders in Washington are echoing his Financial Elite ideology.

> *"Socialism destroys law, morality, prosperity, productivity, education, incentive, and finally, life itself. It creates conditions for dictators to come to power"* (Karl Marx, Father of Communism).

> *"We are on the verge of a global transformation. All we need is the right major crisis, and the nations will accept the New World Order"* (David Rockefeller, September 23, 1994).

> *"But it became clear as time went on that in Mr. Bush's mind the New World Order was founded on a convergence of goals and interests between the U.S. and the Soviet Union, so strong and permanent that they would work as a team through the U.N. Security Council"* (Excerpt from A. M. Rosenthal in the New York Times, January 1991).

> *"Further global progress is now possible only through a quest for universal consensus in the movement toward a new world order"* (Russian leader Mikhail Gorbachev).

Remember in 1989 when the Berlin Wall fell, President Bush Sr. met with Russian leader Gorbachev and Communist Pope Paul II to announce the birth of the New World Order.

"Out of these troubled times, our objective a New World Order can emerge. Today, that New World Order is struggling to be born, a world quite different from the one we have known" (President George Bush Sr., addressing the general assembly of the United States, February 1, 1992).

"It is the sacred principles enshrined in the United Nations Charter to which the American people will henceforth pledge their Allegiance" (President George Bush Addressing the U.N.).

"What Congress will have before it is not a conventional trade agreement but the architecture of a new international system...a first step toward a new world order" (Henry Kissinger, CFR member and Trilateralist, in The Los Angeles Times concerning NAFTA, July 18, 1993).

"The United Nations will spearhead our efforts to manage the new conflicts [that afflict our world]. Yes, the principles of the United Nations Charter are worth our lives, our fortunes, and our sacred honor" (General Colin Powell, April 21, 1993).

"He [President Nixon] spoke of the talks [trade talks] as a beginning, saying nothing more about the prospects for future contacts and merely reiterating the belief he brought to China that both nations share an interest in peace and building a New World Order." (New York Times, February 1972).

"There is a chance for the President of the United States to use this (9-11) disaster to carry out...a New World Order" (Gary Hart, at a televised meeting organized by the CFR in Washington, D.C. September 14).

I end our series of quotes with this quote from the CFR to remind you that most of our top people in Washington belong to this subversive Financial Elite organization.

"The Council on Foreign Relations is the American branch of a society, which originated in England…[and]… believes national boundaries should be obliterated and one-world rule established" (Dr. Carroll Quigley, CFR member, college mentor of President Clinton, & author of *Tragedy and Hope,* 1966). That is why Democrats want to end national sovereignty with their open borders policies.

Why America Needs to Liberate Itself From the Tyranny of Globalism!

Remember, when our children are taught that Capitalism is evil, what they are referring to is the crony Capitalism imposed on the world under the Rothschild banking system of slavery. It is the Free Enterprise System, the American Economic System, which made America the greatest nation the world has ever known! It is fear of this system that makes America the greatest enemy the Financial Elite have ever faced. It is this system we must restore because the world depends on us winning this struggle for fundamental human rights. That is why the Financial Elite are committed to our destruction, and that is why we must stand up and fight. The quote below states exactly why we must win the war! And a war it is!

"If that mischievous financial policy, which had its origin in the North American Republic, should become indurated down to a fixture, then that government will furnish its own money without cost. It will pay off debts and be without a debt. It will have all the money necessary to carry on its commerce. It will become prosperous beyond precedent in the history of civilized governments of the world. The brains and the wealth of all countries will go to North America. That government must be destroyed, or it will destroy every monarchy on the globe" (The Times of London).

The next quote punctuates the fact that our enemy is real, and like the octopus that hides in the cloud of ink, they lurk in the shadows. It is time to oust him once and for all!

"Since I entered politics, I have chiefly had men's views confided to me privately. Some of the biggest men in the United States, in the fields of government and manufacturing. They know there is a power somewhere, so complete, so perverse, that they better not speak about their breath when they speak in condemnation of it" (President Woodrow Wilson).

Remember, America is no longer a Republic. In 1933 the receivers of our bankruptcy morphed America into a Democracy (Mobocracy) and are now working with all dispatch to drive the U.S. headlong into Socialism and Communism.

Following the Civil War, the U.S. was leading the world in the effort to break the chains of the British Free Trade Slavery System. It imposed high tariffs against British goods, was leading the world into the Industrial Revolution, had completed a Transcontinental Railroad, and was sharing its technological breakthroughs with the world in an effort to elevate while equalizing the condition of man throughout the world.

America represented hope and freedom. England and the Rothschild's represented oppression. That is still true today. So why is this important? Because it means that in the Rothschild Financial Elites, America truly has an archenemy who will do literally anything to take us down. I want to make it absolutely clear that it is, as the military strategist Sun Tzu said, *"We are on death ground,"* and you will find out in the next chapter exactly how high the stakes are. It is truly a case of win or die! The Financial Elite intend on imposing their New World Order Dictatorship, and for that to happen, America must fall.

With that in mind, I want to tell you the story of Tsar Nicholas of Russia. In 1814, he opposed the Rothschild's efforts to establish their One-World Government, and then during the U.S. Civil War; he told England and France that if either of them entered the war on the side of the south, he would consider that an act of war. As you will see in a second, the Rothschild's have long memories, and they don't make idol threats.

The Bolshevik Revolution and the Birth of Communism: Why Tsar Nicholas and the Entire Romanov Family Had to Die!

At the Congress of Vienna, 120 years earlier, Tsar Alexander had opposed Nathan Mayer Rothschild's effort to establish a One-World Government. Rothschild swore that someday he or his decedents would destroy the entire Romanov line. For this reason, the Romanov's were obliterated! As the Rothschild Financial Elite have said, they will have World Government by consent or conquest, and for that to happen, America must fall. We need to put aside our differences. The false differences inflicted on us by the Rothschild Financial Elite and their minions in the fake news, our schools, Hollywood, and Washington.

The Financial Elite intend to have their New World Order, and the only way they will stop pushing for it is if we stop them! It's them or us! We talked about how the organized minority pushes up from the bottom and down from the top to inflict the majority with their special interest programs, which are never in the interest of the majority. It is time the *"silent majority"* got organized and push back! There is strength in numbers. We will discuss how we push back towards the end of this book.

The Truth About America's Open Borders Policy!

So how will they end all Nation States to establish their ten servile trading blocs in their place? There are two possibilities. The 1st option has to do with immigration. In the instance of the U.S., they want to merge the U.S., Mexico, and Canada and get rid of our Constitution and give us a new Constitution modeled after the European Union's Socialist Constitution. This is why President George H. W. Bush met in secret at Baylor University with the Presidents of Mexico and Canada. They signed *The Security and Prosperity Agreement*, empowering unelected bureaucrats to write regulations merging the laws of the three nations.

The Financial Elite Are Preparing to Start WWIII

The 2nd way is to take the world into WWIII. After WWI and WWII, the world wanted to end future world wars, and the Financial Elites used that to further their One-World Agenda. As horrific as those wars were, they were nothing compared to what WWIII could be. They have far more lethal weapons at their disposal now, and they won't hesitate to use them if it gets them across the finish line and finally births their New World Order. The Rothschild's have been the cause of untold mischief and misery in Europe and has piled up its prodigious wealth chiefly through fomenting wars between States which ought never to have quarreled.

> *"Whenever there is trouble in Europe, wherever rumors of war circulate, and men's minds are distraught with fear of change and calamity you may be sure that a hook-nosed Rothschild is at his games..."*
> (The British labor Leader, 1891).

We discussed how they engage in wars for profit. To them, the millions who die mean nothing. It is like CFR member Henry Kissinger said:

> *"Military men are dumb, stupid animals meant to be used as cannon fodder."*

With this in mind, I want to finally ask you to look into the face of the 9/11 tragedy and honestly ask yourself if it is possible that some 3,000 American's were sacrificed on the altar of greed to justify a war for profit intended to drive America deep into debt. The following graphic combines the cost of 9/11, the 2008 financial collapse, and the Wars in Iraq and Afghanistan because they are all interrelated and part of a cascade that started September 11, 2001.

The True Cost of 9/11!	
2001: 9/11 Stock Market Crash	$1.4 Trillion
2008 Collapse of Real Estate Market	$3.3 Trillion
2008 Collapse of the Stock Market	$6.9 Trillion
Cost of the War in the Middle East	$7.0 Trillion
Total Cost of 9/11	$18.6 Trillion
Current National Debt	$26.0 Trillion

"If tyranny and oppression come to this land, it will be in the guise of fighting a foreign enemy" (James Madison).

The Grim Reaper Roams the Land!

Rhetoric was flying
Tempers were flaring
Rage was in the air
Nations were posturing
Their leaders were shouting
Insults were flying
Drums were beating
The march was proceeding
Lovers were pleading
Boys were leaving
Hearts would soon be bleeding
Hatred was everywhere
And war was in the air
All were infected
None were protected
For lies were everywhere
War not for honor
War not for glory
But
war for greed was to proceed

Not only did 9/11 cost America $18.6 trillion, but it also laid the foundation for the hatred, which at some point, the Financial Elite will use to try to drag us into WWIII. We have to see the truth about these wars for profit so we can stop being drug in needless wars that kill millions and create massive debt.

I am about to show you some photos which if you examine with an open mind prove emphatically that:

- **The Twin Towers Came Down by Controlled Demolition:** Prior to 9/11, no structural steel building had ever collapsed due to fire. Why, you ask? Because the temperature created by an open combustion fire is nowhere near hot enough to melt or fatigue steel "I" beams. It is scientifically impossible. For that, you would need thermite used in a controlled demolition, which burns at 4,500 degrees.

- **A Boeing 757 Did Not Hit the Pentagon:** The opening in the façade was too small and was more of what you would expect from a military drone than a 757. Also, there was almost no wreckage.

- **The Crash Site in Shanksville, PA Was Staged:** There was an absence of wreckage, and no bodies were found, not even a single drop of blood.

Hitler said that if you want to sell a lie, make it a big lie, and tell it often and use multiple propaganda sources (fake news outlets). So, with the stage set, I ask you to take a good hard look at the photos below and ask yourself the following questions:

1. How is it possible for a fire to cut steel columns on a 45-degree angle, all facing in.? This is what is required to bring down a building by controlled demolitions, and it can only be done with a shaped charge. No fire can do this!

It is a scientific fact that jet fuel does not burn hot enough to melt metal, but thermite used in controlled demolitions does! To take down a building by controlled demolition, you cut the support beams in the basement at a 45-degree angle. No fire started from jet fuel can cut metal at a perfect angle. Also, remember, the plane hit the 73rd floor. How do you account for the beams in the basement being cut? The first two photos are actual photos from the Twin Towers wreckage after their collapse. The third photo is an example of a demolition crew planting a shaped charge for controlled demolition. Notice the angle at which the charge is placed.

2. How can an open combustion fire that doesn't get any hotter than your stovetop melt tons of metal and fuse concrete and steel? The answer is it can't! Why, because it is scientifically impossible.

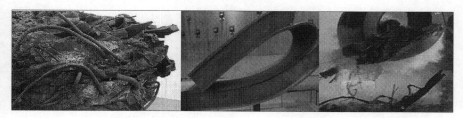

No steel skyscraper has ever collapsed from a fire until the attacks on 9/11. The reason is that a conventional fire is nowhere near hot enough to melt, fatigue, or bend steel girders!

3. How is it Building #5 sustained catastrophic damage and remained standing, and Building #7, with almost no damage, came crashing down? That, too, is impossible. So, was there a reason someone would want Building #7 taken down? You bet there was! Building #7 contained all the records for all the white color crimes committed by the Banker Gangsters!

Look at the photos above. Building #5 sustained catastrophic damage yet remained standing. On the other hand, building #7 had minor damage, with two small fires on two floors, yet it collapsed. What are the chances of that happening?

4. How can a Boeing 757 fit through a hole that small, and where is the wreckage? There should be wreckage, a lot of wreckage from a plane that big.

Experts Say: No Commercial Airliner Hit the Pentagon!

Notice in the photo to the left how the wingspan is much larger than the hole of the Pentagon's façade. French Air Accident Investigator François Grangier said, *"What is certain when one looks at the photos of the facade that remains is that it is obvious that the plane [Boeing 757] did not go through there."* Because of the much larger wingspan of the Boeing 757, the hole would indeed be much larger, and very likely, the wings could have been ripped off, leaving at the very least some wreckage on the ground. The photo on the right shows how, just like Shanksville, PA, there is no wreckage! This is impossible!

5. 9/11 crash site in Shanksville, PA. Again, where is the wreckage? Did it just evaporate, or was it never there?

Crash Site in Shanksville, PA on 9/11   Normal Plane Crash Site

Wally Summerset, County Coroner at the site of Flight 93, said, *"It looks like there is nothing there except a hole in the ground...It looked like somebody just dropped a bunch of metal out of the sky. It looked like somebody took a scrap truck, dug a 10-foot ditch, and put trash in it...I stopped being coroner after about 20 minutes because there were no bodies there. I have not to this day seen a single drop of blood, not a drop."*

So why all these years later should you care? Because this is just one incident in a repeating pattern. Hopefully, the next time they inflict us with a false flag event, we won't be so gullible, and we won't be led into a war for profit that we ought not to be in – inflicted on us by the Financial Elite for political reasons and pure greed.

> *"Beware of the leader who bangs the drums of war in order to whip the citizenry into a patriotic fervor, for patriotism is indeed a double-edged sword. It both emboldens the blood, just as it narrows the mind. And when the drums of war have reached a fever pitch, and the blood boils with hate, and the mind has closed, the leader will have no need in seizing the rights of the citizenry, [who] infused with fear and blinded by patriotism, will offer up all of their rights unto the leader and gladly so. How well I know? For this, I have done. And I am Julius Caesar"* (Julius Caesar, n.d.).

It's Time for You to Decide What You Think!

This is the lightning round. This is where we put it all together, and you decide if you believe the story I have presented is factual or a fairytale. This is where you determine if you can afford to be a bystander or, if you must, out of a sense of self-survival stand up and say no more. It is where you decide once and for all if our elected officials in Washington have sold out to a global banking cartel intent on collapsing America by conquest or consent. It is where you decide if our trade policies of the last fifty-plus years have been an intentional effort to bury America under a mountain of debt. It is where you decide if the Vietnam, Iraq, and Afghanistan Wars were initiated by false flag events and used as wars for profit intended to drive America into unmanageable debt. It is where you decide who the real enemy is; our fellow Americans, who like you, are under the thumb of the Financial Elite, or the Global Banking Cabal intent on collapsing America and establishing a Global Dictatorship. It is where you decide if we are going to allow the Financial Elite to continue enslaving us by printing our money at interest, causing financial collapses at will, and controlling the necessities of life: food, water, energy, health care, and a living wage. It is where you decide if you are going to stand up and be counted or remain passive and suffer under the oppression of the Financial Elite.

Focus Questions: Please, place a checkmark in the box if you agree with the statement, and when you are finished, count your responses. If you conclude that we are indeed facing a genuine and present danger, then the good news is we can drain the swamp and take our country back. If the silent majority comes together in one accord, we will be unstoppable. Here we go.

50 Questions

❑ The news is less about giving us the facts and more about slanting our opinions in a particular direction.

❑ America's moral value system has suffered by taking prayer and the Pledge of Allegiance out of our schools.

❑ Schools have a responsibility to teach our children that America was founded as a Republic, what that means, and why the Republic is the only form of government that protects our property and civil rights.

❑ A nation without borders has no nation to be sovereign over.

❑ Vietnam was a war for profit. It could have been ended any time we wanted by merely mining the Haiphong Harbor as President Nixon did at the end of the war (cutting off the enemies' supply lines, no supplies, no war).

❑ Our Christian values are under attack.

❑ Our welfare system financially rewards single mothers in deference to two-parent households. Not having a male role model in the home contributes to increased school dropout rates, unemployment, gang violence, and makes our inner cities unsafe.

❑ At one time, Lobbyists were illegal, and they should be again because they represent special interest to the detriment of the American people.

❑ Many of our elected officials in Washington have sold out to the Financial Elite and need to be voted out of office as well as imposing term limits.

❑ America lost manufacturing jobs to overseas markets because of excessively high capital gains taxes and burdensome EPA regulations, which other countries were not faced with.

❑ It should be illegal to change the boundary lines of a Congressional District to affect the outcome of an election.

❑ Photo ID's are necessary to prevent voter fraud.

❑ The 1929 Great Depression was intentionally caused by the Financial Elite bankers when they conspired to dry up the credit market.

❑ The Federal Reserve is a private bank that is not accountable to any government office, not even the President. Therefore, they constitute a shadow government that runs the country at the behest of the Financial Elite.

❑ The CFR and T.C. are Financial Elite organizations dedicated to establishing a One-World Government that would end U.S. Sovereignty, so they are a subversive organization that operates against the interest of the American people.

❑ Any politician who belongs to the subversive CFR or T.C. should be voted out of office.

❑ Politicians should be subject to the laws they pass.

❑ Many of the protests we are experiencing are organized by organizations that pay protesters in order to agitate, inflame, and pit us against one another.

❑ Americans are not racists who are against immigration. But it is a fact that there is a limit to the number of people any nation can assimilate without it causing a cultural and economic crisis.

❑ There is an organized attack against family values because the Financial Elite know they are foundational to what makes America great.

❑ There is supposed to be a correlation between productivity and wages. For decades, the Financial Elite have not passed on those increases in productivity in the form of higher wages. They make us slaves without chains.

❑ We need term limits in order to limit the accumulation of undue power by elected officials.

❑ Ever since America opened trade with China, we have suffered under intentionally losing trade policies, and that must stop if America is to rebuild its economy.

❑ We need to get away from electronic voting machines because it is too easy to program them to throw an election.

❑ As Citizens of America, we should all stand for the Pledge of Allegiance. Not to do so weakens us as a nation.

❑ Historical monuments are a part of our national heritage and teach us valuable lessons about who we are.

❑ Super packs should be illegal because they allow the Financial Elite - special interests to unduly affect the outcome of elections.

❑ If America is ever to regain control of our government, the Fed must be put out of business, and the printing of our currency returned to the U.S. treasury.

❑ The Financial Elite have hijacked our educational system in order to promote their agenda.

❑ The U.S., Russian and Chinese leaders have all sold out to the Financial Elite.

❑ America is rapidly moving into Socialism, which invariably leads to Communism.

❑ The Democrats play the race card as a means to divide us and pit us against one another.

❑ Energy is used as a control mechanism. That is why Obama waged war on coal, natural gas, and oil.

❑ We are being lied to about the cause of climate change. That is not to say it is not real, just that our carbon footprint does not cause it. That explanation was just an excuse to impose a carbon tax to enrich the Elite.

❑ A crisis is used as a means to get us to surrender our civil rights to the government.

❑ Key political leaders (particularly our Presidents) are groomed for office by the Financial Elite who finance their campaigns.

❑ It is no accident many politicians go to Washington poor and end up multi-millionaires because they profited by backing policies that favored special interest groups.

❑ We were told the 2008 financial collapse came up unexpectedly, and the stimulus had to be passed immediately. That was a lie because you can't write a 2,000-page stimulus bill overnight.

❑ The 1929 Great Depression and 2008 financial collapse were intentionally orchestrated by the Financial Elite.

❑ The fact that our leaders in Washington repeatedly pass major legislation without even reading it is a clear indication that the special interest groups are pulling their strings, and they get what they want.

❑ It is time to negotiate fair reciprocal trade deals.

❑ We need a balanced budget amendment to keep America from being driven into bankruptcy.

❑ Politicians leaving Washington should be prohibited from leveraging their influence and security clearance in order to get rich as Lobbyists.

❑ Workers should not be forced to pay union dues if they don't want to belong to the union.

❑ The wall needs to be built because it is a national security issue.

❑ NATO members should all pay their fair share of defense costs.

❑ There is a Shadow Government (Deep State) in Washington that serves the Financial Elite's interest.

❑ Race, religion, sexual preference, and socioeconomic status are being used to divide us because the Financial Elite know a nation divided cannot stand.

❑ Sanctuary cities breed crime and are part of the plan to collapse America by inundating it with a criminal element.

❑ It is time to honor our military and police, including our border agents.

Why President Trump Is the Key to Stopping the Next Financial Collapse!

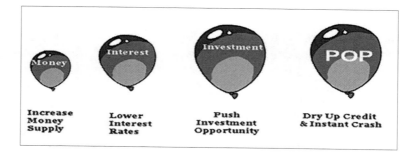

We learned earlier that market manipulation is the key to the Financial Elite's ability to cause financial bubbles and crashes any time they want. But what if there was a kill switch that would disarm their economic doomsday machine?

A miracle of miracles there is, let me explain. Let's look back at the 1929 Great Depression and the 2008 financial collapse. What did they have in common? During both of the most significant financial collapses in history, the Financial Elite had an inside man. What do I mean by that? I mean, they had Franklin D. Roosevelt and George W. Bush. The Financial Elite are not stupid. Their strategy in both instances was to collapse the U.S. economy so they could become the masters of us all. To do that, they had to collapse the U.S. economy, but the trick was to do it without bankrupting themselves in the process. The Financial Elite don't take chances. They are not gamblers as Roosevelt himself said,

"In politics, nothing happens by accident. If it happened, you can bet it was planned that way."

So, what was the plan? It was brilliantly simple, but it would only work if you had an inside man? Let's get to it. In 1929 President Roosevelt declared a bank holiday and confiscated all the people's gold. Then he made them indentured servants under the terms of the receiverships where the Republic was dissolved and replaced by a Democracy and the bailout of the U.S. economy was guaranteed by pledging the assets of the government (the people's assets bought and paid for by the sweat of their brows). **Translation:** The American people lost everything, and the Financial Elite got it all. That's a good deal if you are the Financial Elite and if things go as planned, which you know they will if you have an inside man, especially if that person is the President of the United States!

Regarding the 2008 financial collapse, we learned earlier that President George W. Bush did everything humanly possible to prevent the states from passing anti-predatory lending legislation that would have prevented the collapse. So, now as we know, Bush was complicit in causing the collapse! Then when the collapse occurred, he lied to us. He told us the collapse was completely unexpected and had caught the government off guard. He also stated that if Congress didn't pass the stimulus immediately, he would declare martial law so, a complicit Congress passed the stimulus without reading it. By the way, the stimulus took our money, but the Patriot Act undermined our civil liberties and laid the groundwork for someday legally imposing nationwide martial law. The government was not caught off guard. It was all part of the robbery plan. You see, it would have taken a planeload of lawyers and special interest Lobbyists a year or more to write a 2,000-page stimulus bill. It was all a setup! So, what happened next?

The American people were promised the money would be used to provide credit so they wouldn't lose their homes. Another lie! Instead, the Banker Gangsters got multi-million-dollar bonuses (blood-money) for their part in the theft. Millions of Americans lost their homes and their life savings, and the Banker Gangsters were bailed out by the American taxpayers.

There is a name for what happened in both 1929 and 2008. It's called quantitative easing. The non-sugar-coated definition of that term is collusion and theft on the part of the Fed and both the Roosevelt and Bush Administrations to see that the Financial Elite kept their money and stole that of the American people in the most massive white-collar crimes in history. As they say, *"the den of thieves laughed all the way to the bank!"* Now, do you understand why we have to get rid of the Fed?

I am now going to tell you why the Financial Elite hate President Trump, why the bought and paid for fake news has nothing good to say about him, why the Democrats tried to impeach him, why God put him in office as our President, and why he is the key to America breaking the chains of slavery of the Financial Elite. What a mouth full. But all true.

Trump has foiled their plans. Under President Obama, the stage had been set for another financial collapse, the one that was supposed to finally bring America to its knees. The key was debt, and Obama's *"Fundamental Transformation of America"* had seen him amass more debt than the 43 Presidents that preceded him. The debt trap was set and waiting for Hillary to spring it, but God trumped their plans with a man named Trump. Go figure! How so? Trump is God's man. He owes the Financial Elite NOTHING! So, where is this going? No inside man, no financial collapse. It's that simple.

It goes something like this, the man who would drop the mother of all bombs, the man who would call Kim Jong-un *"little rocket man."* The man who would call NATO to task, the man who would get Mexico and Canada to sign a new trade agreement, and the man who wrote *"The Art of the Deal"* is no man to trifle with. Especially if he is God's anointed – America's Cyrus sent to build the wall and restore America to greatness. So here is the bottom line, should the Financial Elite be stupid enough to cause another financial collapse during President Trump's time in office, here is what would happen. The Bull in the China Shop would say, *"Go ahead, but if you do, I will not bail you out! You may bankrupt America, but I will bankrupt you and put you out of business once and for all."* Trump card played - Match point Trump. Game Over – Winners: The American people! Losers: The Financial Elite! Scriptwriter: God himself!

CHAPTER 6

What Climate Change Has to Do With the Financial Elite's End Game Solution!

WHAT YOU WILL LEARN IN THIS CHAPTER

- Man-Made Carbon Emissions Are Not the Cause of Global Warming!

- The Real Cause of Global Warming!

- The Truly Serious Problem the Financial Elite Are Hiding from Us!

- Looming Water Crisis: What Does It Foretell?

- The Financial Elite's End Game Solution Revealed!

- A Glimpse Into the Financial Elites Brave New World!

Surprise: They're lying to us again! On the one hand, they are lying about the cause of global warming. On the other hand, they are hiding a much bigger, much more serious problem. This chapter exposes the true cause of global warming and the Financial Elite's end game solution! Their end game is more hennas than you can imagine! Hopefully, by the time you finish this chapter, you will truly realize that our lives truly are on the line, and the Financial Elite must be defeated once and for all! It is them or us!

Man-Made Carbon Emissions Are Not the Cause of Global Warming!

We are told that global warming is caused by carbon emissions from manufacturing, automobiles, and factory farming, particularly cattle. All these things do produce carbon emissions, and they do cause problems. But they are not the cause of global warming. President Reagan told us the truth when he said:

> *"Approximately 80% of our air pollution stems from hydrocarbon released by vegetation, so let's not go overboard in setting and enforcing tough emission standards from man-made sources."*

There is no question that we are encountering unprecedented climate change accompanied by erratic weather patterns, severe storms, floods in some areas, and drought in others. Worst of all, rising temperatures are melting the polar ice caps and threatening environmental habitats on both land and the oceans. But the Financial Elite latched onto this very real problem and did what they do best. They used it to create a narrative that furthers their agenda. Their front man, Al Gore, tells us global warming is caused by man, by what he calls our *"carbon footprint,"* and he has a relatively simple solution. He says America needs to drastically cut back it's manufacturing because that is what is causing global warming.

Gore's plan (thank God was not adopted) was to impose a carbon tax on every product made. The legislation proposed to do this was called *Cap and Trade*. But wait a minute, the legislation exempted China and India, the world's largest polluters, so it was apparent it was a bunch of nonsense.

The idea was that placing a tax on every product produced would drive up prices so high that consumption would drop dramatically. Less consumption equals less pollution, problem solved. How simple is that! But as usual, there was a hidden agenda. The real reason for *Cap and Trade* had nothing to do with protecting the environment. The intent was to collapse the U.S. economy because as the leader of the Free Market System, if America collapsed, it would cause a cascade that would collapse the entire Free Market System making way for the birth of the New World Order. This is confirmed by the quote below from the Globalist U.N.

> *"Isn't the only hope for the planet that the industrialized civilization collapse? Isn't it our responsibility to bring that about?"* (Maurice Strong, Founder of the U.N. Environmental Program, Opening Speech, Rio Earth Summit 1992)

Thank God, along came the *"Climate Gate"* scandal, and their lies were exposed! Climate Gate exposed the fact that their science was bogus, made up to fit their narrative. What's new? Below are a couple of hundreds of intercepted E-mails that exposed their scheme to defraud once again the American people and the people of the world.

Their Lies:

> *"We've got to ride the global warming issue. Even if the theory of global warming is wrong..."* (Timothy Wirth, former U.S. Senator (D-Colorado).

> *"A global climate treaty must be implemented even if there is no evidence to back the greenhouse effect."* (Richard Benedict, State Dept. employee working on assignment from the Conservation Foundation)

The Truth:

> *"If the U.S. passed a Cap and Trade and other countries did not, it wouldn't work. It would ruin the U.S. economy, and it wouldn't save the climate either."* (Hannity, November 1, 2009)

"Protecting the environment is a ruse. The goal is the political and economic subjugation of most men by the few under the guise of preserving nature" (J.H. Robbins).

So, their objective was to collapse the Free-Market System and implement the New World Order.

Climate Gate put an end to any hopes of inflicting us with a carbon tax but never mind; they had their man in the White House, so not all was lost. Enter President Obama, and he did behind the scenes what couldn't be done in the light of day. He directed an army of unelected bureaucrats to inflict the U.S. economy with hundreds of job-killing EPA regulations. Though not as devastating as Cap and Trade would have been, it allowed Obama to stall the U.S. economy while intentionally losing trade agreements, Obama Care (which hijacked 20% of the U.S. GDP) and other job-killing initiative allowed him to amass more debt than the 43 Presidents who preceded him combined.

The next step was that under a Hillary Presidency, they would collapse the economy once and for all and usher in the New World Order! But that didn't happen because Hillary lost. Yet neither Hillary nor Obama will go away. Obama is back on the scene, and he has the audacity to claim credit for Trump's unprecedented economic recovery. I want to make this absolutely clear. President Obama was the problem, and President Trump is the solution. The truth is President Trump receded Obama's job-killing EPA regulations, ended the war on oil, coal, and natural gas, lowered the capital gains tax, negotiated fair reciprocal trade agreements with Mexico and Canada, gave the American people a tax cut, and that is just the beginning. President Trump is God's man, he is the people's man, and he is the biggest threat the Financial Elite have ever been up against. That is the truth of the matter. Now back to global warming.

We were told the solution to global warming is to reduce our carbon footprint, but now we know that was a lie. The Financial Elite and their pawns in our government never intended to address the cause of global warming. Neither did they have any intention of telling us just how serious the crisis is. Remember this,

"The New World Order cannot happen without U.S. participation, as we are the most significant single component. Yes, there will be a New World Order, and it will force the United States to change its perceptions" (Henry Kissinger, World Affairs Council Press Conference, Regent Beverly Wilshire Hotel, April 19, 1994).

Translation: The U.S. must fall in order for the New World Order to be birthed

The Real Cause of Global Warming!

The earth is in the midst of a several-thousand-year cycle, which brings it in direct alignment with a 15 million mile wide black hole at the center of the Milky Way Galaxy. This alignment exerts a larger than normal gravitational pull on the sun, which creates a period of maximum sunspot activity. It is a scientific fact that, during periods of maximum sunspot activity, the earth is warmer, and during times of minimal sunspot activity, it is cooler. It is also a fact that what our politicians call global warming coincides with this alignment, which appears to have a considerable impact on earth's temperatures for 100 plus years. If that is the case, we are not quite halfway through this warming cycle, so the problem is very real and very serious. Here is proof that human-made carbon emissions do not cause the problem.

"NASA has determined that every planet in our solar system is experiencing the same warming cycle as Earth, so the cause must be external, i.e., increased sunspot activity and cannot be attributed to man-made carbon emissions."

I have some bad news for you. There is nothing, absolutely nothing we can do to prevent this warning cycle caused by this solar event. That's bad but not as bad as you might think because the real serious problem stems from another source, one the Financial Elite have been hiding from us. What you may ask could possibly be worse than climate change? Well, I will tell you.

The Truly Serious Problem the Financial Elite Are Hiding From Us!

With a catastrophic clean water shortage and depleting natural resources, the collision of overpopulation has caused our planet's 6th mass extinction. This, not climate change, is the real problem. In the span of one generation, the world population has gone from 2 billion to 7 billion. Soon the planet will be uninhabitable! Something must be done, but what? We must find a way short of mass genocide to reduce the population to sustainable levels because population reduction is the only way to restore resource sustainability and eliminate the pollution that is killing the planet!

What sparked this overnight surge in population? The Industrial Revolution, along with mechanized farming and modern medicine, was the cause of this spike. Projections show that by 2050, the planet's population will reach 9 billion. The earth can't sustain that many people. Soon it will be uninhabitable! Not only is there way more of us, but our per capita resource consumption has skyrocketed as we went from an agrarian society to an industrialized society. So, the combination of overpopulation and increased consumption means dramatically increased pollution, which fouls the air and pollutes our rivers and oceans. This collision of overpopulation with out-of-control material consumption, and shortages of natural resources, most notably oil and life-sustaining clean water, has brought the planet to a tipping point, which has ushered in the planet's 6th mass extinction. The underlying problem facing planet earth is overpopulation! There are simply too many of us placing more demands on resources than the earth can sustain. So, we have to find a way to live in harmony with the earth that supports us and use resources at a rate that the earth can sustain. Please make no mistake; this is a severe problem, one that threatens our very existence.

> *"Planet earth is facing a mass extension that equals or exceeds any in the geologic record, and human activities have brought the planet to the brink of this crisis"* (Dr. Peter Raven, Director of the Missouri Botanical Garden and adjunct professor at the University of Missouri, St. Louis University, and Washington University).

An international study published in the science journal *Nature* predicted that *"climate change could drive more than a million species towards extinction by the year 2050."*

> *"By perpetuating the world's sixth mass extinction, mankind may compromise our own ability to survive. We need to steer this nation and lead the world toward a sustainable path"* (David Wilcove, Professor).

Population control is essential to saving the planet that sustains us. Either we develop a plan to reduce the population, or the Financial Elite will do it for us. More on this momentarily, but first, let's explore just how severe the shortage of clean drinking water truly is.

Looming Water Crisis: What Does It Foretell?

The Clean Water Crisis: Approximately 70% to 80% of our water consumption is for agricultural purposes, so when we look at severe water shortages, we are automatically talking about curtailing food production. In a technological society, oil is important, but we can live without it, but the same can't be said for water. It is the quintessential necessity of life. With that in mind, we will be looking at water stress levels worldwide, but I want to start with the U.S.

Fruit, Nut and Vegetable Crops in U.S. and Mexico at Risk Due to Water Shortages: Most of the U.S. fruits, nuts, and vegetables come from California, and those crops are dependent on irrigation from two sources, the San Joaquin Aquifer, and the Colorado River, both of which are under severe water stress. Water shortages are already causing agricultural land to be taken out of production. The San Joaquin Aquifer is in real jeopardy from overuse. It is not an exaggeration to say that most of our fruits and nuts come from California, and it accounts for upwards of 95% of most of our vegetables. So, if water shortages in California were to substantially curtail agricultural production, we would be in big trouble. Not only is California's Aquifer under stress, but its supply of groundwater is also under stress, so there truly is a real crisis.

Water flows in the Colorado River have reached all-time lows and threaten disastrous drought for western states. Beginning in the 1920s, the western states began divvying up the Colorado Rivers water, building dams and diverting the flow hundreds of miles to Los Angeles, San Diego, Phoenix, and other fast-growing cities. The river now serves 30 million people in seven U.S. states and Mexico, with 70 percent or more of its water siphoned off to irrigate 3.5 million acres of cropland. Lake Mead is down 130 feet since 2000. Water resource officials say some of the reservoirs fed by the river will never be full again. Making matters even worse is the fact that other than California, we get most of our fruits and vegetables from Mexico. As the following

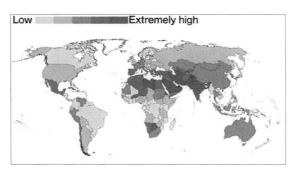

graphic shows, Mexico is suffering a severe water shortage as well.

As you can see, both California and Mexico are suffering from severe water shortages. You will also notice that a significant portion of Europe, China, Russia, and India have severe water stress as well. The water shortage extends across the 40th parallel in the northern hemisphere, encompassing most of the planet's breadbasket. With approximately 50% of our calorie intake from grains and many nations of the world depending on exports from these countries, a water crisis in these northern hemisphere countries threatens a worldwide food shortage and potential famine. By the way, that is precisely what the Bible prophecies.

World's Largest Rivers Also Under Stress

Referring to the next graphic, which lists rivers under stress, I would note that climate change aside, we are taking more water from these rivers than nature can replenish. We are destroying wildlife habitats, but of more interest to humans, upwards of 75% of the water we take from these rivers is for agricultural production. If these rivers continue their decline, global food production will most certainly decline, eventually leading to global famine.

Top River Basins Facing Water Stress (Listed by Highest Population)		
RANK	**RIVER BASIN NAME**	**BASELINE WATER STRESS SCORE**
1	Qom (Namak Lake) (Iran)	5.00
2	Yongding He (China)	4.99
3	Brantas (Indonesia)	4.97
4	Harirud (Afghanistan)	4.91
5	Tuhai He (China)	4.90
6	Sabarmati River (India)	4.83
7	Helmand (Afghanistan)	4.83
8	Sirdaryo (central Asia)	4.78
9	Rio Maipo (Chile)	4.66
10	Dead Sea (Jordan)	4.57
11	Solo (Bengawan Solo) (Indonesia)	4.46
12	Indus (Central Asia)	4.30
13	Daliao He (China)	4.19
14	Colorado River (United States)	4.18
15	Palar River (India)	4.15
16	Bravo (Rio Grande – United States)	4.12
17	Liao He (China)	4.00
18	Huang He (Yellow River – China)	4.00

List of Largest Drying Lakes

• The Dead Sea in Israel and Jordan	Hamun Lake, Iran Afghan border
• The Salton Sea in California, U.S.	Lake Chad in Africa
• The Aral Sea in Central Asia	Tulare Lake in California, U.S.
• Urmia Lake in Iran	Owens Lake in California, U.S.
• Walker Lake in Nevada, U.S.	Mono Lake in California, U.S.
• Fucine Lake in Italy	Poyang Lake in China
• Qinghai Lake in China	White Bear Lake in Minnesota, U.S.

• Lake Meredith in Texas, U.S.	Lake Albert in South Australia
• Lake Hindmarsh in Australia	Lake Poopo in Bolivia
• Lake Copais, in Boeotia, Greece	Lake George, in New South Wales, Australia
• Nainital, in Uttarakhand, India	Bakhtegan Lake in Iran
• Lake Amik in Turkey	Lake Faguibine in Mali
• Lake Chapala in Mexico	Lake Mead in Nevada and Arizona

Climate change aside, we are simply taking too much water from our lakes, rivers, and aquifers, and our overpopulation is setting the stage for a famine of Biblical proportion and WWIII as well.

Pointing Out the Magnitude of the Crisis

- **Threat From Drought and Desertification:** According to the United Nations, drought and desertification threaten the livelihood of some one billion people in more than 110 countries around the world.

- **Major Rivers in Trouble:** The Colorado, Rio Grande, Yellow, Indus, Ganges, Amu Darya, Murray, Nile, and many other rivers have so much water taken from them that they discharge little or no water to the sea for months at a time.

- **Global Perspective:** According to the World Health Organization, more than one billion people live in water-stressed regions. That number is expected to double by 2050 when an estimated 9 billion people inhabit the planet. The Mediterranean, Southern Africa, parts of South America, and Asia also face fresh-water crises. In the Andes Mountains of South America, it is estimated that by 2020 melting glaciers will threaten freshwater supplies for millions of people in Peru, Bolivia, and Ecuador. Australia is in the midst of the worst drought in 750 years. Freshwater is so scarce that ranchers are being forced to sell off their cattle, and the city of Perth is being forced to build desalination plants.

- **Water Crisis Threatens Middle East:** Between 2003 and 2009, the Tigris-Euphrates basin comprising Turkey, Syria, Iraq, and western Iran *"lost groundwater faster than any other place in the world except northern India"* (*Gravity Recovery and Climate Experiment* (GRACE) sponsored by NASA and the German Aerospace Centre).

- **Crisis in Syria and Iraq:** Syria, a nation of 22 million people, is depleting its aquifers. As a result, it is becoming more and more dependent on imported grain. Grain production peaked in 2001 and since has dropped 32%. In neighboring Iraq, as of 2012, it was dependent on the world market for two-thirds of its grain. Besides their aquifer depletion, both Syria and Iraq are suffering from reduced flow in the Tigris and Euphrates rivers as upstream Turkey claims more water.

- **Crisis in Yemen:** Yemen, a nation of 24 million, has one of the world's fastest-growing populations. Over the last 40 years, their grain production had fallen by 50%, and with the water table of their aquifers falling roughly six feet a year, they are facing a very severe crisis.

- **Crisis in Pakistan:** The water crisis threatens the 182 million residents of Pakistan. In a World Bank study, water expert John Briscoe says, *"Pakistan is already one of the most water-stressed countries in the world, a situation which is going to degrade into outright water scarcity due to high population growth."* He then notes that *"the survival of a modern and growing Pakistan is threatened by water."*

- **Saudi Arabian Crisis:** There is nowhere on the planet that has been dramatically impacted by falling water tables and restrictions on irrigation than Saudi Arabia. In 2008 the Saudis announced that with their aquifers largely depleted, they would reduce wheat planting by one-eighth each year until 2016 when production would ultimately end. They estimate that from that point, they will be importing some 15 million tons of wheat, rice, corn, and barley to feed their 30 million people.

- **Famine Looms:** Roughly 40% of the world's grain harvest comes from irrigated land, so it comes as no surprise that irrigation expansion has played a central role in tripling the world's grain harvest over the last six decades. As rivers, lakes, and aquifers dry, agricultural land irrigation must mandatorily be reduced, and those reductions could be dramatic. Today, nearly half of our calories come from grains. Couple that fact with projections that the global population will go from its current level of 7 billion to 9 billion by 2050. The only conclusion you can reach is that a global famine is on the horizon.

How Serious Is the Problem Really?

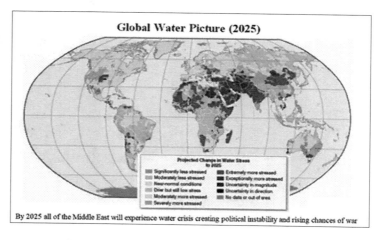

Global Water Picture (2025)

By 2025 all of the Middle East will experience water crisis creating political instability and rising chances of war

By the year 2025, the situation is projected to be extremely serious. I draw your attention to the following graphic. The first thing I want to point out is that by 2025 U.S. food production looks to be severely threatened. The huge high plains aquifer, which supports our grain production, will be under severe stress. Couple that with the crisis we discussed earlier with fruit, nut, and vegetable production in California, Mexico, and North America looks like it will be experiencing a severe food and water crisis. Given that America is one of the world's largest food exporters, this portends very serious problems for the entire world.

Things look equally as dire for Europe, China, India, and Russia. These nations, along with the U.S., provide the bulk of the world's breadbasket. Unless something drastic is done, we are surely looking at a situation that will destabilize the entire world leading to critical food shortages, famine, and wars over water.

Take another look at the previous graphic. I draw your attention to the Middle East and North Africa. As we discussed a short while ago, this region of the world is the most water-deficient region on the entire planet. It also happens to be the most politically unstable region. With this in mind, we will shortly take a look at what God says is in store for this region in the not to distant future. Hopefully, you now appreciate how truly grave the clean water shortage and overpopulation crisis truly is and the fact that there is no exaggeration when I say it is a crisis of biblical proportion that has ushered in the planet's 6th mass extinction. Also, it is no exaggeration to say that by 2025, the Middle East's situation will possibly be serious enough to threaten a widespread famine that could cause WWIII. We could very well be in seven years of plenty to be followed by seven years of famine and tribulation. It would appear the four horsemen of the apocalypse may be on the horizon. Prepare while you can, because when the day of tribulation comes, it will be too late!

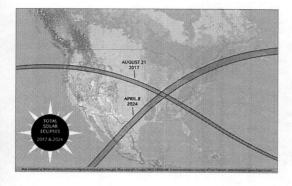

Speaking of warning, *"His people,"* I think God is warning the people of America. In 2017, we had an eclipse that traversed the U.S. from west to east. It traversed the Cascade Seduction Plate in northern California. It then went directly across the Yellowstone super volcano, and it finally passed over New Madrid, the location of the largest earthquake in U.S. history. So, the eclipse went directly over the three most geologically unstable places in the U.S. Do you think that is an accident? Do you think it could be a warning from God?

Wait, it gets better. In 2024, exactly seven years later, we will have another eclipse that passes directly over the New Madrid fault line. **X** marks the spot!

U.S. Navy's Earth Change Flood Map!

Rev 16:18 (NKJ) "And there were voices, and thunders, and lightening; and there was a great earthquake, such as has not been since men were on the earth, so mighty an earthquake, and so great.

Wait, it gets better. The next graphic shows what the U.S. Navy expects the U.S. to look like based on geologic events that it expects at some time in the future. Their map is based in part on the ice caps melting and flooding coastal areas. Still, the worst of what they expect coincides with the water inundation caused by geologic events occurring directly over the path of the two eclipses shown in the graphics above. Let those who have eyes to see, see, and those with ears to hear, hear. God is warning his people!

The Financial Elite's End Game Solution Revealed!

Get ready. We are about to find out what the Financial Elite's end game really is and what it has to do with climate change! I promise you will not like it! The Financial Elite's solution has been staring us right in the face, but very few of us knew about it. It was etched in stone in the form of the Georgia Guide Stones. The Georgia Guide Stones call for maintaining the human population below 500 million.

"The technetronic era involves the gradual appearance of a more controlled society. Such a society would be dominated by an Elite, unrestrained by traditional values" (Zbigniew Brzezinski).

"Global sustainability requires the deliberate quest of poverty, reduced resource consumption, & set levels of mortality control" (Professor Maurice King).

The Financial Elite of the World Are Unified in Their Quest to Drastically Reduce the Planets Population!

"A total world population of 250–300 million people, a 95% decline from present levels, would be ideal" (Ted Turner interview, Audubon Magazine).

"Depopulation should be the highest priority of foreign policy towards the third world" (Secretary of State under President Nixon, Henry Kissinger, 1974).

Is there an actual plan to commit global genocide? Absolutely! And it was authored by our old friends at the globalists U.N. The Financial Elite's end game solution was always about forcibly reducing the population in order to bring consumption and resource utilization back in balance. To them, we are just useful idiots who are utterly expendable! The only thing that matters is that they become the masters of us all! And there are too many of us consuming too many of their precious recourses, so the decision is simple: EXTERMINATE US! Still have doubts anyone would do such a heinous thing. Then let's take a look at precisely what the U.N. is planning. It is all laid out in a document entitled *Agenda 21*.

Agenda 21

Agenda 21 is the U.N.'s plan to forcibly reduce the population, make most of the planet off-limits to human habitation, and establish their One-World Dictatorship. It calls for:

• Reduction of Global Population	from 7 Billion to 1 to 2 Billion
• An End to National Sovereignty	One-World Government
• Abandonment of the Constitution	No Inalienable Rights
• Presumption of Guilt Until Proven Innocent	No Inalienable Rights
• Abolition of Private Property	State Owns Everything
• Education Focused On	Environment and Allegiance to State
• Restructuring of Family Unit	Population Control
• Lack of Privacy	State-Owned Residential Units Along Rail Corridors
• Limitations on Mobility	Upwards of 75% of Land Off-Limits
• Carrier Limitation/State	Controls Education & Employment Opportunities

A Glimpse Into the Financial Elite's Brave New World!

The Financial Elite have absolutely no intention of working with us to solve the population crisis. They have absolutely no intention of working with us to clean up the air or water. They have absolutely no intention of putting into place meaningful conservation programs. They don't have to mess with any of that because they have a much simpler, much faster, much more efficient solution planned. Mass genocide!

All They Have to Do Is:

• Collapse the U.S. economy, causing a global monetary collapse.

- Step to the table and offer to bail us out on the condition that we accept their New World Order (One-world Communist Dictatorship).

- Have the puppets they have placed in the various governments worldwide (their Shadow Government) declare martial law.

- Round up all the dissidents, the poor, the disabled, all the useful idiots, and take them to camps like they do in China and Russia.

- Systematically dispose of 5 to 6 billion of us.

PROBLEM SOLVED, END OF STORY!

The Post Genocide World!

- No more overpopulation.

- Natural resource consumption is at sustainable levels.

- The Financial Elite can implement cheap, clean, renewable energy solutions they have denied us.

- The pollution problems will begin to dissipate.

- The rivers and oceans will recover, and the aquifers will refill.

- Planet earth will be a virtual Utopia.

- All it will have cost is the lives of 5 to 6 billion people.

- They won't need us any longer to do their menial labor because they will have trucks that drive themselves, factories ran by robots. Even artificial intelligence to do much of the thinking for them.

- And oh yes, they will make available computer augmentation, gene enhancement, and a host of other technologies to extend their lives and allow them to be physically fit and youthful for well beyond our current life spans.

- But it would be pure insanity to share any of that with us, useful idiots, so we must die that they may live long and prosper. It's a great deal if you are one of the Financial Elite and a horrible deal for the rest of us!

United We Stand, Divided We Fall!

Now you know why Rockefeller revered Mao and his Cultural Revolution. Now you know why those in our government say that the Free-Market System is nonsense. Now you know why every President since Carter (except Reagan & Trump) has pledged their allegiance to the U.N., the very entity dedicated to collapsing America. Now you know why we were lied to about global warming. Now you know why U.S. Presidents, Russian Leaders, and Chinese Leaders are all committed to establishing a one-world government. Now you know why there is an absolute gridlock in Washington with a do-nothing Congress. Now you know what President Trump is referring to when he talks about the Deep State Shadow Government (the swamp). Now you know why the media, Hollywood, academia, and many of our politicians in Washington, both Republicans and Democrats, are so adamantly against the President. They can't wait for the New World Order to take power because they will be among the privileged Elite. Life will be so much better once all of us useful idiots have been disposed of.

Closing Comments: In summary, we are being lied to about the cause of climate change. It is not caused by human-made carbon emissions. It is caused by a cyclical cycle of the sun, which for a period of approximately 100 years, brings the earth in alignment with a 15 million mile wide black hole at the center of the galaxy. This creates a greater than normal gravitational pull on the sun, which in turn causes an increase in solar flares, which heats up the entire galaxy, not just the earth. Therefore, the cause is external and could not be from human-made carbon emissions.

Climate change is real, but there is a lot more going on than just rising temperatures. The earth is at a tipping point caused by the collision of overpopulation, out of control material consumption, and shortages of natural resources, particularly oil and, most importantly, life-sustaining clean water. This collision has brought about the planet's 6th mass extinction. The situation is so serious that unless we reduce the population and resource consumption, humanity may very well destroy the entire food chain. In the process, we could cause our own extinction along with all the millions of plants and animals that inhabit the earth. Man has become a virus that is killing the planet that sustains us.

The Financial Elite have a straightforward solution for the overpopulation problem and the overconsumption of water, oil, and other natural resources. They have a simple plan for how to return the planet to sustainable levels of resource consumption. All they have to do is collapse the U.S. and the rest of the Free-Market System and then offer to bail us out on the condition we accept their New World Order. Then they round 6 billion or so of us useful idiots and commit mass genocide. End of story, problem solved. The only problem is that most of us are dead. Wake up, America. Don't let the Financial Elite divide us any longer. We are all in this together, and there is only one enemy we should be fighting: The Financial Elite.

Suppose the unorganized majority becomes the organized majority and stands as one nation under God with liberty and justice for all. In that case, we can save our nation, our lives, and the planet. It will not be easy, but God is calling His people. He is opening our eyes that we may see the truth, and the truth may set us free from the bondage of the Financial Elite who have for so long divided us and made us slaves without chains. I promise you that the next chapter will furnish you with a strategy for what we need to do to defeat them, but it will depend on us standing together as one people. United we stand, divided we fall!

God's Plan vs. Man's Plan:

Before I close, I want to change the focus from the Financial Elite's plan to God's plan. What we have been talking about in this chapter, and indeed, the entire book, is God's plan for the harvest of souls. Regardless of what happens, it will not be the end of the earth. It will be the end of the age. What exactly is the end of the age? As the scriptures below tell us, it is the *"time of the harvest,"* the time when the wheat (the righteous) and tares (the wicked) are separated and judged. The righteous who have endured to the end are given their heavenly reward, and the wicked are judged according to their sins. Then there is a new age, a 1,000-year millennial reign on earth when the deceiver (the devil) is bound in the bottomless pit of hell, and a remnant of righteous people inhabit the earth for 1.000 years unencumbered by the temptations of the devil.

> Joel 3:13 (NIV) *"Swing the sickle, for the harvest is ripe. Come, trample the grapes, for the winepress is full and the vats overflow— so great is their wickedness."*

> Matthew 13:30 (KJV) *"Let both grow together until the harvest: and in the time of harvest, I will say to the reapers, gather ye together first the tares, and bind them in bundles to burn them: but gather the wheat into my barn."*

> Revelation 20:4-6 (KJV) *"And I saw thrones, and they sat upon them, and judgment was given unto them: and I saw the souls of them that were beheaded for the witness of Jesus, and for the word of God, and which had not worshipped the beast, neither his image, neither had received his mark upon their foreheads, nor in their hands; and they lived and reigned with Christ a thousand years."*

What does this mean to us as nations and as individuals? In the time soon to come, nations will be judged, but so will each individual. What we do now will affect our nation, and it will affect us. For your sake and the sake of the nation, I urge each of you to search your hearts and seek God and ask for His forgiveness, which He will grant if we truly repent and turn to Him. If America repents and seeks God, then He will keep his promise, and not only will we defeat our enemy: The Financial Elite, but even more importantly, the latter-day rain will fall, and we will see the glory of God and multitudes will be saved and welcomed to the Lord's harvest table. May God Bless you and yours!

Gods Final Warning

The time of the harvest is at hand.
For there is much sin in the land
The wheat and tares they grow together
But the nations and people stand not together

Hatred and war threaten to ravish the land
And hunger and pestilence are upon the land
God calls to his people to submit to him
But most hear not his voice and live in sin

The time of the harvest is at hand
The sickle is ready to be thrust in
Who shall be counted among the righteous?

Who shall be among the first fruit?
And inherit the Promised Land
And live with the spotless Lamb

Who shall know the second death?
And be judged by the Lamb
For he was called and did not head
Choosing instead the wages of sin
And then shall they know
what the blood did purchase!

Choose Wisely!

CHAPTER 7

The Plan to Restore America to Greatness!

WHAT YOU WILL LEARN IN THIS CHAPTER

- Regaining the Reins of Power!

- The American Reformation Program!

- The Plan to Address the Problems That Have Ushered in the Planet's Sixth Mass Extinction!

- End the Division in America and Lay the Foundation for Worldwide Peaceful Coexistence!

Regaining the Reins of Power!

The American Reformation Platform, which will be presented shortly, is intended to restore the foundation stones that made America great in the first place. It's not complicated. Our Founding Fathers got it right. All we have to do is put back in place the economic policies, moral foundation, and balance of power that made America great in the first place, and America will blossom. Unfortunately, the three coequal branches of government have been co-opted, and that balance of power must be restored. That will require more than just electing conservatives in the House and Senate. We must restore balance to the Judicial System and remove thousands of non-elected bureaucrats who are busy writing regulations that are systematically driving us into Socialism. Congressman Ron Paul said,

> *"I think there are 25,000 individuals that have used offices of powers, and they are in our Universities, and they are in our Congresses, and they believe in One World Government. And if you believe in One World Government, then you are talking about undermining National Sovereignty, and you are talking about setting up something that you could well call a Dictatorship—and those plans are there!"* (Congressman Ron Paul at an event near Austin, Texas on August 30, 2003).

So How Do We Restore the Power to the People?

1) We Vote Out All the Carrier Politicians at Local, State, and Federal Levels: The entire house of government must be swept clean except for a very few people whose voting record demonstrates a clear commitment to our founding principles.

If we are to save our country and restore the Republic, then the silent majority must organize with the single purpose of removing the carrier politicians. This is the only way we will be able to make the sweeping changes that are needed.

Our house cleaning starts with sweeping election reforms intended to give us representative government, which means that all the special privileges the politicians have that make them an elected elite must be taken away! That means we must have an unprecedented level of election reform. That will only be possible if all those with a vested interest in the current corrupt political system are removed from office.

> *"The day will come when our Republic will be an impossibility because wealth will be concentrated in the hands of a few. When that day comes, we must rely upon the wisdom of the best elements in the country to readjust the laws of the nation"* (President James Madison).

Pledge of Allegiance to the 2ⁿᵈ American Revolution: Nothing short of a peaceful revolution can save America. No half measures will work. The house of government must be swept clean, or America will fall to the Financial Elite, and we will lose our freedom. We are indeed fighting for our freedom and lives, and this is a battle we must win! Are you ready to take back your country? If so, I ask you to pledge to join the fight to save America! Time to stand up and be counted!

PLEDGE: As my Forefathers before me pledged their honor and their allegiance to this nation, I hereby pledge mine. I **(Name):** _____ will do everything in my power to support the restoration of America's founding principles of *"One nation, under God, indivisible, with liberty, and justice for all!"*

It is not enough to vote out the old corrupt politicians. We must be focused and single-minded. All those we support for office must sign a pledge to implement the planks of the American Reformation Program, and that pledge begins even before they are elected. A condition for endorsement is a commitment to disclose all financial contributions above a certain amount and the individual or organization's name making that contribution. Otherwise, we will be no better off than when we started. This provides a safeguard against the Banker Gangsters, so they can't just buy a new crop of turncoat politicians!

2) We Must Invoke Article 5 of the Constitution: Article 5 allows us to return the power to the states so we can pass a constitutional amendment evoking term limits. The Tea Party movement was our 1st effort to drain the swamp, but unfortunately, it proved unsuccessful. Why? Not because it failed to get some good, well-intentioned people elected because it did. There simply were not enough of them to overcome the carrier politicians (the Political Elite) who serve the special interest, not the people. Also, they had no way of counteracting the imbalance of power that has resulted from the stacking of the courts with Liberal Judges and the appointment of thousands of non-elected bureaucrats. The Progressives have systematically undermined the Constitution and pushed the nation further and further toward Socialism, and they must be stopped, but how?

That brings us to Article 5 of the Constitution. What is it, and how can it solve our problems? We have to end the accumulation of power by carrier politicians, judges who are appointed for life, and non-elected bureaucrats. To do this, we will have to set term limits, and that requires a constitutional amendment. Congress will never call for such an amendment or any of the necessary electoral reforms because to do so will end their status as a Political Elite who are above the laws they pass. That is where Article 5 comes into play; just like our Founders gave us the 2nd Amendment, which provides us with the right to bear arms as the last defense against a tyrannical government, it gave us Article 5 to allow the States to amend the Constitution.

Here is how the process works. 2/3rds of the states (34 states) are required to call a State Convention. If 26 states agree on an amendment, the amendment is sent out to the states for ratification. 38 States are needed for ratification. Currently, 12 states have signed a resolution calling for a State Convention, so 22 more states are required. Please contact your State Representatives in support of this inactive. This inactive is being spearheaded by Dr. Tom Coburn (former (R) Senator Oklahoma & Senior Advisor Citizens for Self-Government) and Mark Meckler (one of the founders of the Tea Party). Mark Levin of *Life Liberty and Levin* on Fox News has proposed the following amendments. Others may be required as well, but this is a starting point for a national conversation.

- Term limits for the Senate and House
- Term limits for the Supreme Court and other judges
- Ability to overturn Supreme Court decisions with a supermajority of 3/5th of House and Senate.
- Spending limits
- Taxing limits
- Borrowing limits

These things would go a long way toward returning power to the people and restoring fiscal responsibility, so America doesn't collapse under a mountain of debt. At our current rate of accumulation of debt, it is estimated that in 5 years, 100% of the Federal budget will be consumed by (interest payments, Medicare, and Medicaid) leaving no money to run the country. That is the definition of financial collapse, which is exactly what the Left wants because that would force us into a One-World Government.

The Constitution in the National Archives Is No More: That beautiful, succinct document written by our Founders is no more! One hundred fifteen years of Liberals undermining our Constitution has ballooned it into a 2,738-page document that has systematically stripped power from the people and the states and created an all-powerful federal government controlled by self-serving carrier politicians! Either we take back our Constitution, or America is destined to fall!

3) We Must Get Back the Ability to Print Our Currency: That means the Federal Reserve must go, and the Treasury must print our currency, which is what our Founding Fathers intended. It's as Henry Kissinger said, *"He who controls the money controls the world."* Suppose we don't take away the Financial Elite's ability to print our currency, the means to inflict us with predatory lending schemes, and the ability to intentionally cause financial crashes. In that case, we will perpetually be slaves without chains, and we will eventually be driven into bankruptcy again and this time into a One-World Dictatorship. A little later, we will discuss exactly how to do that. But for now, I refer you to the quote below from the Director of the Bank of

England. He understood exactly how corrupt the bankers are and what we must do if we want our freedom back.

> *"Banking was conceived in iniquity and born in sin. Bankers own the earth. Take it away from them but leave them the power to create money, and, with the flick of a pen, they will create enough money to buy it back again. Take this great power away from them, and all the great fortunes like mine will disappear and they ought to disappear, for then this would be a better and happier world to live in. But, if you want to continue to be a slave of the bankers and pay the cost of your own slavery, then let the bankers continue to create money and control credit"* (1ˢᵗ Baron Josiah Stamp, Director of the Bank of England).

What you just read are just the fundamentals, the core essentials of what will be required to take our country back. It's time to get into the nitty-gritty and layout the individual planks of the   American Reformation Program.

The American Reformation Program

1ˢᵗ Plank – Election Reform: As we have discussed, our political leaders in Washington have become a Political Elite who are above the laws they pass and who cater to Lobbyists and other special interest groups rather than their constituents. They are more interested in serving their vested interest than ours. Generally speaking, Congress does not serve what is in the best interest of the people. The system has to be changed, so let's get to it.

The Planks of Election Reform:

- **Get Rid of Electronic Voting and Mail-in Ballots:** It is too easy to create election fraud.

- **Vote Out Carrier Politicians:** The political corruption goes so deep that we have no choice except to sweep our political house clean and start over. With few exceptions, those in office must be voted out. That goes for Republicans and Democrats. It includes those holding local, state, and federal offices. We must reboot our political system, which can't be done unless our political house is swept clean. Out with the old and in with the new.

- **Require Candidates to Sign a Pledge:** In order to get our support, they must agree to term limits and all the items listed in the American Reformation Program.

- **Outlaw Gerrymandering:** Restructuring of Congressional Districts for political purposes.

- **Outlaw Lobbyists:** Special interest advocates used to be illegal and should be again.

- **Set Limits on Campaign Contributions and Personal Spending on Campaigns:** So, the Financial Elites can't so easily buy elections.

- **Abolish Signing Statements:** This allows the President to alter legislation passed by Congress unilaterally.

- **Prohibit Presidents From Having Their Records Sealed:** In order to hide what they have done.

- **Congress Subject to All Laws They Pass:** i.e., social security and Obama Care, etc.

- **Legislators Required to Report All Stock Transactions:** So, they are blocked from getting rich from insider trading.

- **Require Legislators to Report Financial Transactions of All Their Relatives and Business Associates:** Right now, there is a huge loophole that allows politicians to do under the table deals and hide them from the American people. For example, Joe Biden and John Kerry's sons struck a $1.5 billion-dollar deal with the Chinese government ten days after a trip to China by Biden according to an exclusive *New York Post* excerpt from the book: *Secret Empires: How the American Political Class Hides Corruption and Enriches Family and Friends* (2018) by Peter Schweizer. As long as this is possible, our government is a sham, political theater, and nothing more!

- **Congress Prohibited From Approving Their Own Salaries**.

- **No Lifetime Pension After One Term.**

- **No Healthcare Program Just for Politicians**: Subject to all laws they pass.

It is as this quote says, *"We can either have democracy in this country or we can have great wealth concentrated in the hands of a few, but we can't have both"* (Louis Brandeis, Supreme Court Justice, 1916-1939).

Closing Comment: I know what I laid out above sounds impossible, but I tell you God is exposing the corruption in Washington and before the dust settles, the American people will realize that the corruption goes so deep that what I have laid out is our only hope of wrenching power from the Financial Elite and returning it to the American People.

2ⁿᵈ Plank - Immigration Reform: Both political parties are playing the American public for fools. Neither party intends to build the wall nor end chain migration and go to a merit-based immigration policy like most other countries in the world. Why? For the Democrats, it's about building their voter base, so they pander to illegal immigrants with their sanctuary cities, open border policies, and entitlements. For Republicans, it's about pandering to their wealthy special interest business owners. The latter benefit because illegals, which by in large, pay no federal income tax or personal property tax, are able to work for lower wages than taxpaying Americans. That benefits the wealthy business owners by driving down wages for blue-collar Americans! These policies are destroying America in five fundamental ways.

1. Like Europe, America is being inundated by more immigrants than it can assimilate. This is morphing America into a 3ʳᵈ world country.

2. Open borders constitute a national security issue. Our southern border is an open conduit for drugs, human trafficking, and terrorists.

3. Many Hispanic immigrants don't want to assimilate. In this instance, they not only don't pay income tax and school taxes, but they also send most of their money abroad, so it never makes it into the U.S. economy where it is subject to sales tax.

4. Illegal immigrants are a drain on the economy. I.E., they burden our welfare system, and noninsured illegal immigrants drive up our healthcare costs. We also have to provide special English emersion classes for their non-English speaking children. Then there is the cost incurred by law enforcement and our courts.

   "The cost of harboring illegal immigrants in the United States is a staggering $113 billion a year – an average of $1,117 for every native-headed household in America" (according to a study conducted by the Federation for American Immigration). These costs accrue in lost taxes, lower salaries, an economic drain on the education system, healthcare system, welfare system, and the added cost to our criminal system.

   Then, there is the staggering cost of the opioid crisis in terms of cost and human suffering. The vast majority of opioids cross into this country from our southern border, and yet our corrupt politicians refuse to build the wall as President Trump wants. Trump is virtually alone in wanting to solve our illegal immigration crisis! He is virtually alone in having a sincere interest in *"Making America Great Again"* because most of our corrupt politicians have sold out to the Financial Elite.

5. Open Border Policies Are a Covert Effort to Birth the Amero Union:
   The biggest problem of all is that the Globalists want to end U.S. sovereignty. As we discussed earlier, they want to merge the U.S., Mexico, and Canada into a servile trading bloc modeled after the Socialist European Union. In that event, we would have a common currency and a common Socialist Constitution. America would be no more. As discussed earlier, Bush Senior attended a secret meeting intended to do precisely this.

   Even today, bureaucrats are busy writing laws intended to merge the three countries. Given this fact, I wholeheartedly believe domestic security is even more important than foreign security, but the Left acts as though this very real crisis doesn't exist and criticizes President Trump when he threatens to use military appropriations to build the wall. The Financial Elite are intent on ending U.S. sovereignty. How could there be a bigger threat than that? We must have a border wall if America is to retain its sovereignty.

The Planks of Immigration Reform:

- **Build the Wall:** Essential to national security. Israel has a wall, and it works. A country without border security has no sovereignty.

- **End Chain Migration and Lottery System:** Because they result in those least educated and least able to contribute to society entering the country and becoming a burden on our already overburdened welfare system.

- **Implement a Merit-Based System:** Like most other countries, applicants must show the needed skillset and be able to support themselves without being on welfare.

- **No Amnesty Deals for Future Illegals:** Allow those here illegally (who have not committed any other crime) to stay as permanent residents, but no path to citizenship and no voting rights ever. The only exception is *"Dreamers"* who were brought here as children.

- **Customs Inspection to Be Conducted by U.S. Customs Agents:** Currently, the 1st customs inspection station after you cross into the U.S. is in Kansas City, and it is sovereign Mexican property. How is this even possible? This could be a major conduit for narcotics and human trafficking.

- **End or Modify Friendly Trader Program:** Where certain Mexican companies are allowed to enter the U.S. using an electronic chip like those used on toll roads. There are no inspections of incoming trucks of companies who belong to this program. This could be a major conduit for narcotics and human trafficking.

- **End Catch and Release:** Catch and deport like Australia.

- **Mandatory Jail Time:** For non-documented people caught entering the country a 2nd time.

- **Change Asylum Laws:** Illegals are being coached to say they are in danger. Must be able to give credible evidence on why they are in danger. If they entered the U.S. through Mexico, they are not eligible for asylum under any condition because they must ask for asylum in 1st country they enter after leaving their country of origin.

- **Proof of Legal Status:** To get benefits or entitlements, i.e., driver's license, health insurance, public education, homeownership, social security, etc.

- **E-Verify:** With substantial fines & legal sanctions for employers who hire illegals.

- **Must Pass English Literacy Test to Get Legal Immigration Status.**

- **Make English the National Language:** No bilingual nation has ever prospered. Stop bilingual marketing and packaging, so people are forced to learn English.

- **Roll Back Immigration Quotas:** Until 1970, the U.S. took in approximately 250,000 immigrants per year. This number of immigrants could be assimilated into the culture, and for that reason, we need to go back to that number.

- **No Automatic U.S. Citizenship for Children Born in the U.S.:** Unless the mother is here legally.

Closing Comment: If we continue with our current open borders policies, the day will come when you will not recognize America. Even worse, the continuation of those policies will lead us headlong into the Amero Union modeled after the European Union. We will have a Socialist Communist Constitution, just like Europe. Your inalienable rights will be taken away, and along with them, your freedom. The stakes couldn't be higher.

3rd Plank - Welfare Reform: The current welfare system is intended to create a racial divide because it serves the political agenda of the Financial Elite. A racial divide is intentionally inflicted on the inner cities and those who reside there by our generational welfare system. If we can fix the welfare system to give people a hand up instead of trapping them in generational poverty, then the racial tension will dissipate over time. As long as those in the inner city feel they are victims of the system, we will never have any hope of ending the racial divide. So, the answer is to implement policies that allow those in the inner city to break the cycle of generational welfare.

How do we do that? We have to provide people a pathway off of welfare into the job market. We can no longer allow policies that make it more lucrative to receive a welfare check than it is to work. We have to fix the education system to prepare students for jobs, so they will feel that staying in school is actually going to benefit them. We can no longer allow policies where single women are incentivized to have children in order to get additional welfare benefits. It is an absolute fact that not having a male role model contributes to higher school dropout rates and antisocial behavior such as drug addiction, prostitution, and crime. Remember, one of the goals of the Financial Elite is to destroy the nucleus family because it, along with patriotism and Christian values, constitutes the glue that holds society together. Unfortunately, until the communities are safe, the financial investment that could provide local employment opportunities simply will not happen. That means that by whatever legal means necessary, gang members must go in order to make way for economic development. So, sanctuary cities that harbor criminals must be done away with.

Unfunded entitlement (welfare) is one of the principle ways the U.S. is intentionally collapsed under a mountain of debt. The current welfare model is simply a restructuring of plantation slavery, where real chains are substituted with welfare policies constituting invisible chains. Our civil unrest will never be put to rest till we fix the broken welfare system. If you want to learn more about this modern-day system of slavery without chains, I recommend the documentary *Hillary's America* (2016) by Dinesh D'Souza. It documents the fact that the Democrats, not the Republicans, were and are, to this day, the party of slavery. For example, that is why sanctuary cities like Chicago are almost all run by Democratic mayors who are trading sanctuary for votes. The big cities' crime rate is due to social and economic problems that accompany the generational welfare system and not racism like we are told. It is like President Trump said on the campaign trail. The Democrats pander to Black Americans every election and then disappear without doing anything. Then when the next election rolls around, they show up with more hollow promises. It is time to fix the problem and to do that, we must restore the economy, so we have the money to do what needs to be done!

The Planks of Welfare Reform:

- **The Incentive to Work:** Benefits are not cut till reasonable earning thresholds are reached.

- **Able-Bodied Persons Required to Work to Receive Benefits:** But eligible for educational programs.

- **No Welfare or Entitlements Benefits for Illegal's:** If they can't make a living, they won't come. It's that simple.

- **Deport Illegal Immigrants That Are Known Gang Members:** Unless the crime rate is reduced, economic development simply will not happen.

- **Aid for Dependent Children:** Benefits for one child only. We have to stop the incentive program whereby single women are incentivized to have babies to get more welfare benefits. This is not only a financial issue but also a social issue because, as we just said, children raised without a male role model have been proven to be more likely to drop out of school and or be involved in criminal activity.

- **Daycare Benefits for Single Moms:** So, they can work and or attend school and eventually get off welfare.

- **Education Programs:** With tax incentives for employers who hire graduates. American corporations need to step to the table and train U.S. citizens like they do in Europe. Work visas should only be given after all efforts to train and hire U.S. citizens have failed to produce qualified U.S. workers.

- **Vocational Training in High Schools:** Inner-city kids who don't see themselves going to college have little incentive to stay in school. But if they were given vocational training and job placement, they would have much more reason to stay in school.

Closing Comment: The objective of welfare should be to give people a hand up. A path to a better life, but instead, it is designed to create perpetual servitude and dependency on the government in exchange for votes. Benjamin Franklin got it right when he said,

> *"I am for doing good for the poor, but I differ in opinion of the means. I think the best way of doing good to the poor, is not making them easy in poverty, but leading or driving them out of it."*

4ᵗʰ Plank - National Security: As we discussed earlier, Europe has been inundated with so many Muslims that the national heritage of the native Europeans will be wiped out in a single generation. There will be no Danish, no Polish, no Italians, no French, no Germans, etc. because Europe will have a Muslim majority. Hand in hand with a Muslim majority population comes the imposition of Sharia Law and the Islamic religion. That means an end to western culture and Christianity in Europe. Europe will have fallen not through war but immigration and an explosion of the Muslim population. That same thing is planned for the U.S. Hillary said if elected, she envisioned *"a borderless America."* As I have said repeatedly, borders define the geographic area over which a nation has sovereignty. If a nation has no borders, it has no sovereignty, and the nation ceases to exist. Suppose we don't secure our borders and slow down the number of immigrants to a level that can be assimilated, like Europe. In that case, our national heritage will be obliterated, and those things that made America the greatest nation in the world will be obliterated as well. America will become a Spanish speaking nation, and the Spanish heritage will prevail. This inundation from Mexico and South America is intended to do to America exactly what the Muslim migration has done to Europe. I ask you, is that what you want for America? There is a reason those countries are 3ʳᵈ world countries, and America is the greatest nation the world has ever known. Our greatness is founded on our Christian heritage, our Puritan work ethic, and the Twelve Foundation Stones I presented at the opening of this book. The simple fact is those are not the values of those coming across our southern border.

Turning to Foreign Policy: The sad truth is that America is deep in debt, and we no longer have the resources to be the world's police force. We have to be wise about the money we spend on foreign wars. It is as James Madison said,

> *"If tyranny and oppression come to this land, it will be in the guise of fighting a foreign enemy."*

Remember, history has now proven that WWII, Vietnam, and the Iraq wars were all provoked by false flag events inflicted on us by the Financial Elite, and they were prolonged to make the Financial Elite richer and the American people poorer. We have to learn the lessons of the past and stop letting the Financial Elite drag us into wars for profit. Our primary security concerns should be domestic security, which includes building the wall.

The Planks of National Security:

- **Secure the Border by Building the Wall and Reducing Immigration Levels to Levels That Can Be Assimilated:** Make no mistake. Securing our borders is as important as or even more important than anything we do on foreign soil. Reflect on the following quotes. They show that our enemy is patient and methodical. The Financial Elite feel they will be more likely to take over America through debt, immigration, and eroding our patriotism, Christian, and family values (i.e., an end-run on national security) than through conquest. Wake up, America! We need the wall, and we need to change our immigration policies, or we will soon go the way of Europe, and American heritage will be lost forever.

  "We shall have world government whether or not you like it. The only question is whether world government will be by consent or conquest" (James P. Warburg [Representing Rothschild Banking Concern] While speaking before the United States Senate, February 17, 1950).

"The New World Order will be built… an end-run on national sov-ereignty, eroding it piece by piece will accomplish much more than the old-fashioned frontal assault" (Council on Foreign Relations Journal 1974, P558).

- **NATO Must Pay Their Fair Share of Defense Budget:** America is broke. We can no longer allow European nations to take advantage of us by not paying their fair share of their defense costs. I applaud President Trump for bringing them to task on this issue.

- **Peace Through Strength:** President Trump has repaired our damaged relationship with Israel. He has changed the rules of engagement in Iraq, and as a result, more has been done to end the war in Iraq in the last year than in the previous 17 years combined. His *Peace Through Strength* policy is reversing much of the damage caused by President Obama's *Strategic Patience,* which was responsible for the Arab Spring and the Syrian refugee crisis that has significantly destabilized Europe.

President Trump's policies have resulted in Arab leaders seeing America as a credible ally in the fight against Al-Qaeda and may yet lead to meaningful peace talks in the Middle East. His sanctions and his credible threat of a preemptive strike on North Korea have brought Kim Jong-un to the table to talk about giving up their nuclear program entirely.

What will not work are more appeasement policies, financial assistance programs, and broken promises like we got with Presidents Clinton, Bush, and Obama. There is no more room to kick the can down the road. Either they disarm or else. Call President Trump a warmonger, if you will, but time after time, we learn that the only thing a dictator understands is strength. In WWII, Prime Minister Neville Chamberlain of England tried to negotiate with Hitler while one country after another fell to the Nazi onslaught. Winston Churchill got it right when he said, *"You can't negotiate with a tiger when your head is in his mouth."* Either we stop North Korea and Iran now or pay the price later.

Regarding the Iran deal, it is just another example of kicking the can down the road. No, in truth, it is worse because President Obama removed the sanctions and gave them billions to fund their nuclear program and to fund terrorism.

Closing Comment: If we don't build the wall, the day will come when America looks like Mexico when our freedom will be taken away from us, American exceptionalism will be no more, and we will be part of the dictatorial New World Order. The border wall is estimated to cost $15 to $25 billion. That is a drop in the bucket compared to the $7 trillion we have spent fighting the Afghanistan and Iraq wars. What do we have to show for it? The threat of terrorism is greater now than before the war. And we now know that 9/11 was a false flag attack perpetrated by the Financial Elite. The movie *Shock & Awe* (2017) clearly establishes this fact. I highly recommend it. I end by repeating this quote from James Madison:

> *"If tyranny and oppression come to this land, it will be in the guise of fighting a foreign enemy."*

5th Plank – Financial Reform: The true cause of America's financial decline resides in three irrefutable facts. 1) The U.S. government is run by the Federal Reserve and IMF. 2) Our elected officials in Washington are Political Elite who serve not the American people but their puppet masters, the Financial Elite. 3) Both political parties have sold out to the Financial Elite and are irrelevant. What we call politics is nothing but political theater. Both party's posture, but when it comes down to decision time, what they always do is spend irresponsibly because their job is to drive the U.S. into unmanageable debt and create so much division that the nation tears itself apart so that the Financial Elite can birth their New World Order. If America is to survive, we must sweep Washington clean of the corrupt carrier politicians and take back control of our monetary system by dissolving the Fed!

Remember, the 1st central bank in the world was in England. It was established when England went bankrupt and was bailed out by the Rothschild's. The bailout was conditioned on being given control over printing the nation's money and its credit system. From that moment, England became a servile slave of the Financial Elites. America likewise lost control of our government in 1913 when the Fed took over the printing of our currency. Then in 1933, the U.S. declared bankruptcy and ceased being a Republic and became a Democracy (a Socialist-Communist Order). We must take back control of our monetary system and sweep Washington clean of the Shadow Government. I ask you to contemplate what Josiah Stamp, Director of the Bank of England, had to say about banking:

> *"But if you want to continue to be slaves of the banks and pay the cost of your own slavery, then let them continue to print money and control credit... The modern banking system manufactures money out of nothing...Banking was conceived in iniquity and born in sin."*

The Planks of Financial Reform:

- **Balanced Budget:** To force fiscal responsibility.
- **National Usury Law:** To protect consumers from predatory credit card practices. We used to have usury laws. They need to be reinstated because they would literally stop predatory lending in the credit card industry.

- **Mortgage Tied to Borrower Not Property:** To end predatory mortgage practices that require a new mortgage when refinancing or buying a new home. Your job and credit score determine your creditworthiness. The house is only the collateral. It makes no difference what the property address is as long as the house appraises, so there is absolutely no reason other than greed that your mortgage should have to start over every time you refinance to buy a new home.

- **Repeal Illegal Income Tax:** 100% of the tax goes to the (private) Fed as debt service for printing our fiat currency.

- **Return to Smaller Government:** More control in the states & less in Washington (Article 5).

- **Reinstate Financial Safeguards:** Such as the Glass Steagall Act, etc.
- **Capital Investment Fund with Low-Interest Rates:** To stimulate job growth, rebuild infrastructure, and make capital investments.

- **Get Rid of the IRS:** A simplified tax structure could enable the elimination of the Internal Revenue Service, but it will require that we stand up and demand it!

- **Dismantle the Fed, Establish a National Bank and Return the Printing of the Currency to the Treasury Department:** So, money can once again become the servant of humanity rather than its slave master.

Closing Comment: President Jackson got rid of the 1st Central Bank, and President Kennedy would have gotten rid of the current Fed if he had not been assassinated. So how can it be done this time? In order to replace the fiat currency of the Fed, we must be in a position to print a new currency back by gold, silver, oil, or some combination of tangible commodities. That is what Kennedy did when he issued the Silver Certificates that were pulled out of circulation by President Johnson immediately following Kennedy's assignation.

Where does that leave America when we are so deeply in debt. We must stand behind President Trump and his *Make America Great Again* policies intended to end our debt cycle and restore America to financial solvency. It will take time, but I honestly believe his economic policies can turn America's debt crisis around. All of the financial policies we have been discussing will play a part in our financial restoration. Still, the two that hold the potential of allowing us to become debt-free are President Trump's policy of 1) Establishing fair trade agreements and 2) His policy of becoming not only energy self-sufficient but becoming an exporter of energy. These are the two foundation stones of any sound economy.

6th Plank - Trade Reform: This book opened with the historical account of how trade is the basis of wealth. We saw how the colonizing nations of the world, particularly England, were able to take their colonies' natural recourses and then manufacture products in sweatshops and produced finished goods so cheaply that non-colonizing nations couldn't compete and were literally driven into bankruptcy. This system of slavery was called *"British Free Trade."*

We discussed how as these European Feudal Monarchies fell, they took the vast sums of money they had amassed from controlling global trade and set up a global network of Central Banks through which they control the world's sovereign nations. We also discussed how, through their banking network and the likes of J.P. Morgan, they invested in the emerging corporations and got a stakeholder position in most of the emerging corporations. In the words of Henry C. Carey, Economic Advisor to Abraham Lincoln,

> *"It the British System* [free trade system] *is the most gigantic system of slavery the world has yet seen, and therefore it is that freedom gradually disappears from every country over which England is enabled to obtain control."*

Change the name to Chinese Free Trade, and you can see how the Financial Elite and their puppet politicians in Washington are inflicting intentionally losing trade policies on America in order to bury us under a mountain of debt. We also learned how Wilson was put in office by J.P. Morgan and a European banking cartel and then how he repaid them by establishing the privately-owned Fed who took over the printing of our currency. Then we discussed how by controlling the amount of money in circulation, the interest rate, and the credit market, they could create financial collapses on demand.

Then just 16 years after the Fed's establishment, they caused the 1929 Great Depression, which led to the U.S. declaring bankruptcy in 1933. That event precipitated the confiscation of our gold. But most importantly, it ended our Republic, which was replaced by a Democracy. That event allowed the Fed and IMF to take over the U.S. government and control it from the shadows.

We then discussed how the CFR and T.C. were formed to end all nation-states' national sovereignty to establish the New World Order, which is to be a highbred Capitalist Communist Government modeled after China. We looked at the ranks of the CFR and T.C. and saw that it is a veritable who's who of Washington politics. We learned how the CFR and T.C. were embedded in the CIA, FBI, Justice Department, and U.N. So, with this said, you now know how the Shadow Government of the Financial Elite has been embedded in the legitimate government of the U.S. and countries all around the world.

This brings us full circle back to where we started, which was with the British Free Trade System of slavery, which our Founding Fathers fought the Revolutionary War to escape. In modern times, that system of slavery has once again been imposed on America to drive us into unmanageable debt. That came about when President Carter was put in office by Trilateralist Zbigniew Brzezinski. President Carter paid him back by placing twenty-six T.C. members in his administration, particularly in the Treasury and in areas that controlled trade. So immediately, President Carter opened trade with China. On cue, the U.S. economy tanked, and a period of corporate raiding ensued in which major corporations were bought only to be broken up and sold off in pieces. That set the stage for China to emerge as the new face of Free Trade, that old system of economic slavery imposed on America so many years earlier by Britain. It is the same system of slavery, just a different name. Now you know why we must end our intentionally losing trade policies and negotiate Fair Trade Policies. The fate of America rests on our doing this!

The Planks of Trade Reform:

- **Get Out of Globalist United Nations:** Work to form a new global body dedicated to working together to solve the issues which have ushered in the planet's 6th mass extinction event. The very survival of the planet and all life on it depends on us solving this crisis!

- **End Intentionally Losing Trade Deals:** Negotiate fair reciprocal trade deals so we can reduce or eliminate our trade deficit.

- **Eliminate Fast Track Treaty Process:** It makes it too easy to impose intentionally losing trade deals on the U.S. by those in our government who support the globalist agenda.

- **Make it Illegal to Incorporate Outside the U.S.:** To reap, trade, or tax benefits.

- **Support U.S. Sovereignty:** No participation in initiatives imposing Global Governance, i.e., Cap & Trade, Codex, Agenda 21, Amero Union, etc.

- **Capital Investment Fund:** With low-interest rates to encourage capital investment projects, i.e., infrastructure.

- **Crackdown on Corporations Aiding Our Enemies:** i.e., Google opened Artificial Intelligence Center in China while at the same time threatening to end a similar program with the Pentagon (Fox, The Next Revolution).

Closing Comment: Please don't let the Left tell you that we have to continue our losing trade policies. It took over 200 years to accumulate a $660 billion national debt & all of a sudden, thanks to intentionally losing free trade agreements, our debt has skyrocketed to $22 trillion. Yes, there will be blowback from China on tariffs imposed by the U.S., but the price of backing down is much more costly in the long run. If we continue our intentionally losing trade policies, they will absolutely bury America under a mountain of debt. Make no mistake; China needs America as much or more than we need them. Why? Because when it is all said and done, China is a Communist country, and the mass of China's population is a poor peasant class. With this said, China's economy depends far more on trade with America and Europe than domestic consumption. Please take a stand!

7th Plank - Intellectual Initiatives:

1) **Organize the Silent Majority:** I open with some quotes for you to contemplate:

> *"I believe that if the people of this nation fully understood what Congress has done to them over the last 49 years, they would move on Washington; they would not wait for an election....It adds up to a preconceived plan to destroy the economic and social independence of the United States!"* (Senator George W. Malone [Nevada], speaking before Congress in 1957).

"The one aim of these financiers is world control by the creation of inextinguishable debts" (Henry Ford, Industrialist).

"The real menace of our Republic is the invisible government which like a giant octopus sprawls its slimy length over city-state and nation. Like the octopus of real life, it operates under cover of a self-created screen. At the head of the octopus are the Rockefeller Standard Oil interest and a small group of powerful banking houses generally referred to as international bankers. The little coterie of powerful international bankers virtually run the United States government for their own selfish purposes. They practically control both political parties" (John F. Hylan, Mayor of N.Y. 1918-1925).

"We shall have world government whether or not you like it. The only question is whether World Government will be by conquest or consent" (James P. Warburg Representing Rothschild Banking Concern While speaking before the United States Senate February 17, 1950).

"The New World Order will be built… an end-run on national sovereignty, eroding it piece by piece will accomplish much more than the old-fashioned frontal assault" (Council on Foreign Relations Journal 1974, P558).

So now we know who the enemy is and what he has planned for our great nation. The question then becomes, are we going to stand by and allow it to happen? But we can't just go off willy-nilly. As I said earlier, we must revolt and take back our nation, but it must be a peaceful revolt. Violence plays into the Financial Elite's hands because their strategy is to create order out of chaos, and violence creates chaos.

The problem we face is that the Financial Elite have vast amounts of money to spend on organizing their army of followers. Some of them have communist leanings, but some of their followers are well-intentioned people who have just been sold a bill of goods. It is like the Bible says in Romans 1:28 (KJV), *"… God gave them over to a reprobate mind, to do those things which are not convenient."* In either event, they represent the organized minority, and here is what Vladimir Lenin, founder of the Soviet Union, had to say about them:

> *"The organized minority will beat the disorganized majority every time."*

We discussed how the Rothschild's bought the nation's 25 largest news-papers and put in their own editorial staff in order to control public opinion and how the Financial Elite went on to buy Hollywood studios as well. Hollywood is an even more powerful propaganda machine than news outlets because their message reaches us on a subliminal level while we think we are being entertained. Consider this quote from Joseph Stalin, a Russian leader, and a mass murderer.

> *"If I could control Hollywood, I could control the world."*
>
> *"If we understand the mechanism and motives of the group mind, it is now possible to control and regiment the masses according to our will without them knowing it... Those who manipulate the unseen mechanism of society constitute an invisible government, which is the true ruling power of our country...In almost every act of our lives, whether in the sphere of politics or business in our social conduct or our ethical thinking, we are dominated by the relatively small number of persons who understand the mental processes and social patterns of the masses. It is they who pull the wires that control the public mind."* (Edward Bernays, Father of Public Relations).

What can we do to organize the silent majority? We have to organize. We have to help President Trump help us. We can't afford to miss this op-portunity to stand as one voice and let our concerns be heard. We need to rally around a platform that we want to see implemented and require polit-ical candidates to sign a pledge to support that platform, and if they get in office and don't keep their pledge, then we have to vote them out. It is time we take control of our government and see to it that it serves: *"We the People."*

We must stop looking at the government as our savior and take our future into our own hands. It is as President Ronald Reagan said,

"In the present crisis, government is not the solution to the problem, government is the problem."

But how can we stand against the vast wealth and the army of organizers the Financial Elite can field? President Trump did it with a tweeter feed! I want to signal an alarm. The Democrats want President Trump out no matter what. That is why we are seeing so many allegations of voter fraud during this election. We need to have a groundswell resurgence of the Tea Party or some organization like it, and we need to give generously to it. With President Trump still in office, we won't have to worry about the IRS coming after us like what happened under Obama. Lastly, we sanction rogue countries and those who fund their agendas. It seems to me there ought to be some way to go after the George Soro's of the world and freeze their assets and maybe even uncover their treasonous actions and put them in jail. That would put a real crimp in the Financial Elites ability to control us.

2) Revamp Our Educational System: The educational system, like most of our governmental institutions, has been taken over by the Progressives. Over half the positions in our schools are nonteaching positions filled by bureaucrats put in place to make sure the liberal agenda is implemented. I hate to say it, but our educational system is used as a means of control. It is used to indoctrinate our children in liberal ideology, and it is no accident that college graduates can't get jobs in their field of study.

Europe, in particular Germany, doesn't have nearly the unemployment problem we have here in the U.S. Currently, we have an estimated 6 million high-tech jobs available for which we don't have qualified workers. So, what do we do? We give work visas to foreign nationals to come to America and take jobs from our citizens. At the same time, we have $1.5 trillion in school loans for a college-educated workforce that can't find work in their field of study. Many of them are working at menial jobs, unable to pay their school loans, in many instances living at home because they don't have enough money to live on their own, and don't have enough money to get married and start a family.

We need to follow Germany's lead, and if we do, we could address many of the problems in the inner cities and the suburbs. We could also curb the opioid crisis because when people are depressed and feel hopeless, they often turn to drugs to escape their plight. Couple these policies with building the wall, ending chain migration, sanctuary cities, and implementing merit-based immigration. The racial tension in America would begin to subside because people would have dignity and the hope of a meaningful life.

What Can We Do to Fix the Education System? The system is broken, but there is a solution.

The German Apprenticeship Program: In Europe, Unions, Corporations, and Schools cooperate in designing training programs that turn out a workforce for which there are guaranteed high paying jobs. Here is how it works.

Youth unemployment for those under age 25 in Germany is 8%. Why? 2/3rds of youth in Germany participate in an apprentice program. **Note:** 2/3rds of their workforce are not college-bound, but they are guaranteed good-paying jobs. Not only will they have a job, but they are also high paying jobs. Isn't that better than a handout? A job gives you dignity and makes you self-reliant, while a handout lowers your esteem and makes you dependent on your government slave masters. The German apprenticeship program is a cooperative effort between corporations, vocational schools, the government, and trade unions to train a skilled labor force that meets employers' needs.

Unfortunately, here in America, the politically correct rhetoric and divisiveness propagated by the media, our school system, and those in Washington make such cooperation impossible. If we hope to survive as a nation, we had better put the word cooperation at the forefront of everything we do. We better get our vocational schools, the government, and trade unions to cooperate, or else! A nation divided can't stand, and neither can its people get jobs!

Participants in Germany's Apprenticeship Program Receive:

- 3 ½ years paid training.

- Guaranteed job offers.

- Free vocational school (paid for by the government, unions, and employers). This means they graduate debt-free.

- Graduates receive a certificate good throughout the industry and may work for any company they please. 85% chose to stay with the company which trained them.

Note: Germany's success as an exporting country is attributed to its apprenticeship program and the skilled labor force it provides. Automation and technology are how you compete with the cheap slave labor from China and elsewhere. Additionally, Germany has placed tariffs on Chinese imports (something President Trump is finally doing). They have set limits on the number of Chinese imports allowed into the country, so (unlike America) they don't have entire industries driven out of business. The population doesn't become dependent on cheap goods from China (like America is).

This is pretty simple stuff. It is basic common sense, so why hasn't America done what Germany has done? As we have discussed in detail, the U.S.'s wealth is to be redistributed to other nations. Our exceptionalism is to be ended, and we are to be driven into the One-World Government. We can't allow that to happen.

> *"The New World Order can't happen without U.S. participation, as we are the most significant single component. Yes, there will be a New World Order, and it will force the United States to change its perceptions"* (Henry Kissinger (CFR member), World Affairs Council Press Conference, Regent Beverly Wilshire, April 19, 1994).

Ben Franklin said, *"By failing to prepare, you are preparing to fail."* That is exactly what America is doing—preparing to fail.

It is as Jefferson said, *"The Democracy will collapse when we take away from those who are willing to work and give to those who will not."*

"You cannot help men permanently by doing for them what they could and should do for themselves" (Rev. William J.H. Boetcker).

So, the answer to most of our racial issues is to give people in both the inner city and the suburbs meaningful employment so they can have dignity and hope and stop feeling like victims.

The Danger Imposed by Robotics and Artificial Intelligence: I don't see a solution to this threat because it would require a global initiative where every nation on the planet cooperated, and we know how difficult that would be. But I want to issue a warning anyway. Robotics and artificial intelligence have the capability of causing catastrophic levels of unemployment that could utterly destabilize modern civilization. But that is exactly what the Financial Elite want. If they have robots to do their work for them, it makes it that much easier to exterminate 6 billion of us and usher in their Utopian New World Order.

3) Put God Back in Our Families, Schools, Public Institutions, and Churches: We stood by and allowed President Obama to say America is not a Christian Nation. This released the Abrahamic curse on America. But God is merciful, and he still has plans for America. He wants to restore America. He has promised that he would pour out on the earth a *"Latter Day Rain"* that would be greater than the former. The greatest revival the world has ever seen is about to break out, and America has a key role to play. But 1st we have to repent, stand up and boldly proclaim that America was dedicated to God and still serves Him. Then the blessing will fall. We have to take a stand against the liberal rhetoric and boldly proclaim that America serves God. We have to put prayer back in our schools and our public affairs. And you Pastors, President Trump has removed the 501c restriction so you can speak freely from the pulpit. Get your house in order. Get out from under the 501c and start professing the ungodliness in Washington, our schools, and society. Enough with the feel-good, seeker-friendly, prosperity messages of the mega-churches. God is not coming back for a watered-down material-istic lukewarm church. He is coming back for a spotless bride. The day of the lukewarm church is fast coming to an end. God is about to send out an army into the streets to gather the harvest of souls, and if the churches get in the way, he will deal with them just like he is getting ready to deal with the corruption in Washington. America turn back to God or else!

8th Plank – Climate Change: The simple truth is we are being lied to about the cause of climate change and global warming. Humans are indeed fouling the air and water, which is a serious problem, but it is not the cause of climate change. As we discussed earlier, all the planets in the solar system are experiencing the same warming trends, so this rules out our carbon footprint as the cause. As we discussed, the probable cause is increased sunspot activity caused by alignment with a 15 million mile wide black hole at the center of the galaxy. This alignment affects our weather for decades, so it is truly a serious problem, but it is not caused by human activity.

Our political leaders have seized on this issue in order to use it to collapse the U.S. and the Free Market System as part of their plan to birth their New World Order. They tried to impose *Cap and Trade* in an effort to place onerous taxes on U.S. manufacturing that would not be placed on other countries. The result would have been to make the U.S. unable to compete in the global market. When they couldn't get *Cap and Trade* passed, President Obama imposed job-killing EPA regulations and attempted to take the U.S. into the *Paris Climate Treaty*, which like *Cap and Trade*, was designed to render the U.S. unable to compete in the global market.

The problem which the Financial Elite are not telling us is that planet Earth is in the midst of its 6th mass extinction, caused by the collision of overpopulation with shortages of clean water and natural resources, the most important of which is clean water and oil. The Financial Elites have a simple solution to this problem: Impose a global dictatorship and then exterminate 6 billion of us. Problem solved. The planet returns to sustainable levels of resource utilization, and the water and air stop being fouled because we are gone.

The Planks of Climate Change:

- **Access to Cheap Clean Renewable Energy Solutions Which Are Being Withheld From Us:** If we want to address the problems facing the world in the 21st century, we can no longer allow critically important technologies to be withheld by greedy corporations and self-serving politicians, to the detriment of the planet that sustains us. We must demand access to hydrogen on-demand at the point of use, generators powered by permanent magnets, cars powered by compressed air, oil made from our garbage, etc.). These technologies are being withheld from us to protect the revenue of the oil and electric companies. The time is quickly approaching where these technologies will be essential to our survival as a species. Think about it. We could have energy-efficient, environmentally friendly factories capable of producing products at a fraction of current costs. We could build cost-effective desalination plants and pipe water to where it was needed. If we added in hydroponic technology, food could be grown at the point of consumption instead of, as is the case now, where it is transported an average of 1,500 miles to market. We could drive nonpolluting cars powered by permanent magnets, solar, or hydrogen on demand (no gas stations). Homeowners could have electric generators, which would allow them to be off the grid.

- **We Must Transition From a Disposable Economy to One Based on Product Longevity and Reusability:** If we are to survive as a species, we have to figure out how to voluntarily reduce the population to sustainable levels while simultaneously lowering resource utilization to sustainable levels by transitioning the economy from the disposable, planned obsolescence economy typified by the Free Market System into a sustainable economy that focuses on resource conservation and product longevity and reusability. This process will fundamentally change our economic system and will require extensive planning and a long-term implementation strategy. But if we don't face these issues, the Financial Elite will do it for us simply by committing mass genocide. Drastic changes will be required to implement a holistic approach to reengineering society that integrates humankind's needs with the long-term sustainability of the planet that sustains us.

The problems we face in the 21st century are too big, too critical, too life-threatening to allow greedy bankers, corporations, and self-serving politicians to withhold the very solutions that could solve them. It is time for the 2nd American Revolution. The unorganized majority must unite their voices in one refrain and demand access to life-altering cheap, clean energy technology. Remember, the Financial Elite have no intention of solving these problems. They do not need to. All they have to do is sit back and wait for things to get so bad that we will come crawling to them for help. At that point, they will make available to us these life-altering technologies, but it will come at the cost of accepting their One-World Dictatorship. Once that is in place, they will simply go about the process of exterminating 6 billion of us useful idiots, and all their problems will be solved. We are all in the same boat: Liberals, Conservatives, and people of all religions and races worldwide. As Americans, our best hope is to stand together shoulder to shoulder as one united people and demand access to life-altering technology.

- **Patent Reform:** We need legislation that declares energy and medical patents that have been intentionally shelved be returned to the public domain. Our ecological crisis demands that cheap, clean, renewable energy solutions be made available.

- **Planned Obsolescence:** We need a long-term strategy to convert our economy from one based on planned obsolescence to one based on resource conservation and product longevity and reusability. In a society where population must be reduced, constant economic growth is impossible, which, by the way, is why our government says, *"The Free-Market System is nonsense."* A new economic model is imperative!

- **Clean Water and Agricultural Production:** We need to change clean water and agricultural practices, so they are more sustainable. We are using the water in aquifers that took thousands of years to fill in a matter of decades. We take so much water from our rivers and lakes for industrial and agricultural use that they are literally drying up. Water conservation is required, but that alone will not be enough.

We must reduce the population, so demand is reduced. We must put restrictions on aboveground irrigation, where much of the water is lost to evaporation.

We need to follow Israel's example of using less wasteful drip irrigation. We must also grow as many crops hydroponically as possible. Hydroponics drastically reduces water usage, fertilizer, and pesticide usage, and as discussed a minute ago, it allows products to be grown at the point of consumption. Suppose I am correct about the hydrogen technology that creates cheap, clean, renewable energy that burns at the temperature of the sun. In that case, we need access to this technology so we can build massive desalination plants on the coast and pipe water to wherever it is needed. Israel has built commercial desalination plants based on reverse osmosis. They are state of the art today, but my money is on hydrogen, which burns at the temperature of the sun and uses saltwater, the most abundant resource on the planet.

> *"Planet earth is facing a mass extinction event that equals or exceeds any in the geologic record. And human activities have brought the planet to the brink of this crisis"* (Dr. Peter Raven, Director of the Missouri Botanical Garden and adjunct professor at the University of Missouri, St. Louis University, and Washington University).

> *"The time has come when cheap, clean, renewable energy solutions must be taken out of the hands of the Financial Elite and made available to all of humanity. And real conservation measures must be taken to save the planet, not to line the pockets of the Elite and to enslave us"* (Larry Ballard).

9th Plank - Intentionally Caused Division: We must end the intentionally caused division in America and lay the foundation for worldwide peaceful coexistence? How do we do that? We restore the 12 Foundation Stones that made America great in the first place. When all is said and done, we have the ultimate blueprint. Just restore the things that made America great, and

America will come back as strong as ever. Isn't that simple? Our politicians try to make it sound impossible, but it isn't.

The Planks of Intentionally Caused Division:

All of the things listed below cause division, and they must be changed if we are to end the intentional division that is being inflicted on us!

- **Culture:** America's greatness was based on family and Christian values. Today these core values have been undermined and are used to divide us!

- **Patriotism:** America has a lot to be proud of. But instead, our flag and our heritage are maligned and used to cause racial and ethnic division!

- **Politics:** The American people were supposed to be in charge of the four centers of power. Monetary, political, intellectual, and religious, but they have been hijacked by those who, as Kennedy said, *"Want to be the masters of us all."* When these things are controlled by the people, there is peace and harmony, but when the Financial Elites control them, they are used to cause division!

- **Economics:** America's greatness was based on creativity as the basis of wealth and on the American Economic System, which shared the fruits of our innovation with the world to elevate while equalizing the condition of all humankind. By contrast, the British Free Trade System, which has been replaced by Chinese Free Trade, controls natural resources and wages in order to make us *"slaves without chains!"* When there is intentional income inequality, there is always division!

- **Messaging:** The media, Hollywood, and our corrupt politicians all insight discourse and division. In particular, the Democrats messaging is centered on racism and division!

Our only hope as a nation is if we can see through these intentionally divisive tactics and come together as one nation, one people! We must recognize that we all share a common enemy, the shadow government of the

Financial Elite. They want to divide us, enslave us, and ultimately kill most of us to restore the planet to what they consider sustainable resource levels. They and they alone are our enemies! We are on death ground, and if we don't wake up, we will lose our freedom and our lives!

If we restore the values that made America great, the entire world will benefit. If there is more economic equality in the world, there will be less reason for humankind to exterminate ourselves in senseless wars. If we work together as a species to solve the overpopulation and ecological crises that threaten all life on earth, we may yet save the planet, and in the process, learn to live in peace. These are the lessons God wants to teach humankind. It is all scriptural. We are to be our brother's keeper and love our brother as we love ourselves and do unto others as we would have them do unto us. When we learn these lessons, we will have peace on earth, and the planet will be a wellspring of beauty instead of a dying garbage dump!

We have more power than you think. We can vote out corrupt politicians, the unorganized majority can unite and become the organized majority and take our demands to Washington, we can organize peaceful protests, we can use our economic clout to boycott where necessary, and we can unleash the creativity that made America great in the first place. If we stand united and demand change, it will come, and we can have a better, more prosperous, and secure future. It is time to come together and take a stand. This entire book has been laying the foundation for a Great Awakening, where us Useful Idiots, us Mindless Sheep, finally know the truth and come together in unity and take back the reins of power from the Financial Elite and join together to solve our mutual problems so our children will have a future. It is time to take a stand. This is a call for the mass of humanity to join together before it is too late. The time is short. Either we win this battle or else.

CHAPTER 8

Flash Point:
How the Pandemic, Our Debt Crisis, and the Riots Hold the Key to Making America Greater Than Ever!

WHAT YOU WILL LEARN IN THIS CHAPTER

- Acknowledging the Wound of Inequality That Divides Us!

- Understanding Who Our Enemy Is and His Strategy for World Dominance!

- The Rise of China and the Decline of America Is No Accident!

- Time for America to Make a Resurgence!

- How to Bring Back Our Manufacturing From China and Simultaneously Heal the Wounds of Socioeconomic and Racial Injustice That Divide Us!

Acknowledging the Wound of Inequality That Divides Us!

"Those that make peaceful revolution impossible make violent revolution inevitable" (President John F. Kennedy).

The streets of America are ablaze as lawless mobs of frustrated people of all nationalities and walks of life smash storefronts, loot, burn businesses, and savagely bludgeon those who try to stop them. We are told it is over the wrongful death of George Floyd, a Black American man killed by a White Police Officer, but that is just the excuse to release generations of pent-up frustration.

Sadly, these riots are not about the appalling actions of one man who took another's life. They are only superficially about claims of police brutality. They are not exclusively or even primarily about racial inequality. Those who are protesting are of all races and ethnicities, so this cannot be minimized by playing the race card. What truly motivates these protests is systemic anger and distrust of a political and economic system that people see as disenfranchising. But what has turned the protests into riots is paid anarchists whose goal is to bring about a political coup while the protesters hide behind their 1st amendment rights, groups like Antifa and Black Lives Matter secretly want to suppress your free speech. Doubt what I say, go to their websites. They are part and parcel of the political correctness and cancel culture movements that have infected our Universities and brainwashed our kids. *"The freedom of speech may be taken, and dumb and silent we may be led, like sheep to the slaughter"* (George Washington). Make no mistake; that is precisely what they are doing to us, wake up America!

This political correctness and cancel culture rhetoric is spreading like wildfire, threatening to divide Americans and turn them against one another with the goal of collapsing America from within. This is exactly what Adolf Hitler did when he galvanized Germany with his racist hate message vilifying Jews and enshrining and glorifying the Arian race! What started in our public schools and Universities has now spread to our corporations, the government, including the FBI, the military, even breaching the walls of West Point. In all these institutions, critical race theory indoctrination is mandatory! These brainwashing indoctrination seminars teach about toxic masculinity, microaggressions, gender bias with the overarching message that America is inherently racist, that our founders were racist, that America is evil, and that White people should apologize for their White privilege. Heads up, not all White people were born with a silver spoon in their mouths. I lived in the ghetto growing up, so it is hard for me even to imagine what privilege of any kind looks like. All I ever understood was that the American dream that has brought millions of immigrants to America is that in America, if you work hard and keep your nose clean, anything is possible. Take, for example, the renowned neurosurgeon and Presidential candidate Ben Carson. He worked hard, got an education, and got his ticket out of the ghetto. What differentiated him from those that remain trapped is that he believed in the American ideal of rugged individualism, which is to say we can accept what we are handed or study and work to make our dreams come true. America is the land of opportunity, not the land of oppression. That is just a lie out of the Left's playbook.

As Hitler said, the bigger the lie, the higher it flies (paraphrased). If you want to blame someone for the riots and actions of the peaceful protesters who are intimidating local residents, beating those who dare to oppose them, and killing innocent bystanders, look no further than the political correctness and cancel culture movement that takes their inspiration from Mein Kompf (Hitlers anti-Semitic Nazi manifesto). It used hate and division to bring the world to the brink of destruction. Then along came the Financial Elites, and they are using racism to get us, Useful Idiots, Blacks and Whites to rip each other's throats out to collapse the most powerful, most free nation the world has ever known. Why would they want to do that other than because they are maniacal, megalomaniac, narcissist, and power-crazy tyrants? I will tell you why! They want to create a utopia where the earth is a pristine lush garden, where they are in control of absolutely everything and everyone and where we are not consuming their natural resources faster than the planet can replenish them, where us useful idiots have either been exterminated or put on the reservation or in work camps so they can harvest our organs should they need to! Think of your worst nightmare, and I guarantee it is child's play compared to what these monsters have conjured up so that they may rule over the earth and everything and everyone in it. In truth, they are minions of Satan!

It is a tragedy when anyone is killed, but the real culprits in this tragedy are not the police. The police are not racist, especially not the Black and Hispanic police officers. In truth, more Whites die at the hands of police than Blacks, but that doesn't matter to the enraged protesters. The police are task with managing a problem they didn't create and can't resolve. It is a fact that the poverty of our inner cities makes them a breeding ground for violent crime, so every time a police officer responds to a call, he is putting his life on the line. Tragically, mistakes are made in the heat of the moment, and sometimes those mistakes result in wrongful death. But the police are not targeting Blacks; they are just human beings resounding to a dangerous stressful situation.

Is it true that if you are a Black, especially living in the inner city that you are more likely to be stopped by police and patted down? Yes! But the reason is not that the police are racist, especially not the police officers of color. So, why are inner-city Blacks so much more likely to be stopped? The truth is that the inner cities are where gangs and drugs are the most prevalent, and it is where the vast majority of violent crimes occur. The truth is that these violent crimes take far more Black lives than incidents involving the police. It is also true that a visible police presence keeps down violent crime, and their presence keeps local residents safer. In fact, though the stop and frisk policies are intimidating and degrading and a source of anger, they actually save Black lives in the final analysis. So, this rhetoric from Democrat politicians threatening to cut police funding or get rid of them is lunacy. The result is that our inner cities' streets are becoming lawless, killing zones where law-abiding citizens are prey forced to cower in fear in their homes.

If you want to know what that will look like, look no further than Communist China, the nation the Financial Elite have chosen as their model for their New World Order Dictatorship. Under Chinese leadership, religious freedom is not allowed; dissent is not allowed; there are no inalienable rights. If you challenge the government's authority in any manner, you may well end up in a work camp where you will have your blood typed and cataloged so that your vital organs can be sold to the highest bidder. There is no such thing as personal freedom. There is just a surveillance state that monitors your every move and controls you with a social credit score that rewards compliance and punishes any form of personal expression. Is that what we want for America? If not, we had better once and for all address the socioeconomic injustices that the Financial Elite are using to tear America apart from the inside out.

In 2016, then-candidate Donald Trump said to the Black community, *"What do you have to lose by giving me a chance?"* He was elected, and he has established *"Opportunity Zones"* to encourage economic development in the inner cities. He also implemented *"Prison Reform,"* which has seen the release of many Black inmates! This is more than any of his predecessors have done. Trump's support among Black voters has increased somewhat. However, thanks to the biased media, the vast majority of Blacks are still loyal to the Democratic granny state that buys votes with handouts rather than giving people the dignity that comes from having a good job and being able to have a family and provide them with a decent standard of living. Without knowing it, they keep themselves in bondage to the very people who brought their ancestors to America in chains.

But less you think the Socialist-Democrats are anything but equal op-portunity oppressors. They are busy in the suburbs, teaching the middle-class to hate America, that marriage is an outdated institution, and there is no God! Then they send their brainwashed middle-class suburbanites off to college to finish their brainwashing. The real agenda is not to educate them so they can get a good-paying job but to teach them to hate America so that at the right time, they can be used to tear it down from within. The agenda is also to indenture them with student loans, which they will struggle to pay back because their slave masters saw to it that their degrees were worthless. After all, they intentionally failed to prepare them for a good-paying job. But no matter, they are ready to play their part. They can go home and live in their parent's basement and get a job as a waiter or waitress and let their frustration fester into hatred for the system that has failed them. So, you see, the Financial Elite are equal opportunity oppressors because their goal is to end the middle-class and enslave all of us useful idiots. In their minds, they are superior to us and are destined to rule over us all: Black, White, Hispanic, etc. It doesn't matter. This system of indentured servitude is the enemy of all of us, and unless we come together as one nation and one people, the Financial Elite will kill most of us and make slaves of those of us whom they believe they can use to serve them.

Racial discrimination as an official policy has ended, but it is still well and thriving in the bowels of our inner cities as a socioeconomic reality. A system of generational welfare is inflicted on disenfranchised inner-city dwellers (Black, Whites, and Hispanics) that create a system of slavery without chains. Comply, and you will be given a handout intended to make you dependent on supporting the very system that oppresses you.

Socialist Democrats pander to Blacks, but in truth, they are just interested in buying votes. Every election cycle, they make promises to make things better, but as soon as the election is over, their promises are conveniently forgotten until the next election cycle when they make the same hollow promises. People are fed up with being used as political pawns. They are tired of broken promises, tired of being forgotten and abandoned. They are tired of politicians who intentionally take legitimate political and economic issues and label them racist to create division because those who want to destroy this country know a nation divided cannot stand.

Make no mistake, the violence in our streets is being allowed by Democrat Mayors and Governors because they think it will help defeat President Trump in the election. What does it say when politicians are willing to let cities burn, be looted, and people be killed to win an election? How evil is that? But this is no ordinary election. The Financial Elite and their pawns, the Socialist Democrats, are afraid that if Trump wins a second term, his policies will, in fact, *"Make America Great Again."* On the other hand, they are confident that if China-friendly Biden wins, their power and graft will be intact and to hell with the rest of us. After all, they think they will have a seat at the table after their coup is over! Little do they know that they are just useful idiots like the rest of us!

Our progressive-leftist school system is the incubator for the rage in our streets. Our children are taught that America is an evil nation, that it is inherently racist, and that the police are analogs to Nazi storm troopers. This flies in the face o f reality. D id America have slavery? Yes, but virtually every nation had slavery up till the birth of the Industrial Revolution, which was spearheaded by America, whose economic goal was to create an economic system *"That elevated while equalizing the condition of all mankind."* America was successful in achieving that goal until 1933 when in the depths of the Great Depression, it declared bankruptcy, and the Globalist Bankers became the receivers of the bankruptcy and abruptly terminated our Republic. At that point, America became a Democracy - a Socialist Communist Order. At that moment, Capitalism died, replaced by crony Capitalism responsible for the repression that has festered into the anger and hatred that is responsible for the burning of our cities. That was also the moment when *"The Deep State Communist Shadow Government"* infested the bowels of our government in Washington, and our schools and other institutions were likewise filled with an unelected army of socialist intent on systematically dismantling America from within. It is they who lit the fires that are burning America. It is they who are behind this political coup masquerading as a protest.

The Pledge of Allegiance says, *"I pledge allegiance to the Flag of the Unit-ed States of America and to the Republic for which it stands..."* But these days, America is always referred to as a Democracy. That is no accident! As you just learned, we have not been a Republic since 1933 when we became a De-mocracy, and the Deep State Shadow government was birthed in secret in the shadows. Consider the following words of wisdom from those in posi-tions of power where they have access to the Financial Elite's secret agenda.

Speaking of the secret shadow government, Patrick Henry said,

> *"The liberties of a people will never be secure when the transactions of their rulers may be concealed from them."*

President Kennedy also warned us of the dangers of secret governance when he said,

"The very word secrecy is repugnant in a free and open society, and we are as a people inherently and historically opposed to secret societies. Even today, there is little value in ensuring the survival of our nation if our traditions don't survive with it! And there is a very grave danger that an announced need for increased security will be seized upon by those anxious to expand its meaning to the very limits of official censorship and concealment..." (JFK, address before the American Newspaper Publishers April 27, 1961).

"Today the path of total dictatorship in the United States can be laid by strictly legal means, unseen and unheard by the Congress, the President, or the people. Outwardly we have a Constitutional government. We have operating within our government and political system, another body representing another form of government – a bureaucratic elite" (Senator William Jenner, 1954).

Congressman Ron Paul told us that there is, in fact, a shadow government, and they are secretly working to establish a One - World Dictatorship.

"I think there are 25,000 individuals that have used offices of power, and they are in our Universities, and they are in our Congresses, and they believe in One World Government. And if you believe in One World Government, then you are talking about undermining National Sovereignty, and you are talking about setting up something that you could well call a Dictatorship—and those plans are there!" (Congressman Ron Paul at an event near Austin, Texas on August 30, 2003).

America is unique in that it fought a war (the Civil War) to end the inhumanity of slavery, and in that war, more Americans (most of which were White) were killed than in either WWI or WWII. America also passed legislation giving Black people the right to vote, but unfortunately, the Democrat Party (the party of slavery) has, up till this moment in time, managed to take plantation slavery (slavery with chains) and turn it into inner-city slavery (slavery without chains). Instead of using whips to control their slaves, the (Socialist Democrats) use generational welfare and an intentionally underperforming educational system to suppress the inner-city dwellers (most of which are black) in order to keep them dependent on them for their welfare checks. The Socialist Democrats use education as an instrument of slavery. *"Education is dangerous. Every educated person is a future enemy"* (Herman Goering, Hitler's designated successor). *"Give me four years to teach children, and the seed I have sown will never be uprooted"* (Vladimir Lenin, Founder, Soviet Union).

By contrast, President Trump wants to give those in the inner cities a good education because he knows that education is the ticket out of the ghetto and off the plantation. It is the best way to heal the wounds of social injustice and make America truly great. That is why he is for Charter Schools where your children can escape the brainwashing of the public schools.

Education is also the key to keeping our Constitution and the freedoms it guarantees. *"If a nation expects to be ignorant and free, in a state of civilization, it expects what never was and never will be"* (Thomas Jefferson, 1816). Our Republic requires an educated public capable of making an informed decision based on what is in the nation's best interest as a whole. Generational welfare is a trap for those receiving it and for those from whom the money is extorted, *"The Democracy will cease to exist when you take away from those who are willing to work and give to those who will not"* (Thomas Jefferson).

I am a product of the inner-city ghetto and can recall a conversation between two black women. One said to the other: *"I have to find me a man to get me pregnant because my oldest is turning 18 and I will lose my child support, and I depend on that, so I have to have another child."* This points out how the Financial Elite keep their slaves on the plantation. Their policies assure that the majority of black families are single-parent families because they know that when a child is raised without a male figure, that child is statistically prone to dropping out of school, becoming a gang member, turning to crime, drug addiction, or prostitution and that is how you keep the slaves on the plantation. *"The family is the nucleus of civilization"* (Ariel & Will Durant). The Financial Elite know this to be true, which is why they intend to destroy the family because it stands in the way of their Communist takeover of America. I would add that education is what got me off the plantation. I worked my way through college as a construction worker, mover, shipbuilder, and janitor. No job was too hard, too dirty, too dangerous, or too demeaning because they represented my ticket to the American dream! I didn't want to be a ward of the state-dependent on their handouts. I wanted dignity and self-sufficiency because even back then, I knew handouts were a trap. Consider what Senator Barry Goldwater said about the welfare system, *"Remember that a government big enough to give you everything you want is also big enough to take away everything you have."* I worked hard, and I got my dignity and the American dream, and you can too!

President Barack Obama was elected twice with overwhelming White support hoping he would bring Blacks and Whites together and end our racial divide. But the sad truth is that he was groomed by the Financial Elite. Like so many Presidents before him, he was put in office to do their bidding, so his legacy was that instead of bringing the nation together, he fanned the flames of racial hatred and became perhaps the most inflammatory President in modern times. He served the agenda of his Masters, the Financial Elite, and was handsomely rewarded for betraying those he claimed to champion. His campaign slogan was *"Hope and Change,"* and the American people bought his lies hook, line, and sinker. In his acceptance speech, he said: *"We are just five days away from fundamentally transforming America."* Like all of his rhetoric, it was inspirational and did indeed fill people with hope. The intent behind the meaning of *"fundamental transformation"* is exposed by this quote by George Bernard Shaw, *"A government policy to rob Peter to pay Paul can be assured of the support of Paul."* Unfortunately, Obama is a radical with an agenda to destroy America, and he is backing Joe Biden!

- He was mentored by Bill Ayres, a member of the Weather Underground that bombed the Pentagon.

- He taught *"Rules for Radicals,"* a doctrine outlining how to topple governments by burying them in debt. Incidentally, he has the distinction of having amassed more debt than the 43 Presidents who preceded him combined.

- While a community organizer at SEIU, he sued Citi Bank and was responsible for the *"predatory lending policies"* which underpinned the 2008 financial collapse, which bankrupted millions, took their homes, and left them disenfranchised. For the first time in our history, he made it possible to buy a home with no money down and no income verification. Without these policies, the 2008 financial collapse could never have happened.

- His Pastor, Jeremiah Wright, is famous for saying, *"God D--- America."* Despite having sat in his church hearing such hate-filled messages for 20 years, Obama disavowed his radical pastors' rhetoric.

- Frank Marshall Davis is believed to have been Obama's father. But what we know for sure is that he mentored under this man who was an activist and a card-carrying Communist who was instrumental in formulating Obama's world view.

- For several years, he lived in Indonesia, where he attended school, becoming a student of Islam and a devotee to Mohammad. He called the Islamic call to prayer *"The most beautiful sound he had ever heard"* though it was politically necessary to claim to be a Christian, he was not. He disavowed Christianity on many occasions.

  ○ He said: *"America does not consider itself a Christian nation."* And he criticized The Sermon on the Mount.

  ○ He said, *"We will never be at war with our Muslim brothers. I intend to disarm America to a level acceptable to our Muslim brothers."* and he did. When he left office, the military was utterly depleted, and Trump spent $2 trillion rebuilding it.

  ○ He ended the Christian Day of Prayer but invited his Muslim brothers into the Whitehouse to pray. The point, in fact, when a person says the *"Call to Prayer"* that is the initiation into Islam, and Obama acknowledged that he had done just that.

  ○ When Obama was elected, his wife, Michelle, said it was the first time she had ever been proud of America.

America put into the Whitehouse a man who hated America and was secretly a Communist, a Globalist, a Muslim, and whose wife shared his disdain for America. The Left's propaganda machine is powerful, and with the help of the fake news, sold-out politicians, and a Socialist - Progressive education system, they could dress a traitor up in a suit and sell you on the fact that he was the greatest thing since sliced bread. And that is exactly what they did with Obama. There is evidence that with the exception of Kennedy, Reagan, and Trump, all our Presidents since Wilson have, in fact, been puppets of the Financial Elite and have used the Office of the President to covertly collapse America from within. They, along with most of our politicians, are Manchurian Candidates groomed, financed, and placed in their positions to systematically dismantle America from within, slowly transforming it into Socialism – Communism. Consider the following quotes:

> *"A crisis is an event that forces democracies to make decisions they wouldn't otherwise make"* (Timothy Wirth, former U.S. Senator, D-Colorado).

A crisis is a tool, real or staged, used by people in power to manipulate political events. This is what the protests, riots, and looting in America's cities are really about. They are the opening volley in a coup intended to collapse America and the world and enslave us all.

> *"We are on the verge of a global transformation. All we need is the right major crisis, and the nations will accept the New World Order"* (David Rockefeller, September 23, 1994).

Folks turn your T.V. on or, better yet, go to one of the cities under siege, and you will quickly realize that these riots are nothing short of a coup orchestrated by the Financial Elite. They are funded by Hollywood and many global corporations, and it is sad to tell many of our politicians. And the fake news and the Socialist Democrats are their propaganda outlets.

> *"Out of these troubled times, our objective a New World Order can emerge. Today, that New World Order is struggling to be born, a*

world quite different from the one we have known" (President George Bush Sr., addressing the general assembly of the United States, February 1, 1992).

Folks, this revolution has been going on a long time, and most of our political leaders are part of the Shadow Government and are the enemies of freedom-loving people.

"We shall have world government whether or not you like it. The only question is whether World Government will be by conquest or consent" (James P. Warburg, Representing Rothschild Banking Concern while speaking before the United States Senate, February 17, 1950).

As the military strategist Sun Tzu would say of America, *"We are on death ground, and we are fighting for our lives"* (And I would add our freedom).

"The case for government by Elites is irrefutable" (William Fulbright, US Senator).

"The real truth of the matter is, as you and I know, that a financial element in the larger centers has owned the Government ever since the days of Andrew Jackson" (A letter written by FDR to Colonel House, November 21, 1933).

"We can either have democracy in this country or we can have great wealth concentrated in the hands of a few, but we can't have both" (Louis Brandies, Supreme Court Justice).

"Our government will soon become what it is already a long way toward becoming, an elective dictatorship" (Senator J. William Fulbright).

"The size of the lie is a definite factor in causing it to be believed, for the vast masses of a nation are in the depths of their hearts more easily deceived than they are consciously and intentionally bad. The primitive simplicity of their minds renders them a more easy prey

to a big lie than a small one, for they themselves often tell little lies, but would be ashamed to tell big lies" (Adolf Hitler, Mein Kompf, 1925)

"What is being sold to the American people today as Americanism, if you peel off the label, you find so much similarity to what we were fighting against when we were fighting Communism, Nazism, and Fascism... The media controls the information a person gets. In various ways can make sure that the average American watching the tube, reading the newspaper is going to come out with a certain mindset. This is good. That is bad." (G. Edward Griffin Author, Creature from Jekyll Island).

"We can't expect the American People to jump from Capitalism to Communism, but we can assist their elected leaders in giving them small doses of socialism until they wake up one day to find that they have communism" (Russian Leader Vladimir Lenin).

This is President Obama's *"Fundamental Transformation of America"* in Action! Wake up, America! Wake up. For God's sake, wake up your life depends on it!

"Communism is the death of the soul. It is the organization of total conformity – in short, a tyranny – and it is committed to making tyranny universal" (Adlai E. Stevenson, Ambassador to United Nations).

"Every Communist must grasp the truth; Political power grows out of the barrel of a gun" (Mao Tso-Tung).

"Whatever the price of the Chinese Revolution, it has obviously succeeded not only in producing more efficient and dedicated administration, but also in fostering high morale and community of purpose. The social experiment in China under Chairman Mao's leadership is one of the most important and successful in human history" (David Rockefeller, statement in 1973, N.Y. Times 8-10-73).

Remember, what Rockefeller is talking about here is the execution of an estimated 67 million Useful Idiots who were slaughtered to birth Communist China. The country the Financial Elite want to model their New World Order after! Think about that all of you protesters, all of you who have been brainwashed into hating America. In the 20th century, communism exterminated an estimated 100 million people, and now in order to protest what they consider to be *"their precious natural resources"* (according to Agenda 21 and the Georgia Guide Stones), they are prepared to exterminate the bulk of humanity reducing global population to between 500 million and 1 Billion. As horrific as that sounds to them, it's just a few decimal points because we are sub-humans whom they consider to be a virus that must be eradicated. Let that sink in! It is horrific, but none the less true!

Perhaps Carol Quigley, Georgetown professor, member of Trilateral Commission, and mentor to President Bill Clinton, expressed the threat that the world faced at the reemergence of Feudalism when he said that the goal of the Financial Elite who control central banks around the world are,

> *"...nothing less than to create a world system of financial control in private hands able to dominate the political system of each country and economy of the world as a whole...controlled in a feudalist fashion* (Communist Fashion) *by central banks of the world acting in concert by secret agreements arrived at in private meetings and conferences."*

This is a perfect description of the Financial Elite's dream of establishing a Super Capitalist – Communist Government modeled after China, the nation that was birthed on the graves of 67 million of its citizens who were considered Useful Idiots and nothing more! Wake up, America, this is coming to a town near you and into your homes!

> *"The most powerful clique in these [CFR] groups have one objective in common they want to bring about the surrender of the sovereignty and the national independence of the U.S. They want to end national boundaries and racial and ethnic loyalties...What they strive for would inevitably lead to dictatorship and loss of freedoms by the people. The CFR was founded for the purpose of promoting*

*disarmament and submergence of U.S. sovereignty and national in-
dependence into an all-powerful one-world government"* (Harper's
Magazine July 1958).

President Trump understands this, and that is why he wants to close
our border, why he supports our military and our police, why he stands for
America first, and against the Financial Elite. He is America's last best hope
of retaining our freedom!

> *"The Rockefeller File is not fiction. It is a compact, powerful and
> frightening presentation of what may be the most important sto-
> ry of our lifetime—the drive of the Rockefellers and their allies to
> create a One-World government combining Super-Capitalism and
> Communism under the same tent, all under their control...not one
> has dared reveal the most vital part of the Rockefeller story: that the
> Rockefellers and their allies have, for at least fifty years, been care-
> fully following a plan to use their economic power to gain political
> control of first America, and then the rest of the world. Do I mean
> conspiracy? Yes, I do. I am convinced there is such a plot, interna-
> tional in scope, generations old in planning, and incredibly evil in
> intent"* (Representative Larry McDonald).

President Trump understands that China is the only Super-Capitalist –
Communist Government in the world and represents an existential threat
to not only the U.S. but also the entire world. By contrast, Biden is China's
pawn bought and paid for. Just ask his son (No Experience Hunter) why he
got a $1.5 billion deal with the Chinese government. Never mind, he was
already asked that question, and the answer was because he was Joe Bidens'
son. Go figure! This alone should disqualify Biden from ever being President!

> *"The New World Order cannot happen without U.S. participation,
> as we are the most significant single component. Yes, there will be
> a New World Order, and it will force the United States to change
> its perceptions"* (Henry Kissinger: World Affairs Council Press

Conference, Regent Beverly Wilshire Hotel, April 19, 1994). Here you have it: The New World Order can't happen unless the U.S. falls!

"I think there are 25,000 individuals that have used offices of power, and they are in our Universities, and they are in our Congresses, and they believe in One World Government. And if you believe in One World Government, then you are talking about undermining National Sovereignty, and you are talking about setting up something that you could well call a Dictatorship—and those plans are there!" (Congressman Ron Paul at an event near Austin, Texas on August 30, 2003).

This is your Deep State Shadow Government, which is why we have a do-nothing Congress. By in large, they represent the Financial Elite and the banks that are too big to fail, and they're global corporations and not the people who elected them.

President Kennedy said, *"There is a plot in this country to enslave every man, woman, and child. Before I leave this high and noble office, I intend to expose that plot."*

They killed him before he exposed that plot but hopefully, if I have done what God ordained me to do, you now understand what Kennedy was talking about. Hopefully, you know who our mortal enemy is and his plan for America and all us Useful Idiots. May God bless you and yours!

Understanding Who Our Enemy Is and His Strategy for World Dominance!

Before we jump into the solution to our common problems, we need a quick review of how we got into this mess that threatens our national sovereignty and that of the entire world! Let's go all the way back to the founding of America. America was founded to escape the oppression of the British Colonial Empire. Britain was called the nation upon which the sun never set, signifying it as the world's preeminent global empire. It is important that we understand just how England became so powerful. They were one of the most ruthless empires in human history. Money and power were their gods, and they were and still are willing to commit any atrocity in order to be the rulers of the world. They plundered their colonies' natural resources while making certain they lacked the essential infrastructure that would be necessary to achieve any degree of independence. Much of their empire was built on the slave trade and the trafficking of opium, but that was not the real basis of their wealth and power. They were the masters of the sea. They controlled all the key seaports of the world and used them as choke points to control trade (the basis of all wealth).

They took the plundered natural resources from their Colonies and refined them and manufactured them into finished goods that they sold worldwide. Because they stole their raw material from their Colonies and manufactured their finished goods in sweatshops where they used child labor, they were able to produce goods cheaper than any non-colonizing nation. This system of slavery without chains was referred to as *"The British Free Trade System."* Of this system of slavery, they proudly boasted, saying,

> *"...Slavery is but the owning of labor and carries with it the care of labors, while the European plan...is that capital shall control labor by controlling wages"* (Hazard Circular, July 1862).

Understanding the Enemies Strategy Is Essential in Defeating Him: What follows is a repeat from the introduction, but we need to repeat it here, so we fully understand what we are up against when it comes to fighting our mortal enemy: The Financial Elite and their pawns.

Let's take a step back and see how the Rothschild Globalists created their Deep State Shadow Government in the U.S. Rothschild Jacob Schiff is sent to America in 1905 with orders to establish a banking network for the explicit purpose of gaining control of the United States Government.

His Orders Were To:

- ❑ **Establish a Central Bank to Print the Nation's Money:** Because he who controls a nation's money supply controls the nation (the privately-owned Fed was established in 1913).

❑ **Take Control of the Four Centers of Power:** Monetary, Political, Intellectual, and Religious buy buying the loyalty of powerful decision-making and influencers at all strata of society.

❑ **Place Their Recruits in Key Positions:** In strategically important corporations, universities, Hollywood and the media, the federal government, the Congress, Supreme Court, and all federal agencies! This includes selecting and financing the Presidential Candidates of their choice. This became what today we call, *"The Shadow Government – The Deep State."*

❑ **Create Racial, Ethnic, and Class Strife:** In order to create division and tear the country apart from within! This is the basis of the Democrat's identity politics and what underlies the riots that are literally destroying our cities and threaten anarchy.

❑ **Destroy Religion, Patriotism, Morality, and the Family:** Because they are our core values. They are the glue that holds the fabric of society together! *"America is like a healthy body, and its resistance is — its patriotism, its morality, and its spiritual life. If we can undermine these three areas, America will collapse from within"* (Joseph Stalin, Russian leader, and mass murderer).

❑ **Buy Media Outlets:** To control public opinion and literally brainwash the masses! They bought a controlling interest in the 25 largest newspapers in America to control public opinion, and today they also control the three major network news outlets.

❑ **Endow Universities:** In order to control their curriculum and steer our youth toward progressive socialist ideologies.

❑ **Establish Organizations Such as the Council on Foreign Relations (CFR):** And charge them with ending national borders and national sovereignty.

Last night, while watching the reporting on the riots in California, I witnessed something that made me finally realize just how effective and pervasive the propaganda and brainwashing of our would-be masters have become. I saw what looked like a couple thousand mostly White people lying prostrate on the ground dutifully repeating a mantra that apologized for their supposed White privilege as if they had any control whatsoever over the color of their skin or the circumstances into which they were born.

That made me think of the thousands of Useful Idiots protesting, rioting, and looting, oblivious to the fact that they supported originations and ideologies that threatened our Constitution and all the freedoms it provides. They were mindlessly demonstrating chaos, anarchy, and surrender of their freedom!

Then Along Came America: We fought a war to gain our independence. By the end of the Civil War, we were finally ready to challenge England for global supremacy. Abraham Lincoln oversaw the building of the world's first Transcontinental Railroad in order to gain access to America's vast treasure-trove of natural resources. Then America sparked the Industrial Revolution, which created the automation that allowed America to manufacture products cheap enough to compete with England on the global stage. In order to protect domestic manufacturing, President Lincoln imposed high tariffs on England (just like President Trump is doing to China and other countries which take advantage of unfair trade agreements).

Then America did something extraordinary. It shared its railroad technology and industrial prowess with the world in order to *"Elevate while equalizing the condition of men throughout the world."* Henry C. Carey, Economics Adviser to Abraham Lincoln, put it this way,

> *"Two systems are before the world. One is the English system; the other we may be proud to call the American System of Economics... The only one ever devised the tendency of elevating while equalizing man's condition throughout the world."*

By contrast, the British Economic System was one of oppression and a system of slavery without chains: Again, in the words of Henry C. Carey,

> *"It [the British System] is the most gigantic system of slavery the world has yet seen, and therefore it is that freedom gradually disappears from every country over which England is enabled to obtain control."*

America turned England's tactics on them, and in the span of thirty years, replaced England as the world's global superpower. Would you like some proof that President Trump's policies work? On September 5, 1901, President Mc Kinley made a speech at the Pan - American Conference in Buffalo to 50,000 North and South Americans espousing the virtues of the American Economic System. The quote below is from that speech.

> *"Thirty years of protectionism have brought us to 1ˢᵗ rank in agriculture, mining, and manufacturing development. We lead all nations in these three great departments of industry. We have outstripped even the United Kingdom, which had centuries head start on us...30 years the Protective tariff policy of the Republicans has by any measure by any standard vindicated itself."*

Just think of it. Had all the nations of the world been allowed to develop their natural resources and infrastructure and develop their manufacturing capabilities, this would be a very different place. WWI and WWII would probably never have happened, and the world would be a far more peaceful, more prosperous place.

Unfortunately, America's dream of *"elevating while equalizing the condition of man throughout the world"* was squashed by a series of events. The two strongest supporters of the American Economic System, Presidents Lincoln, and McKinley were assassinated. After nearly twenty-five years of plotting, England was successful in starting WWI with the intent of destroying all of Europe because they had adopted the American Economic System and were busy developing their manufacturing capability and building an intercontinental railroad system which when completed, would have ended England's control of trade by sea because rail transportation was faster and cheaper.

That is how England dashed America's dreams of a better, more peaceful world. The world was left with the crony Capitalism controlled by the Financial Elite, which is the cause of the socioeconomic inequities responsible for the riots and luting occurring in America.

President Woodrow Wilson sold out America to the Financial Elite. He was responsible for the emergence of crony Capitalism and the death of the dreams of a better world envisioned by Presidents Lincoln and Mc Kinley. Wilson came to regret his actions, and he made the following confession of the damage he had caused.

> *"Our great industrial nation is now controlled by its system of credit* (referring to the establishment of the Fed). *We are no longer a government by free opinion, no longer a government by conviction and the vote of the majority, but a government by the opinion and duress of a small group of dominant men...Our great industrial nation is controlled by its system of credit* (crony Capitalism). *Our system of credit is privately centered. The growth of the nation, therefore, and all our activities are in the hands of a few men...Who necessarily by very reason of their own limitations chill and check and destroy genuine economic freedom. We have become one of the worst ruled, one of the most completely controlled and dominated governments in the civilized world"* (President Woodrow Wilson).

What you just read is in a matter of speaking Wilson's confession for his part in the death of *"The American Economic System"* and the birth of crony Capitalism, which is the root cause of the riots which today are tearing America apart. In truth, these riots are less about racial prejudice and more about the economic injustice and oppression that is systematically destroying the middle class and small business. The riots are making way for a Corporatocracy comprised of the alliance of big business and big banks which use their wealth to suppress the middle-class and enforce a system of slavery controlled by wage suppression, which was exactly the tactic used by the British Free Trade System to enslave the world. Make no mistake, those that are orchestrating the burning and looting of America have the objective of destroying the middle-class in order to solidify their stranglehold on us, Useful Idiots! When the dust settles, millions of small and midsize companies will be gone, replaced by the corporate giants of the Financial Elite's Corporatocracy! The noose tightens, and if we don't stand up against our common enemy soon, it will be too late!

Along Came China: The nation the Financial Elite have designated as the model for their New World Order Dictatorship. England achieved global dominance by controlling natural resources, inflicting the world with the British Free Trade System of Slavery, and buying power and influence, destroying patriotism, Christian and family values, buying media outlets, etc. China is doing exactly the same things England did!

Then America turned the tables on England and, as you just read, in the span of 30 years, surpassed England as the world's economic superpower. Then in 1977, Jimmy Carter was elected President with financial backing from the Financial Elite. All of a sudden, a series of events unfolded that made way for China to make its move toward economic superpower status. There was an oil embargo that gave the Fed the excuse to raise interest rates to a staggering 18 to 21% during all of President Carter's term in office. As if that wasn't bad enough, inflation was also 18 to 21%. This phenomenon was referred to as stagflation, which brought the U.S. economy to a screeching halt. Then on cue, there was an unprecedented period of corporate raiding in which perfectly sound companies were bought only to be broken up and sold off in pieces so they couldn't compete with China's emergence. None of this was by accident. It was planned and orchestrated by the Financial Elite and their pawn in the White House, President Jimmy Carter. China became the Financial Elite's pawn in what was a frontal assault on America intended to seed global power back to them as the power behind China.

The Rise of China and the Decline of America Is No Accident!

I want you to see how the Financial Elite have intentionally orchestrated America's decline and China's Rise. It was no accident. If we can see what they have done to us, it will go a long way toward uniting us against our common enemy!

The U.S. In 2001: The 9/11 attack was used to drag America into a war that persists to this day and demoralized the nation and cost us over $7 trillion (money we could have used to rebuild our infrastructure and re-vitalize our inner cities). We were told that Iraq was behind the attack and that Saddam had weapons of mass destruction, but none were ever found. We were told that the Twin Towers came down because of the planes that crashed into them. But the facts indicate they were taken down by controlled demolition. The entire event was a false flag event orchestrated by The Financial Elite, who used Osama bin Laden as the face of terror. It just so happens that Osama bin Laden had close connections with the Bush family, and on 9/11, all of his relatives were allowed to fly out of the U.S. at a time when all other U.S. air traffic was grounded. It seems more than coincidental that President Bush's brother was a principal in the security company with the security contract for both the Twin Towers and Dulles airport.

China In 2001: China joins The World Trade Organization and is given favored nation status. It immediately deploys its plan to gut U.S. manufacturing and implement Free Trade Policies used by the British, which allowed it to rule the world for hundreds of years. On cue, the U.S. experienced a long-term economic shutdown referred to as stagflation, which brought the U.S. economy to an absolute standstill during Carter's entire term of Presidency. It took the U.S. over 200 years to amass a scant $660 Billion national debt. All of a sudden, we engaged in intentionally losing trade agreements with China, and our debt skyrocketed, and today June 2020, it is a staggering $25.9 trillion.

The U.S. In 2008: Leman Brothers goes bankrupt, causing a cascade that leads to the worst financial crisis since the Great Depression. We learned earlier that the financial collapse would never have occurred had it not been for actions taken by Presidents Bush and Clinton and then-Senator Obama, whom it is my contention were all put in office by the Financial Elite and were their puppets.

China In 2008: China hosts the Olympics and spotlights its economic accomplishments to the world. As America reels from the largest financial collapse since the Great Depression, China takes a leadership role in leading the world to economic recovery. This marks a shift in the balance of power between the U.S. and China.

The U.S. In 2013: The U.S. government was completely polarized, making it increasingly difficult to pass legislation on a bipartisan basis. The government has become little more than political theater, with each side unwilling to work with the other. In the pandemonium that ensues, unable to agree on a budget, the U.S. Government is shut down. As much as I hate to say it, most of our Congressmen and Senators have sold out to the Financial Elite and no longer represent the people and need to be voted out.

China In 2013: Xi Jinping announces *the "One Belt One Road"* initiative, which is an ambitious plan to extend Chinese influence throughout the rest of Asia and into Europe and Africa. It provides land and sea infrastructure and develops trade relations, making it difficult for the nearly 100 participating nations to oppose China because of their dependency on them.

2020 sees America on the razor's edge, teetering on the brink of financial collapse and anarchy. As insane as it sounds, lawless mobs burn our cities while Democrat politicians call for defunding the police that protect our communities. They don't for a second think that would make those cities safer. Quite to the contrary. They intend to create chaos hoping their insane policies will keep President Trump from being reelected. The Financial Elite and their pawns, the Socialist Democrats, are petrified that President Trump's policies are making America great again. That is the last thing they want because it threatens their plans to birth their New World Order Dictatorship modeled after China. I tell you in all sincerity! If Trump is not elected, anarchy will prevail in America, and we will lose our freedom to our mortal enemy, the Financial Elite! A situation is developing where for the first time in U.S. history, neither party will be willing to concede the election, and we will not have a peaceful transition of power!

I make no apology for being a Christian, and this may be a good time to remind you how this book came to be. Some 50 years ago, I had a near-death experience, and I was shown that when my hair was salt and pepper (which is now), America would face the greatest crisis in its history. The crisis would shake America to its core so He, God could use the crisis to remove the scales of deception from our eyes so America could unite as one nation one people and once again emerge as the nation He, God ordained to lead the world to a better tomorrow. If we want God to intervene on our behalf, we have to turn to Him in prayer, and when we do, He will hear our prayer and come to our aid. But as is the case in story after story in the Bible, we must demonstrate that we are willing to take a stand against the evil forces arrayed against us. Please, America, let us stand united against our common enemy. I remind you of President Kennedy's words when faced with the threat of war with Russia over the Cuban Missile Crisis, *"In the long history of the world, only a few generations have been granted the role of defending freedom in its hour of maximum danger. I do not shrink from this responsibility; I welcome it."* It's time to stand and be counted!

Time for America to Make a Resurgence!

To do that, we finally have to stand up to China and level the playing field. We must protect our intellectual property and natural security interest and make sure China can no longer control us by controlling the global supply chain. China is vulnerable for several reasons.

- **China Is Dependent on the U.S. Dollar:** The governments of the world do not want their currency controlled by a Communist nation. Less than 9/10th of 1% of global commerce is conducted in China's currency.

- **China Is No Longer the Cheapest Supplier of Manufactured Goods:** Even before the pandemic rallied support for redistribution of the supply chain China was losing manufacturing to Vietnam, Laos, Cambodia, Mexico, and that trend will continue and almost certainly accelerate.

- **Control by the Chinese Communist Party:** China has Nationalized some companies, making investors reluctant to risk investing in China. There is also resistance caused by the forced transfer of intellectual property.

- **China's Extraordinary Growth Is Coming to a Halt:** Their cheap labor pool is shrinking due to an aging population. This is causing factories to close and unemployed workers to seek work in nearby Vietnam or return to their villages. Countries that relied on China for revenues from the sale of commodities are seeing these revenues shrink appreciably.

- **The Masses No Longer Believe the Communist Parties' Promise of a Better Life:** Millions of what has become known as the *"Ant People"* live subsistence lives in the big cities. These are college graduates who had dreams of living the good life, but that is not the case. Evidence of widespread disillusionment is seen in the suicide rate, where the number one cause of death for people 15 to 34 is suicide.

- **The Backlash Against China Based on the Perception They Could Have Contained the Virus and Instead Intentionally Allowed It to Spread Around the World:** Such perceptions are exacerbated by perceived hoarding of personal protection equipment (PPE) and a bold statement threatening to *"Burry the U.S. under the sea of the Coronavirus."* Most importantly, when China's factories closed, the global supply chain was disrupted, and countries worldwide realized that it was untenable to have one country control the supply chain, so it is almost certain that countries worldwide will be bringing home at least some of their manufacturing. This will almost certainly hurt an already slowing Chinese economy.

- **Concerns Over Security Issues Associated With the Emergence of 5G Technology:** This has led President Trump to say to our allies that they either get on board to prevent China's dominance in technology, or we can no longer be a military ally because their actions are threatening our national security.

- **Movement by the U.S, India, and Others to Forbid Domestic Acquisition of Companies by China, Particularly of High-Tech Companies:** The concern is that when China acquires a domestic company, they acquire their technology, and this is one of the ways China is acquiring foreign intellectual property.

- **U.S. Tariffs on Chinese Goods:** Remember tariffs are how the U.S. leveled the playing field against England following the Civil War and, in the span, of 30 years, emerged as the world's economic superpower. The Bible says, *"There is nothing new under the sun."* So, it should come as no surprise that President Trump's tariffs caused a slowdown in the Chinese economy and an uptick in ours.

- **Pandemic Highlighted the Fact That Global Pharmaceutical Production Must Be Distributed Amongst Several Countries**: So, this sector of the Chines economy is almost certain to contract amidst global pressure.

- **Debt Associated with Belt and Road Inactive and Ghost Cities**: China has gone deeply into debt betting on two future development strategies. 1) The building of huge urban cities in the interior in the hopes of attracting resettlement to them. 2) A mammoth investment in what is called "One Belt and Road," which is a land and sea route that is intended to open trade routes with an estimated 100 countries from China to the Middle East, Europe, and Africa. This project is vital to China for several reasons ranging from trade to national security. Still, perhaps the most important reason is that China is the world's largest importer of oil and this land and sea route gives them access to oil and other natural resources in Africa and the Middle East. However, many building projects in both China and along the Belt and Road have been stopped as China is faced with the slowest growth rate in half a century, and post-pandemic, the slow down can be expected to get even worse. China is vulnerable for the first time since the 1980s.

- **Infrastructure Loans Are Seen by Many Countries as a Debt Trap**: This is yet another strategy used by the Financial Elite where they loan money to developing nations ostensibly to develop infrastructure projects and then, through a variety of tactics, see to it that the country defaults on the loan then they get control of their natural resources or get control of the project they had funded. This relates to the Belt and Road Initiative and creates yet another concern about the success of the project.

China has made two huge back-to-back political blunders, which have finally united the world against them. First, through a number of provocative actions, they have alerted the world to their intentions to establish a Global Communist Dictatorship. Second, their handling of the recent pandemic has shown the world just how ruthless they truly are. The world now understands that it is too dangerous to allow China to control the global supply chain. This creates an opportunity for America to take back our manufacturing and strengthen our global leadership role. As we just discussed, China has a number of systemic issues that make it vulnerable to economic competition that it was previously impervious to.

President Trump's Make America Again Agenda in Action: As the sun sets on one nation, it invariably rises on another. For the last 50 years or more, the Financial Elite have bet against America and placed their bets on China. They thought that with their help, they could manage the decline of America and the rise of China. But they didn't count on President Trump and his *"Make America Great Again Agenda."* President Trump correctly sees China as an existential threat to America and the entire free world! He is the first President in decades whose loyalty has not been bought by the Financial Elite. His Make America Great Again Policies are tried and true because they are based on the very policies which made America great in the first place. As the saying goes, *"There is nothing new under the sun."* Put another way, *"What worked before will work again."* We know that the British achieved economic dominance by controlling the three pillars of the economy: natural resources, manufacturing, and trade.

Following the Civil War, the U.S. turned the economic tables on Britain by using their own economic policies against them. America imposed high tariffs on England, just like President Trump is doing to China. As a result, prior to the pandemic, China had the worst economic numbers in 50 years.

Following the Civil War, America built the world's first Transcontinental Railroad to gain access or natural resources. Trump has eliminated job-killing regulations and ended the war on oil, gas, and mining, and brought many factories back to America. Perhaps most importantly, he has ended America's dependence on foreign energy. As a result, those jobs which Obama - Biden said would never come back have come roaring back.

President Trump has turned the tables on our intentionally losing Free Trade Policies by negotiating Far Trade Deals with China, Mexico, Canada, South Korea, and Japan and others are in negotiation. After decades of trade deficits, America has finally stopped hemorrhaging billions of dollars due to our insane intentionally losing trade deals.

We still labor under the Fed's oppression, but President Trump has thus far managed to force them to go along with his policies. Before the pandemic, Trump's economic policies had invigorated the U.S. economy, the stock market, and resulted in record-high employment for all demographic. As the saying goes, *"A rising tide raises all boats."* Importantly, Trump's economic policies created a strong dollar, which gives Trump vitally important leverage against China. We previously discussed how the nations of the world don't want to conduct business in Chinese currency. That, along with Trump's tariffs, gives America leverage with China, which we didn't have under previous administrations. Lastly, Trump's strong pre-pandemic policies have made the U.S. more resilient than Europe and most other countries. The Obama – Biden's recovery from the 2008 financial collapse was the slowest since the Great Depression. Even in the face of lockdowns, President Trump's policies are responsible for creating a V-shaped recovery!

How to Bring Back Our Manufacturing From China and Simultaneously Heal the Wounds of Socioeconomic and Racial Injustice That Divide Us!

Again, Trump has been proactive. He has invested in opportunity zones, which have stimulated economic opportunities and employment in our inner cities. But it may just be that the very crisis that has so shaken America may provide an unprecedented opportunity for an American economic resurgence which could simultaneously heal the wounds that have for so long divided us. The 64-thousand-dollar question is, how do we accomplish this task?

We Develop Manufacturing Revitalization Zones: What I am suggesting is a combined infrastructure project, redevelopment project, educational project, and urban planning project designed to:

1. Bring essential manufacturing back to America.

2. Help restore our trade balance and reduce our debt.

3. Restore blighted property to the tax rolls.

4. Educate inner-city residents so they can get off generational welfare.

5. Attract private investment in retail and housing as a result of the economic stability provided by building factories.

6. Reduce crime and drug addiction because we know that automatically happens when there is economic stability, and the family unit is restored.

7. Eliminate the hatred of the police because the things that cause that hatred has nothing to do with race and everything to do with people having a reasonable standard of living, a stable family, and hope for a better life for the future.

If America is to survive as a nation, we must stop the decay of our inner cities. That is not an option, and it is not impossible. What I have just suggested is exactly what China did to America with the Financial Elite's help, and their bought and paid for cronies in the deep state shadow government. What China did to America was to use our greed to economically and socially destroy us. Now the opportunity has been presented to us to turn the tables on them and restore America's wealth and dignity.

Putting It All Together: What I am proposing would require an all-government approach. For starters, let's say we go into Detroit as a pilot, which has an 84% black population and has probably been hit harder by the loss of our manufacturing than any city in the nation. There are acres and acres of shuttered buildings that are literally falling down. I propose we bulldoze them and then offer the land to companies that agree to build factories and bring strategically important products back from China to America. These companies would get the land for their factory for, say, $1, and they would also get tax breaks to be phased out over a specified number of years.

In exchange, developers would agree to provide inner-city residents with any necessary training to employ them. They would agree not to hire illegal immigrants or hire people from overseas upon penalty of loss of tax credits and fines. The factories in the redevelopment zones would agree to share the cost to provide daycare so single moms could get off welfare and provide their children a better standard of living. In order to incentivize workers, those on welfare would for a specified period of time be allowed to keep their welfare payments, which would be gradually phased out over time.

A portion of the reclaimed land would be set aside for residential and retail development with similar private investors' incentives. No public housing would be allowed, only private development. Storefronts would have housing units above them, and in order to get the max utilization of the land, all housing units would be condos or low to midrise buildings. With the exception of grocery and hardware stores and perhaps a variety store such as Target, no other big box stores would be allowed. That way, local entrepreneurship of small businesses can be maximized. The property would also be set aside for schools, and for efficiency, elementary, middle, and high schools would be built in one location and where practical resources would be shared. School choice should also be an option for residents.

Recreational sites would be set aside to be developed after the community was fully developed and self-supporting. Looking forward toward the future, we might want to set aside space for a factory farm that could provide produce at the point of consumption. The model for such factory farms are multistory aquaponic towers that can grow up to 40 different varieties of vegetables in water using fish to provide nutrients. Such facilities use minimal water, little to no chemicals, and are very labor efficient. Eventually, if proven to be cost-effective, the widespread use of such facilities could reduce the water stress on our acquirers, which are being depleted at an alarming rate.

This may sound extraordinarily expensive, but not so. The factories come online first to solve our supply chain problem and generate revenue for the project's subsequent phases. The only cost to the government would be the cost of demolishing the land and putting in the infrastructure necessary for redevelopment. This is very similar to what China did to America when they hijacked our manufacturing, and it made them an economic superpower. This can be the key to not only reinvigorating the U.S. economy but also to, once and for all, healing the wounds of economic and social injustice that are tearing America apart from the inside out. This could unite America and provide the means for it to be greater than ever! It is not a matter of whether or not we can afford to do this! We cannot afford not to do it! Our future depends on it.

We Can Have Meaningful Socioeconomic Change and Social Justice, or We Can Have Riots and Looting: What happened to George Floyd was horrible. If the evidence supports it, the officer's responsible need to be prosecuted to the fullest extent of the law. But as discussed, police violence is just a symptom of the real problem, which is the socioeconomic inequities that have existed in America since its founding. I hope you will champion the plan I just laid out by sharing it on social media and by contacting your Congressmen and Senators. This injustice needs to be solved, and right now, we have a unique opportunity to bring about real change. Please don't squander this opportunity by allowing this movement for social justice to be usurped by radical anarchists. Calling for the abolishment of ICE and the police will not correct the injustice. Still, it will discredit the movement, and it will most certainly result in increased violence and deaths in Black communities.

Please don't let Democrat Mayors and Governors placate you with hollow promises, and don't let radical Communist organizations like Antifa tear this country apart. Antifa has adopted the manifesto of the Weather Underground, which was prevalent in the 1970s. Their manifesto was published in a booklet entitled *"Prairie Fire."* Its manifesto calls for:

1. **Destroying Capitalism:** This is tantamount to a political coup.

2. **The Weapon of Choice Is Systemic Racism and Political Racism:** So, in their own words, they don't want to solve the problem; they want anarchy.

3. **Identifying a Victim Class and Organize a Protest and Other Forms of Resistance:** Again, they are not interested in making the lives of inner-city residents better—all they want is to incite protest and riots.

4. **Engaging in Solidarity with the Global Movement:** Translation, they want to end our U.S. sovereignty and surrender to a socialist – Communist Dictatorship.

5. Attacking and Dethroning God: They are atheists and are against God, the family, and patriotism.

This manifesto is a weapon of the Financial Elite, dedicated to destroying America to birth their New World Order Dictatorship modeled after Communist China. Please don't let yourself be used by radicals who are only interested in using your movement to destroy this nation. Yes, America has flaws, but it is still the freest nation in the world. The plan I just laid out is a win for inner-city residents, manufacturers, and the government. Please support this plan, and let's see if we can't end the division that is tearing America apart.

We Must Protect Our High-Tech Industries and Provide White Color Jobs: China not only took our blue color jobs; it also took strategically important white color jobs. It was a technological innovation that allowed the U.S. to become the world's leading economic superpower. But today, China has caught or surpassed the U.S. in several key technologies, most importantly, A.I., 5G, robodocs, and nanotechnology, which are the technologies that will define the 21st century. If China gains superiority in these technologies, they will undoubtedly realize their dreams of becoming the world's undisputed economic superpower. And the Financial Elite will have their Super Capitalist Communist Slave State. We cannot let that happen.

Since China released the COVID-19 virus on the world, the U.S. is in an undeclared war with China (a new cold war), and in that war, perhaps their most effective weapon is good old-fashioned American greed. Given this, the same type of incentives proposed for inner-city factory sites could be offered to high-tech companies, for example, in the medical field. Additionally, the government must consider antitrust action and any and all types of restrictions that make it cost-prohibitive for U.S. based corporations to engage in business ventures with foreign entities if such activities are injurious to U.S. vital interest. For example, Google is working with China to develop A.I. applications that are clearly not in the best interest of the U.S. I leave it to the lawyers, but surely something can be done to prohibit Such activities.

POSTSCRIPT

This book has opened your eyes to the truth of what is being done to destroy our great nation, and hopefully, you will join in the fight to restore our God-given freedom. There are men in our government who have sold out to the Financial Elite, and they are enemies of freedom! We must remove them at the ballot box if possible. If that is impossible, then we must initiate a 2nd American Revolution in order to protect our Constitution and our inalienable rights to life, liberty, and the pursuit of happiness.

> *"We the people are the rightful masters of both Congress and the courts, not to overthrow the Constitution but to overthrow the men who pervert the Constitution"* (President Abraham Lincoln).

I leave you to ponder the words of President Franklin D Roosevelt, *"In politics, nothing happens by accident. If it happened, you can bet it was planned that way."*

So, with this quote in mind, do you think the events leading up to the 2020 election have just been an extraordinary string of coincidences, or is it more likely we are in the midst of a political coup attempt of the United States and efforts to birth the Financial Elite's New World Order headed by China? I see the number of coincidences we have supposedly experienced to be a mathematical impossibility! Given that they all in one way or another destabilize the U.S. and the world. My conclusion is this is all part of a carefully planned and executed coup! Are the following events coincidences, or are we in the middle of a coup attempt, and if so, what do we do?

- **Release of Virus by Our Global Adversary China:**
  - Do you think it was a coincidence that President Trump takes on China in a trade war, and China releases a virus on the world and says, *"We will bury America under the sea of the Coronavirus?"*
- **Create a Global Debt Crisis:**
  - Do you think it is a coincidence that the lockdowns have doubled global debt and the Financial Elite's agenda for world dominance calls for driving the world's sovereign nations into unmanageable debt and then stepping in and bailing them out conditioned on accepting their New World Order?
- **Collapse of the Middle Class:**
  - Do you think it is a coincidence that under Communism, the middle class is utterly crushed, and that is exactly what the virus is being used to do to our middle class?
  - Do you think it is a coincidence that while big chain stores are open and making record profits, small businesses around the country are forced to close their doors and are being driven out of businesses?
  - Do you think it is a coincidence that the lockdowns are crippling small businesses and the middle class and ceding power to Wall-street and the Corporatocracy?
  - Do you think it is a coincidence that outdoor dining is forbidden, but mass protests are allowed and encouraged?
  - Do you think it is a coincidence that keeping kids out of school also keeps their mothers from being able to go to work, which financially hurts middle class families all over the country!
  - Do you think it is a coincidence that Democrat Mayors and Governors are issuing draconian lockdown orders, but they turn around and disregard their own orders?

- **Attack on Patriotism and Christianity:**

  ◦ Do you think it is strange that mayors joined in with Black Lives Matter protesters to demonstrate and paint murals on city streets, but Christians having outdoor services were arrested?

  ◦ Do you think it is a coincidence that liquor stores and marijuana shops are allowed to be open without draconian restrictions, but churches, no matter how large, are restricted to ten people?

- **A Coup Attempt With Riots and Looting:**

  ◦ Do you think it is a coincidence that a long list of global corporations has made donations to Black Lives Matter groups and that the money has been used to bail out rioters so they could go back to their rioting and looting?

  ◦ Do you think it was just an oversight that the media called the riots "*mostly peaceful protests*" while we could see businesses burning in the background?

  ◦ Do you think it was an oversight that for months the Democrats were mute on the subject of the riots occurring across America and failed even to mention the violence during the Democratic Convention?

- **Censorship and Election Interference:**

  ◦ Do you think it is a coincidence that the tech giants censored conservatives' voices and even President Trump in the run-up to the election? Could it have anything to do with opposing President Trump's Make America Great Again Agenda because they are in bed with China and the Financial Elite?

  ◦ Do you think it was a coincidence that YouTube labeled any claims of election fraud fake news and banned any such content? Doesn't that make them just a Communist propaganda machine that denies the American people free speech so we can decide for ourselves what is truth and what is lies! That isn't for them to decide! Doesn't that make them traitors to the Constitution?

○ Do you think it was a coincidence that Rahm Emanuel, Obama's Chief of Staff said, "*You never want to fail to take advantage of a crisis.*" Then amid the pandemic, Black Lives Matter and Antifa decided to burn and loot American cities and intimidate Trump supporters?

- **Election Fraud and an Attempted Coup:**

    ○ Do you think it is a coincidence that Nancy Pelosi tried to eliminate any requirement for voter IDs as part of the COVID relief package put forth by the Democrats?

    ○ Do you think it was a coincidence that in the critical swing states, Joe Biden got a statistically improbable higher percentage of votes than in the rest of the country?

    ○ Do you think it was a coincidence that swing states made backroom deals that bypassed the state legislatures in order to change voting rules regarding mail-in votes?

    ○ Do you think it was just a coincidence that it was only in the swing states that voting was suspended, and during that time, more votes were counted for Biden than the voting machines were mathematically capable of counting in the allotted time?

- **One Justice System for the Elite and a Different One for the Rest of Us:**

    ○ Do you think it was just a coincidence that Democrats and the media did everything they could to ignore Hillary Clinton's involvement as the originator of the Russia Collusion Hoax? It has been established that she paid for the Russia hoax dossier in order to divert attention from her pay for play server scandal!

    ○ Do you think it was a coincidence that Hunter Biden's involvement in pay for play in Ukraine and China was ignored in the run-up to the election? Now post-election, we find out from e-mails on Hunter's laptop that Joe Biden lied when he said he had no knowledge of his son's business dealings. In fact, he participated in meetings regarding those deals and was to share in the proceeds from those criminal deals!

○ Do you think it was a coincidence that Jeffry Epstein conveniently died under mysterious circumstances while in prison, taking his secrets to the grave with him?

○ Could it be that all these scandals and others have been ignored because if the truth were to come out about the many people in high place would be exposed and the Financial Elite's diabolical plot to as President Kennedy said, *"Enslave every man, woman, and child"* would be exposed for all to see?

Well, this is not a coincidence. God is a way maker. He knows the ending before the beginning. He sees all, and in due course of time, all will be revealed. A veil of deception has been allowed to be placed over our eyes for several decades, but it is time for that veil to be removed so the truth can be revealed, and our division can be ended! America made a covenant with God on the day of its consecration as a nation, and God intends to use America one more time to champion a Great Awakening then comes judgment, but that is not now. President Trump is a man after God's heart, and he has been chosen to stand in the gap for America and the world. He will serve a 2nd term, and America will be greater than ever!

I want to leave you with an excerpt of a speech by a Chinese economics professor from Fox News' Tucker Carlson broadcast on December 7, 2020. What he says comes about as close to a smoking gun as we will ever get to a confession that Wall Street and our Political Elite, including Biden, have sold out to China! It acknowledges that since the 1970s, China has had Wall Street and the U.S. Political Elites in their pocket, and they consider Joe Biden to be the friend of China and has financial entanglements with China. Entanglements that, in my opinion, make Biden an operative of China and a traitor, potentially guilty of treason! Read what follows and decide for yourself!

America's Elite Political Class Have Sold Out to China: They See Trump as an Obstacle and Biden as an Ally!

"The Trump administration is in a trade war with us (China), *so why can't we fix the Trump administration? Why, between 1992 and 2016, did China and the U.S. use to be able to settle all kinds of issues? We had people at the top. At the top of the American core circle of power and influence. We have our old friends for the past 30 years, 40 years we had been utilizing the core power of the United States. Since the 1970s, Wall Street had a very strong influence on the domestic and foreign affairs of the United States, so we had a channel to rely on, but they couldn't do much during the U.S. – China Trade War, they* (Wall Street) *tried to help* (To use their words, they couldn't fix Trump)...*But now we're seeing Biden was elected, the establishment they're very close to Wall Street...there are many deals out there... so you see that, right?"*

The way I interpret this quote is, President Trump is not for sale, but Biden is! As Biden put it, *"Come on guys, China is no threat,"* we are just beginning to get to the truth! It looks like good old Joe allowed his son (Hunter) to peddle access to him (the Vice-President), and he was in for a share of the money his son got.

Time to Take Our Country Back!

The people of the world must stand united and defeat our enemy. We are many, and they are few. We have more power than we think! Please, now is the time! It is now or never! Either we stand up and take our country back from those that would be the masters of us all, or we will surely lose our freedom, never to get it back. This is the hour when Patrick Henry is shouting from heaven, saying, *"Give me freedom, or give me death."* Winston Churchill cries out, *"Victory at all cost,"* and Abraham Lincoln is reminding us of his prophetic warning from so long ago when he said,

"I see in the near future a crisis approaching that unnerves me and causes me to tremble for the safety of my country. . .corporations have been enthroned, and an era of corruption in high places will follow, and the money power of the country will endeavor to prolong its reign by working upon the prejudices of the people (the false narrative of systemic racism) until all wealth is aggregated in a few hands, and the Republic is destroyed" (President Abraham Lincoln November 21, 1864, letter to Col. William F. Elkins).

This is exactly where we are today! Our political leaders have sold out to China and the Financial Elite. Biden is their pawn willing to usher in their New World Order, and the media and tech giants are in on the betrayal as well! God is exposing the truth, and there is more to come. Nothing will remain hidden!

Made in the USA
Columbia, SC
08 April 2024

34113543R00126